The Standout

Laurel Osterkamp

Drama, Drama

The Standout

A novel by
Laurel Osterkamp

Part 1: Robin

Chapter One

I wanted to jump but I didn't have the guts.

It was one of those moments that I knew would never leave me. I was clinging to the trunk of a solid elm, praying that the rickety old tree house underneath my feet wouldn't collapse. "You whore!" Clara screamed, her face as red as her hair. I looked to Robert, fruitlessly hoping he might help, but all I saw was his backside, just a pair of khaki shorts and a blue Polo jersey retreating through the freshly mowed back yard. I was paralyzed in equal parts by fear and guilt, wishing I could take it all back, wishing I could be someone else, wishing I could jump.

It started innocently enough. I met Clara in a fashion design class at a community college that was like a strip mall with classrooms. The arts building was big and stretched out, with lots of lounges and study areas, and there was a coffee shop at the north end that had a fireplace against a picture window.

On the first day I was early, so I stopped to buy a latte, and I noticed a guy noticing me. You know the type: tall, dark hair, sparkling eyes, well-built. I couldn't even a find a slight, personality-defining imperfection, like a crooked nose or a chipped tooth, to give his face an endearing dose of uniqueness.

I gave him a half-smile, secured a cardboard sleeve around my coffee cup, and went on my way to class.

Before the second class, I stopped for coffee again, and Mr. Tall, Dark and Handsome sat in the same spot as before. This time he had an architecture textbook and a sketch pad, and every few seconds he would absently draw something. Then he looked up, met my eyes, and grinned like he knew me.

I smiled back. With a flick of his head he gestured me over and I responded.

"What's your name?" He asked.

"Robin."

"Really? That's so funny. My name is Robert. It's like we're the same."

That was the beginning. Before every class I would get coffee, and Robert would always be there, studying architecture, and we would always say hello. One night he asked me out and I said yes. There was no ring on his finger, after all. He seemed put-together, driven, and interesting. I'd thought I hit the jackpot.

And for a while, it was like I had.

He didn't ask much of me. His schedule was busy and mine was too. He had roommates, he said, so he always came to my place, but he never stayed the night. I enjoyed the reprieve from loneliness, but I wasn't in love, so I didn't question it.

And then there was Clara. She was the star pupil in our little fashion design class but she should have been the teacher. I didn't even know people with her sense of style existed in Des Moines. And with her lovely hair and slim frame, her clothes look fabulous on her. At first I was intimidated, jealous even. She'd come up with these incredible, couture-worthy designs, and I wanted to pick her brain. Perhaps, just by osmosis, I could absorb some of her brilliance.

Yet she always left before class got out. "Sorry," she said to the instructor the first time this happened. "My husband is waiting." They took class at the same time but his got out sooner than hers did, so to accommodate him, she always left early.

I talked to her every chance I got. "I really like what you did with the last assignment," I said one time. "The collar is amazing. How you'd learn to create lines like that?"

She blushed in pleasure, and told me how she'd learned from her grandmother, who used to work with Diane Von Furstenberg and who also owned a whole closet-full of wrap dresses.

"God, I'd love to see them."

"You should!" She cried. "My husband is out of town this weekend. We should have a girl's night. Come over and see my gramma's dresses. It's not just stuff by Diane Von Furstenberg. She was quite the fashion plate."

I brought two bottles of wine and a box of chocolates, and Clara's gramma told us stories about living and designing in 1970's NYC. Meanwhile we tried on dresses by Tomas Maier, Kenzo, and Halston. By the end of the evening we were giddy and tipsy. Clara's gramma had gone to bed, Clara was lying on the floor and I was on the couch.

The room was spinning so I spoke to the ceiling. "When I grow up, I want to be your gramma." If I could sit up and focus, I'd have looked again at all her photos: women with large sunglasses, holding cigarettes and emanating chic. Nothing in her apartment seemed post-1980, except for me and Clara.

"She's had quite the life," Clara responded. "Lots of lovers, lots of adventure, and she was always well dressed."

"How did she end up in Des Moines?"

"She met my grandfather. He convinced her to marry him and he brought her out here for work. Then he screwed everything in sight while she grew bored and depressed."

My buzz started to dissipate. "Why didn't she leave him?"

Clara let out a loud sigh. "It's harder than you think, to leave your husband when he's cheating on you."

I turned my head towards her. Her neck was arched, her hair was fanned out, and she looked like Sleeping Beauty. What prince wouldn't value her? "What are you saying?" I asked.

"Nothing. Just a feeling, I suppose."

And we left it at that. Eventually, she got up and slept in the bed with her gramma while I slept on the couch, blissfully drunk and unable to think too hard.

Because I could have put two and two together. Instead, I remained willfully oblivious while my friendship with Clara grew strong and my fling with Robert grew stale. Then, Easter came and Clara invited me to eat with her family. The day was lovely and warm. Clara's gramma was napping, her mother didn't need help in the kitchen, and Clara's husband was yet to arrive to the celebration.

"Come outside," said Clara. We went out onto the porch. I thought we would sit on the patio chairs and absorb the sun's rays, but Clara was too squirrely to be still. "Look!" she pointed to her tree house. "My dad built that for me when I was seven. When Bobby and I have kids, I want him to build one. Tree houses are, like, a requirement for childhood, don't you think?"

"Sure," I replied, though I'd never had a tree house and I'd never actually wanted one.

"Let's climb it right now!" Clara, who seemed to operate at extremes, ran towards the trunk with its rickety steps. "Come on," she cried, and I followed even though I could already taste fear on my tongue.

I wouldn't say that I'm afraid of heights. Sure, I feel nauseous and dizzy whenever I'm up high without a barrier to prevent me from falling to my death, but who doesn't get that way sometimes? So I climbed the half-rotted wooden steps of Clara's tree house that was built in the early nineties, and I silently repeated the mantra, "You're safe, you're safe, you're safe," while we sat up among the branches.

Then we heard him call. "Clara? Babe, are you up there?"

And Clara answered, "Hey Bobby! Here we are!"

I didn't want to look down but I had to. There he was, freshly showered after his tennis match, looking up while his face fell. Robert was Clara's husband, and the horrible knowledge of our situation pulsed like a living thing between us.

"Robert?" I uttered, before I could censor myself, before I thought better of admitting to knowing him.

Robert was mute. He stood below, his mouth gaping wide and his cheeks flaming red. Clara looked back and forth between us. "What's going on?" She demanded. "Do you two know each other?"

Neither of us answered, but Clara was not okay with silence. "Bobby! Is she the reason you've been so busy lately?"

I should have put Clara's feelings first. I should have stayed silent. But the betrayal was too fresh.

"You lied to me the entire time?" I said to Robert. "How could you do that?"

Robert muttered something about not wanting to hurt anyone.

"No!" Clara cried. "Bobby! Tell me you didn't fuck her."

Instead of answering he just walked off, and Clara turned to me with tears in her eyes.

"It didn't mean anything," I said. "He doesn't have real feelings for me. Maybe you can talk this through…"

"You whore!" she cried, her face changing from wounded doe to angry wolf. She grabbed the planks of the tree house and started shaking them.

"Clara, please stop." I pictured falling, landing in a heap of broken wood, my head hitting the ground, my body as fractured as the tree house would be.

"You bitch! You man-stealing slut! You pretend to be my friend while you're screwing my husband!"

She continued to shake the tree house and I wrapped my arms around the trunk, certain that I'd tumble down, lose my breath and die. Nobody would think I didn't deserve it.

"I'm sorry Clara, I didn't know. I'm sorry, I'm sorry, I'm sorry!" I could barely get the words out; they were little more than whispered pleas. Clara kept on shaking the tree house and calling me names, yelling accusations, and instead of jumping to safety, I screamed so loud that her father came out and told her to stop.

"And I'd never felt worse about myself," I tell Nick now. He's on the couch with his feet in my lap, listening to my awful tale.

"You didn't even know he was married," Nick answers. His voice is low and gravelly, and he barely flinches as I recount all the details.

"But I should have known." I tug on his big toe, which is safely ensconced in a hole-free sock. "So yeah, that's the worst thing I've ever done."

"Seriously?" His voice squeaks in question. "That's all you've got?"

I scan my brain over a litany of parking tickets, overdue library books, and botched Secret-Santa gift exchanges. None of it compares to the shemozzle I just described. "I'm afraid so."

Nick sits up and kisses my cheek. "I can totally live with that." His smile is big and I feel myself smiling back. "Okay," he says, "my turn. I was fourteen, at summer camp for the first time..."

Happily, I settle in and listen to his tale of lies, deceit, and stolen arts & crafts. Now he knows the worst of me. This intimacy thing isn't so bad, after all.

Chapter Two

"So are you sorry you ordered the trout?"

Nick's eyes, which had been darting around the candle-lit dining room, restlessly settle on me. "Huh?"

"You barely touched your meal," I say. "Didn't you like it? Maybe you should have gone with the steak."

Nick tugs absently on his dark brown necktie, which happens to match his hair and eyes perfectly. But underneath his normally tan complexion he's sort of pale. "The trout was fine." His answer sounds forced. "I just wasn't that hungry."

"Then why did we come here tonight? It's not like it's a special occasion."

We're at one of those low-lit steak houses, where people sip G&Ts while carving into huge hunks of meat. The only thing that makes this place unusual is that on weekends, Nick plays swanky lounge music to complete the posh atmosphere. "Besides," I continue, "I would think you'd get enough of this place."

As he reaches to scratch his temple I notice that his hand is shaking. "I have to get up for a minute." His voice cracks like he's in puberty.

"Are you okay?"

Nick suddenly becomes serious, solemn almost: the calm before a storm. He blinks, widens his eyes and stares into me. "I'm fine. But forgive me, Rocky, for what I'm about to do."

"Huh?"

He nods to someone; I turn and there's a sound guy by the piano. Nick jumps up, strolls over in broad steps, and the sound guy hands Nick a microphone. Then the restaurant lights dim to practically black, except for one light, that's turned up directly over Nick's head. "Excuse me, please!" Nick's voice is still raspy but he's determined to command the room. "Excuse me! I need everyone's attention."

The low murmur of dinner conversations diminishes and heads swivel towards Nick. "Thank you," he says. "I hope you all don't mind if I play just one song tonight. I'm not much of a singer, but you see...." He gestures towards me and my jaw drops as a light comes on over my head. "...This beautiful woman here is my love, Robin. I like to call her Rocky." He pauses and looks at me like we're the only two people in the world. "Rocky, you once told me that you're a sucker for a guy who can carry a tune, so this one's for you."

Then he sits down and tickles the keys with a combination of joy, competence, and frenzy, and all the while his eyes are glued to me. In his lilting voice, he croons the classic Beatles song *In My Life*.

I have heard this song many times but tonight Nick is reinventing it for me; heck, tonight he's reinventing music in general. When Nick reaches the song's bridge he has to look down at the keys for a moment, and his dark head is bowed while his fingers both glide and pound out this beautiful, haunting melody that lodges itself in my heart. When he looks up I feel an electric jolt. His cheeks are flushed and his voice cracks on the high note as he declares his undying love. Then Nick abandons the piano, comes straight over, crouches down on one knee and takes out a ring.

My heart's in my throat.

Time stands still. I want to memorize every single one of his laugh lines, the curve of his mouth, the way his hair slopes over his ears, the strength of his jaw and the warmth of his eyes. "So," he mumbles, breaking the silence. "Will you marry me?"

"Yes." My cheeks are wet and I didn't even know I'd been crying. Nick slips the ring over my finger, and we stand, wrapping our arms around each other, indulging in the sweetest of kisses. When the room erupts in spontaneous applause, I'm convinced: Cinderella has nothing on me, with her glass slipper and pumpkins at the stroke of midnight.

I found my prince, and even if he's sweaty from nerves, his body heat could keep me warm until the day I die.

Chapter Three

I suppose this sort of thing happens every day. People fall in love and decide to get married and it's ordinary, expected even. So maybe it's also ordinary and expected to believe that I am the only person who's ever felt this way, to want to grab every stranger I pass on the street and dictate a list of Nick's attributes. Said list would always end with, "and can you believe it? He's in love with *me*." But reciting the outward manifestations of Nick's goodness still wouldn't capture the contents of his heart, and this is how I know I am unique. I am the only person who has ever fallen in love with and gotten engaged to Nick Davies. Simply put, I'm the luckiest woman in the world.

Somebody was filming Nick's proposal and it went viral, even making the local news. Nick's song was brilliant and sweet and adorable and everything he does is newsworthy, but he insists that we got coverage because of my stint on the survival reality-TV show, *The Holdout*. I have my doubts because I'm less than yesterday's news; I'm last week's news, now used to line someone's bunny rabbit cage.

"People have totally forgotten about me," I tell Nick.

But he always says the same thing back: "That's just what you want to believe."

And I have to concede, that at least here in Des Moines, some people still pay attention to me. Nick believes that's why there were photos in

The Register, and why the footage was played on a local TV station. So for the last week, people at the grocery, the gas station, and the deli stand have been congratulating me. But today I haven't been out much and there's not a lot of traffic in my studio/store either. That suits me because I'm in a reclusive mood, happy to do some beading on the *Downton Abbey*-style cocktail dress I'm working on.

Eventually I get bored and take a break by checking my email. There is a message from an unknown source: FashionQueen_82@mail.com. The subject line says, "You need to read this."

I click it open.

"Robin,

I'm giving you options. You never gave me any options before you stole everything I had, so consider yourself lucky!

You can...

Dump Nick. You're not good enough for him and you know I am right.

Leave the country and never come back. (You can't tell anyone where you're going!)

Be honest about who you are. Let the world see you are a worthless whore and then you won't have to dump Nick because he will dump you.

Do one of these things and I will give you back all your accounts and delete the pictures and videos. If you simply ignore this email then I will be forced to make the choice for you and I guarantee you won't like it.

Stunned, I stare at the words, and after a while they blur together, forming into dark clumps of pixels that have no real meaning. I take a deep breath, hit "reply" and type out my response:

I'm going to the police the second you try anything. Don't screw with me. You won't like it.

I hit send before I can think too long about the wisdom behind it. It doesn't matter, because a second later I get a response: _Mailer-Da emon@Bricker_Robin.com_

This message was created automatically by mail delivery software. A message you sent has not yet been delivered to one or more of its recipients...

I press delete and then it's just my inbox that's displayed on my computer screen, with Fashion Queen 82's message at the top. I Google "Fashion Queen 82" but find nothing.

Looking off, out the window, I see that it's begun to rain. Gray clouds hang low and heavy in the sky and I feel like there's one directly over my head. That email could be from anyone. It could be some random person who has seen me on TV, someone who knows about Nick's proposal, someone who knows how to send email from an anonymous address, and who has now arbitrarily decided that she hates me.

Or it could be from Clara.

Chapter Four

The rain never lets up, and it's one of those afternoons when I'm wet and shivering just from darting from my car to the front door. I unlock it and enter, and a chill rolls through me right as there's a loud clap of thunder and a flash of lightning.

"Hello?" Only the emptiness of the house answers back. That's okay. I'm dreaming of a hot shower followed by some mac & cheese and bad television. Then my cell phone rings.

I'm still dripping in the entryway as I answer. "Hey, Saul" I say, recognizing Nick's father from my caller ID. "How are you?"

"Irritated," he replies. "I don't know why stores don't value their coupons. I was going to buy steak today but they lied about the price and there's no way I'm paying twelve bucks for a piece of meat."

Nick's dad likes to gripe about things, but really, don't we all? I know that Saul tests the limits of Nick's patience, but personally I prefer a crusty temperament to an overly cheerful one. "So were you able to find anything to eat?" I ask.

"Tuna," he grumbles. "I suppose I'll have tuna again."

This is my cue. "Why don't you come here for dinner tonight? We'd love to see you."

He mutters his assent and promises to be over soon. I text Nick: *Saul is eating dinner with us. You have to pick up steak.*

Later, Nick and I are in the kitchen while Saul watches television in our living room, several feet away.

"I'm really not in the mood for my dad tonight." Nick speaks low, grimacing while he seasons the steaks. Nick pretty much represses all of his Oedipal anger and resentment in the name of sonly duty, but he wants freedom from his Dad's harsh criticisms and neediness.

I take a paper towel and wipe the counter. "Sorry, but what was I supposed to do? I kind of had to invite him."

"No you didn't. But he knows you're a soft touch, which is why he called you instead of me."

I throw the paper towel away, and find a corkscrew so we can break out our most expensive bottle of wine, the one that cost twelve bucks on sale. "Don't you think it's important to have him over, Nick? We need to keep our family close..."

"...and our enemies closer?" Nick retorts. "With my dad it's the same thing." Impatient, Nick grabs both the bottle and the corkscrew from me.

"I was going to open that," I protest.

"You were messing it up. It was going in crooked."

"No it wasn't."

Nick sets his jaw as he opens the wine and he looks so miserable that I can't even be annoyed. "Hey..." I step close and brush my lips against his. "I love you."

"I love you too," he concedes, but he doesn't let go of his tension. Instead, he sets the uncorked bottle down and looks at his watch. "When is Andrea getting back?"

"I don't know. Why don't you call her?"

"I did already and she didn't pick up." When he exhales I can feel the pressure lingering in the air. "She'd better be home for dinner. I need her for reinforcements."

"Why? We'll be fine."

"He's just on better behavior when she's around." Nick sighs again, softer this time. "I swear, something's up with her. She used to be so responsible, now half the time I can't even reach her."

Years ago, after Nick's mother died of breast cancer, Nick became Andrea's guardian and he's basically raised her on his own. Saul sort of suffered a breakdown, so now he spends most of his time online, reading about conspiracies and running his own blog, *Conspiracy News Today*. Nick also has an older sister, but she was a groupie until she got married and became busy with her own family. Now Andrea's a senior in high school and Nick is her hero. He adores her as much as she adores him, so that's a lot of adoration to compete with.

Did I say compete? No, no... It's not a competition. Actually, Andrea and I get along great, in that we don't fight and she lets me be nice to her. There are absolutely no problems there.

Andrea doesn't pick up when Nick calls her again, so he cooks those steaks and I make a salad and pour the wine, and soon we're sitting in our dining room, just an ordinary dysfunctional family enjoying dinner on a rainy weeknight.

"Is there going to be more food?" Saul grunts, pushing the chopped zucchini around on his plate. "Not that this isn't delicious, but a few vegetables and one small piece of meat aren't enough."

"The steak's big, Dad." Nick taps his fork against his plate. "And with the walnuts and the feta in the salad, you'll be plenty full. Just give it a chance."

"I'm not criticizing," Saul answers. "I was just asking."

"I could make you some toast," I say. "Would you like some toast?"

Saul twists his mouth at the idea. "I'm not trying to be a bother, but usually with steak you serve potatoes."

He says this looking only at me, his voice measured and overly patient.

"Sorry," I tell him. "I didn't think about potatoes."

"Actually, I was in charge of dinner," Nick interjects. "Robin volunteered to make a salad and I handled the main course."

"You two need to work on your system." Saul scratches his neck, his skin flaking off and sprinkling our dark blue tablecloth with tiny white specs.

Nick clears his throat. "Robin and I have news, Dad. We're getting married."

Saul's craggy face doesn't even flinch. Maybe he already saw the proposal on TV? He blinks a couple of times, as if he's thinking slightly harder than usual, and says, "Congratulations. That's great. What are you going to do about money?" He directs his words only at Nick. "I have no idea how you managed to snag someone so pretty, but Son, be realistic. Robin could be a trophy wife if she wanted to, spending her days spending some rich guy's money. You'd better have a plan."

If Nick was capable of forcing steam out of his ears, he would do so right now. "That isn't funny, Dad."

"Of course it is," Saul laughs. "It's hilarious! Robin's going to marry an aspiring high school music teacher with massive student loans." He turns to me. "Have you looked in the mirror lately, sweetheart? Don't you know you could do much better than becoming a Davies?" I know answering his hypothetical question will only incite him, besides, he redirects his attention back to Nick, jabbing his fork in his direction. "You need to be careful. It's always the pretty ones who take you for everything you have. It's the pretty ones who will steal your soul. I should know. Your mother stole my soul before she died."

Nick's mouth drops open, probably because he can't decide who to defend first: me, or the memory of his mother.

I step in. "By 'stealing your soul,' don't you mean that you just really loved her?"

Saul's face is disarmed for a mere moment before I see his guard go back up. "Of course I loved her. Still do and always will. But if I had it to do over I'd be more practical." He reaches over and pats me on the hand in a semi-fatherly gesture. "You're a lovely girl and I'll be lucky to have you as a daughter-in-law. But marriage is the most difficult thing in the world, so before you make the jump you both want..."he waves his hand in the air, grasping for labels, "to be successful at teaching, or at sewing, or whatever flaky things the two of you are calling your careers this week. Otherwise, I give you two years, tops."

Nick becomes more and more like a coiled up spring with every word his father utters. He's clenching both of his fists and his jaw, and I'm afraid that one more wrong word will send him bouncing around in a conniption.

Then, mercifully, the front door opens and Andrea calls out, "Hey, sorry I'm late. I had an AP study session."

She comes in, her long braid swishing back and forth as she walks. "Is there any food left? I'm starving!" But she senses the tension in the room, and asks, "What's going on?"

"We told Saul about our engagement," I answer.

"I expressed a couple of concerns," argues Saul, "and now I'm the bad guy."

Andrea's cheeks turn pink. "Well then let's talk about something else, okay? Because I'm super-happy about Robin and Nick getting married, and I don't want you to spoil it with negativity."

If she's "super happy" that we're getting married, it's the first I've heard of it. "Begrudgingly accepting" is a better term and Nick is right; ever since we told her, she's been quiet and rarely home.

Saul slaps the table. "How am I negative? Negative and practical are two separate things! You'd be wise to learn that, young lady!"

"O.M.G!" Andrea cries. "I can't take this tension!" But she sits down, shoves a bite of zucchini and walnuts into her mouth, and speaks while she chews. "Dad, tell us about the latest ploy by the government to bring down the working man. Please! Anything to change the subject."

Saul wrinkles his forehead and purses his lips. "I don't like your sarcasm. However, you should all know that Obama's parents were both actually Communists and he plans to turn the U.S. into a Communist regime."

"Dad, that's ridiculous," Andrea answers. "I just came from my AP US History study session, and we were talking about communism." She explains, they argue, and Nick leans over and whispers in my ear. "If you can't marry into this family, I totally understand."

I lean away, look at him with wide eyes, and Nick shrugs. "I mean," he mumbles. "I'll be heartbroken, but I will understand."

Chapter Five

As soon as Saul leaves Nick pulls me into the bedroom and pounces, smothering me with kisses and pressing himself against me. I don't exactly push him away but I do hold back a little. "Andrea will hear us."

"I don't care." He plants rough kisses along my neck and gropes me in a way that would feel inexpert if Nick didn't hold an advanced degree in my body. The pleasure is distracting. "I have to make love to you, now," he says, "or else I'll explode."

"Umm... isn't exploding the goal?" I laugh.

But Nick doesn't crack a smile. His lips are bright red and parted, and lust pools in his eyes as he tugs my clothes off. "God, I hope so," he says. He undresses me completely and I comply, happy to be what he needs. As we come together on our squeaky-springed bed, I'm able to forget about that horrible dinner; I forget about everything except the glorious feel of him.

Afterwards we're lying side by side and I'm breathing in the musky scent of his skin, when he murmurs something.

"What'd you say?" I raise myself up so I can see his face.

"I said I was sorry."

"For what?"

He scratches at his thick eyebrow, squints and breaks my gaze. "Where do I begin? I'm sorry for my dad and everything he said, I'm sorry that all I have to give you are my student loans..."

"Oh come on, Nick. I thought we were past all this."

"We're not. We'll never be past it." I search his face for a sign that he's joking but there's neither a twitch of his lip nor a gleam in his eye. "I wish I had more to give you and I'm incredibly flawed. You should know what you're signing up for."

"Okay... I'm pretty sure I do. Do you know what you're signing up for with me?"

He reaches over and turns on a reading lamp. The hard light does little to soften the growing darkness. "I think so. Unless there's stuff you're not telling me."

I pause for a second. There was a time when I didn't talk much about my past. Yes, early on Nick and I compared stories about losing our mothers and it was Nick's warmth and resilience that made me fall in love. But I kept my tragic college romance locked away, and I certainly didn't tell him about the string of guys that came later, ones I specifically chose because they didn't value me. I still feel the urge to shower when I think about my low standards and poor judgment but I'm even more horrified that several months ago, my tight-lipped stubbornness almost made me lose Nick. Since then I have resolved to expose my heart to him, every chance I get.

"I might have heard from Clara today."

Nick turns his body sideways, toward me, and props his head up on his elbow. "What do you mean?"

"I got this weird email." Nick raises his eyebrows, urging me to continue, so I do. "It was anonymous and it seemed like it could be from her. But it could have been from someone else too, like some crazy person who hated me on *The Holdout*. Whatever; I don't think it's a big deal. I mean, I changed all my passwords and everything so I'm really not worried, but it's a reminder of all the terrible choices I've made."

He kisses my forehead. "You're human, Rocky, and most of your choices have been good ones. After all, you're with me, aren't you?" He smiles so devilishly that I reward him with a grin and a kiss. Then he gently rubs my temple, like his love could alleviate all our fears and negative thoughts.

And maybe it can.

But that doesn't stop me from wishing I'm a better person; that no gap of integrity stretches between Nick and me, that our thoughts, actions and temperaments hold less of a discrepancy. And as I drift off to sleep, I'm struck with a realization. Whether or not Clara is responsible for that email, I should find her and apologize. I may be years too late and volumes too lame, but it's what a good person would do.

No. A good person wouldn't have anything to apologize for. But apologizing is what a decent person would do, and I can at least try to be decent.

Chapter Six

I google Clara for a current home or work address, but I can't find anything. I don't even know if she and Robert are still married. So I drive to her parents' home, and now I'm sitting in my car, which is parked along the curb, trying to work up the nerve to get out and ring the doorbell.

What will I say if her mother answers? *Sorry about that mishap several years ago, when I had sex with your son-in-law and ripped your daughter's heart out. Could you put me in touch with her so I can offer a real apology and appease my guilt?*

I lean my head against the seat-back and realize that's pretty much exactly what I'll say, leaving out the sex part. No need to go into specifics. *Be brave*, I tell myself, and I release my seat belt and open the car door.

My heart is beating so hard there's an echo in my ears, but I carry myself up to their front step and demand that my finger press their doorbell. For a moment it's just silence, and I think, *Oh well, I tried*, but then I hear footsteps and the door opens.

The face that greets me is older than I'd expected. I'm pretty sure it's Clara's mom, but it's like she's aged decades in the last few years. "Mrs. Thompson?" I ask.

She nods her head, which is sparsely covered with gray, thin hair. Years ago her hair was thick, wavy, and chestnut brown, like Clara's. "Hi," I stutter. "I don't know if you remember me. I was a friend of Clara's -"

"I remember you." Her firm voice doesn't match her diminished appearance and my head snaps back in shock. "You're Robin. You came for that awful Easter, years ago."

"Yeah…" I shift my weight, aware that she's not going to ask me in. "Sorry about that. Actually, that's why I'm here. You see, I'm engaged now, and I've been thinking about marriage and the sanctity of it and, well, I would love an opportunity to really apologize to Clara. I tried before, but I think it was too fresh, so, um…"

Mrs. Thompson rolls her eyes. She seems like I woke her from a nap and she just wants to crawl back into bed. "You're too late." She grips the doorknob, pulling the door close as if in protection. "Clara passed away a few months ago."

"Oh my gosh! I'm so sorry! What happened?"

"*I'm* sorry. I'm not feeling well today, so forgive me if I don't give you the details of my daughter's death." Then Mrs. Thompson yanks the door and slams it in my face.

Chapter Seven

I fill Nick in as we get dinner ready. "I can't believe she's dead," I tell him. "God, she was so young and talented. It's just awful, you know? And I wonder how she died. I mean, was it an accident, like with my mom? Or was it cancer, like with your mom? Or, what if..." I swallow back my words because they're too terrible to utter.

Nick is standing at the stove and he looks away from the food he's preparing, toward me. "What if, what?"

I stare at the apples I'm slicing. Little bits of core and seeds are splayed across the cutting board, victims of my knife. "What if I caused it, somehow? Like, she never recovered from her husband's betrayal, and that led to her death?"

"No," Nick states flatly. "Don't think that way. Even if that's what happened, it would be her husband's fault, not yours." Nick flips the grilled cheese sandwiches over with one hand and stirs chicken soup with the other.

I grip the edge of my kitchen knife like I'm using it as a weapon. "Yeah, but I still played a part in the whole thing. And I'm pretty sure that I knew he was married, you know? Maybe I just chose to ignore it."

"Even still, you didn't know he was married to her."

"Yeah, but -"

"But, nothing." Nick turns off the stove and puts sandwiches on our plates. "I get why you feel bad, but Rocky, you have to let it go."

I nod and separate out the sliced up bits of apple cores, which I then send down the disposal to their violent, pulpy end. "So who sent that email, if it wasn't Clara?" I say this as I flip on the disposal switch, raising my voice to compete with the grinding.

"Some crazy *Holdout* fan, most likely."

I turn off the disposal and the silence is like the end of a headache. "Yeah, I suppose." But my gut tells me something different, something I can't articulate. I decide not to try when I look at Nick, and notice that his hair is sticking up a little and he has a big crease between his eyes, a sure sign of his own bad day.

We carry our food into the living room and eat in front of the television. A new episode from the current season of *The Holdout* is on and Nick insists that we watch it. Most of it goes by in a blur because I'm still thinking about Clara's mom. But I pay attention when the contestants mention me and my historic freak-out at Island Assembly.

"I'm never going to live that show down." By now we're sitting on the couch, dinner dishes cleared and our feet resting on our blue crate coffee table.

An advertisement for their twin fashion survival-themed show, *The Standout*, pops up.

"That's the show you ought to go on," Nick says, pointing at the screen. "You'd be great. You could design dresses made from skittles or shower tiles, or whatever weird thing they'd make you do."

"Nope. I'm never going on another reality show again. It's you and me, here in Des Moines." I pat Nick on the knee to emphasize my resolve and use the remote to shut down the TV.

The front door slams and Andrea comes stomping in. She heads straight for her bedroom, but our house is small and the only route is through our cozy, cramped living room. "Why are you home so late?" Nick asks.

"What are you talking about? It's not even nine!" Andrea keeps walking, but Nick gets up and follows her down the hall. Her bedroom is only a few feet away and our walls are thin, so I can hear their conversation clearly, no matter where they stand.

"It's just after nine, but that's not the point. You weren't home for dinner and I have no idea where you've been."

"I was studying at Callie's house." Andrea's tone broadcasts her resentment; obviously Nick's interrogation is *extremely* unjust. "Is that okay with you?"

I pick at a loose thread in our couch cushion, while in the other room Nick is forcing himself into deliberately patient, measured breathing. "It's fine; I simply want you to let me know."

"Don't worry about it," she answers, and as I tug the stubborn cushion thread free, I can picture Andrea's eye roll. "I'm a big girl. Besides, you and Robin need your alone time."

Nick's voice is unyielding. "Come on, Andrea. We're talking about returning a phone call or a text. That's not too hard, is it?"

I yank out that thread, and now - oops - more threads come out and I just created a little hole in the fabric. Meanwhile there's a pause. Andrea must be struggling to find some argument against Nick's extremely reasonable request. After a moment she gives up the fight. "No, that's not too hard. Sorry."

He mumbles something, and as he comes back into the living room, I shift my seat so that my bottom covers the scene of the couch crime. Nick sighs and collapses into me. "I love my sister; I do… but is it wrong to wish that you and I were living on a remote island, just the two of us?"

"It's not wrong." I run my fingers soothingly through his hair. "You're so noble; it's really kind of hot."

Nick lifts his head and looks into my eyes. "What the hell are you talking about?"

"I'm serious. I love how you take care of Andrea. If my dad had wigged out after my mother died, neither of my brothers would have let me live with them."

"Well, Ian would have been too young. But you don't think Ted would have taken you in?"

There's a precarious moment of silence as we both consider Nick's hypothetical question. Then the bubble pops and we both laugh at the ridiculousness of the idea. Ted has never been the warm, cuddly sort. I push Nick off me, sit up, and pull both of us to standing. "He'd maybe have taken me in, but only if there was something in it for him."

"Have you told him about the wedding yet?" Nick asks.

"No, not yet." I guide Nick towards our bedroom, where there's no danger of Andrea disturbing our privacy.

"Don't you think you should?"

"I'll call him," I murmur, pulling Nick inside and shutting the bedroom door. For now, I can shut out the rest of the world as well, and that's all I want to do. As long as I'm here with Nick,

I am happy like a bride should be happy, one who doesn't question how the world works or what else, besides love, compiles her destiny. I have what I need.

Chapter Eight

A couple of weeks go by and I become consumed with wedding plans, which includes sketching out designs for bridesmaid's dresses. Isobel is tall and curvy, Lucy is petite, and Andrea is a beanpole. I'm at my studio, trying to design something that they'll all look good in, when my phone buzzes with a text from an unknown number.

You're too good in the bedroom.

Okay, strange, but not exactly threatening, so I figure it's some failed attempt at sexting, meant for someone else's phone. I delete the message.

Minutes later, another text:

You're also too late.

I start to respond with a *Who is this?* But I drop my phone. Every cautionary tale I've ever heard about cyberstalking ends with the same moral: Do. Not. Respond.

Instead, I call Nick. He picks up on the first ring. "What's up, Beautiful?"

Even the sound of his voice relaxes me. "Hey, remember a couple of weeks ago, when I told you about that email that could have been from Clara?"

"Yeah..."

"Well, it was sort of threatening, like she'll destroy my life if I don't dump you, and - "

"Wait." He inhales and I picture him rubbing his temples. "She threatened you? Why didn't you say so before?"

"Because, it seemed stupid and I didn't want either of us to worry. Plus, I changed all my passwords, so it's not like she can do anything. Plus, I mean, well, she's dead."

"Forward me the email," Nick insists.

"Sure, if I didn't delete it. But Nick, I'm getting these weird texts. You don't think the two could be related, do you?"

"I don't know. Forward them to me too."

"Okay."

I don't know what Nick is going to do about this, how he's going to protect me in ways that I can't protect myself. But that's the joy of being in a relationship; you can share your concerns so they dissipate and lessen in intensity. After I find the original email still in my inbox, and forward that and the texts to Nick, I'm able to forget about it all for a while. Why worry when there's nothing I can do?

But I do worry about letting my brother Ted know that I'm getting married. Nick is right. I need to contact him. So after work, once I'm home, I give him a call.

Ted doesn't even start with hello. "What?" he demands. His voice is dangerously cold, like licking a fence in winter.

But I make some initial small talk and then forge on. "I, um, well...I just wanted to let you know that I'm getting married."

"Good luck!" He punctuates this with a cynical laugh. Then he tells me that he already knew I was getting married because he saw Nick's proposal online. I wonder if he's hurt as he berates me for not keeping him in the loop. No congratulations, only recriminations, and once

I'm off the phone I can't stop crying, which only makes me angry, because who cares what Ted thinks?

He doesn't even want to come to the wedding.

I lie back on the bed and stare at the ceiling. Ted and I have never been close, so it shouldn't bother me that he doesn't want to come. I mean, sure, I could have invited him sooner, but everyone else who may come lives here in Des Moines and it's not like our wedding is going to be the social event of the season.

I turn my head and gaze over at the open closet, where the wedding dress I made hangs. It's a light pink cotton candy cloud, but I figure my wedding day is the only day I can get away with wearing anything like it. Nonetheless, Nick and I are trying to be practical, frugal even. The ceremony will be in the huge backyard at my cousin Monty's house, and I've been combing thrift stores for old china plates and champagne glasses. Dinner will be from pizza trucks, and Nick's music buddy, Dave, is going to DJ.

It's all so economically perfect, with the focus on economically, because Nick has tuition bills and although my clothing business does okay, I'm not rolling in it, not by any stretch of the imagination.

I take one last self-pitying sniff and get up. Nick has music theory class until 6:00, and I'm going to make dinner in our limited-counter-space kitchen, so that when he comes home, he'll be greeted by a piping hot plate of chicken Marsala.

About an hour later he walks in and dinner is pretty much ready.

"Hey," he says, smiling slightly. His hair is sticking up, which means he's been running his hands through it a lot, which means he's stressed. I kiss him on the cheek and he goes to wash up, comes back, thumbs through the mail (meaning bills), and then helps me set out the food.

"So I looked at that email and those texts," Nick says. "Did you get anything new since we last spoke?"

"No."

"And you changed all your passwords?" Nick brings out the salad but the serving spoon that rests inside the bowl falls, landing on the table with a thump. "Shoot," he mumbles, and puts the spoon back.

"Yeah, I changed my passwords. *Again.*"

There's a spot of salad dressing on the table and he dabs at it with his napkin, keeping his gaze on the task and not meeting my eyes. "Then you have to be fine."

"So I shouldn't break up with you?" I say it as a joke, hoping he'll laugh, and he does, but his laughter sounds empty.

"I mean, the other option would be to go the police," he answers.

Using potholders, I place the sizzling casserole dish onto the hot-plate in the middle of our table. The spicy smell emanates out, causing my stomach to growl. It's hard to think about anything as nefarious as cyber-stalking in the midst of such aromatic domesticity.

"I thought of reporting it," I tell him. "But I found this About.com article. It said that unless you can meet the criteria of being a victim, the police won't do anything. And since nothing else has happened..."

"There's probably no point," Nick finishes my statement.

I nod. "How was your day?" I ask, as we sit down to eat.

"Fine." He rolls up the sleeves of his oxford shirt then picks up his fork. "Class was fine. I showed a couple of houses this morning, so work was fine too."

"Then what's wrong?"

His lower lip juts out ever so slightly. "Tuition is due." Nick momentarily squeezes his eyes shut. "I don't know how that slipped off my radar. I mean," he clears his throat, "I can pay it. It will be fine, but..."

"But we'll have to cancel cable?"

He nods and takes a bite of chicken. "This is really good." His smile while he chews is genuine.

"Well," I say, "I had an interesting day. I called Ted and he..." I'm cut off by the ringing of my cell phone. Thinking it might actually be Ted calling to apologize, I grab it and see a number I don't recognize. But the area code makes my stomach flip flop.

"Who is it?" Nick asks.

"I'm not sure." I press answer. "Hello?"

"Hello, Robin?"

"Yeah."

"Hi! This is Quinton, from the network. How are you? It's been so long!"

Quinton was one of the producers of *The Holdout*. He first discovered me at a casting call at the Mall of America. "Umm, I'm fine," I say. "And you?"

"Great, great. I have actually switched shows. I'm now co-producing *The Standout*. You've heard of it, right?"

"Sure."

"Yes, yes, of course you have. You design clothes, after all. Well, Robin, we loved having you on *The Holdout*, and the viewers loved you too. And as it turns out, there's an unexpected vacancy on this season's *Standout*, because a contestant had to drop out for personal reasons. So we were thinking: why not get Robin Bricker in? America would be thrilled! What do you think? Filming starts next week and runs through the summer."

Nick stares at me as I listen to Quinton, and all the while my mouth goes dry as my palms grow damp. "I'm getting married in June," I say.

Quinton takes a measured pause. "Oh. Well, could you postpone the wedding? I'm not sure you realize how big this opportunity is.

Most designers would kill to get on *The Standout*, and we're willing to bring you on, without even seeing your portfolio or doing background checks."

"You already did background checks," I say, thinking about *The Holdout* audition process, which took months. That must be why they're "willing to bring me on" now. They need someone fast, and I've already passed all the psychological tests they need to administer.

"Who is it?" Nick mouths.

"Can I call you back?" I ask Quinton. "I need to talk to my fiancé about this."

"Yes, yes, of course. But Robin, call me back soon, okay? We need a decision and time is of the essence."

I hang up, take a look at Nick's confused face, and dive right in. Nick's jaw just hangs there while he struggles to respond. "Oh, you should go," he manages to say. "No question. Why wouldn't you?"

"Because filming begins soon. We'd have to postpone our wedding."

Nick's chest heaves up and down, but before he answers the front door opens and Andrea calls out. "Hello? I'm home."

We exchange a frustrated eye roll, but I force a smile into my voice. "Hey, we're in here! Are you hungry? I made chicken."

Andrea steps into the tiny dining room. "You mean you made chicken with pasta." She says *pasta* like it's *cancer*. "I wonder how much sodium and carbs are packed into one just serving." Still, she plops her skinny butt down and grabs the serving dish and a fork, forgoing the niceties of a plate.

"I thought you had rehearsal until late," Nick says.

"We got out early because everyone learned their parts so well." Andrea flips her long brown braid over her left shoulder and takes a bite.

She doesn't let a little thing like chewing keep her from continuing to talk. "Ms. Paulson says there's a violin scholarship I should apply for."

Nick dejectedly pushes the food on his plate around with his fork. "You'd better get a scholarship. It's not like Dad will pay your tuition."

"Well, I'll just go to Iowa State, like you, and I'll keep living here. We could even commute together!" Andrea smiles sweetly and I see Nick melt, like sugar in water.

"You're always welcome here, Andrea," I say. Nick obviously feels this way, and at least if it's coming from me, I feel some amount of power. But her face falls and I feel like I crashed her birthday party.

"Thanks," she replies, her voice flat.

I mean, I get it; her mother is dead, her dad's a disaster, and her sister is busy with her own kids. That leaves Nick, who has always belonged to her, but now that I'm here, her headliner status has changed to the opening act. Of course she resents me. My job is to not take it personally, to be the adult.

But I've always been the younger sibling, and I've never had a sister, so there's a learning curve.

"So Andrea," I say, "Nick and I have a tough decision to make."

"What?" She asks.

"I have a chance to go on that reality show, *The Standout,* but if I do, it would mean postponing our wedding."

Andrea squints at me. "When did you apply to be on it?"

"She didn't apply," Nick says. "They called her."

"But that's incredible! You have to go! Forget about winning! Just being there, and the connections you could make, and all the people who will know about your internet business—my God, Robin! It's like sitting on a gold mine!" Andrea's enthusiasm is this Jedi force and I'm unsure if she's genuine or leading me towards the dark side. Maybe she just wants me to disappear for a few weeks.

Nick, who is ignorant about his sister's ambivalence towards me, shrugs. "She's got some good points, Rocky."

"But the wedding…" A lump forms in my throat.

Nick reaches over and grabs my hand. "We can do the wedding any time. Andrea's right. This is too big an opportunity for you to pass up."

Chapter Nine

L ife becomes a flurry of contacting people: contacting wedding guests because the big day has been postponed, contacting the network because I'm doing the show, and contacting all my current clients with their completed projects, so I can leave without a heavy heart.

Today, after an epic stretch of long days at my studio, I take time off. It's raining and the sun is taking a nap, so I may as well too. Actually, I don't nap; I stare at the television instead. I've recorded a marathon of last season's *The Standout* and I take notes on what I learn:

One, never assume that a half-assed effort is enough. For example, in the opening challenge a designer draped a tablecloth into a toga dress and called it a day. The judges couldn't kick him out fast enough. Meanwhile, the person who wove a gown from straw coasters won.

Two, always listen to Jim Giles: He's the salt-n-pepper haired, impeccably dressed mentor who offers advice. His catchphrase is "You can do this!" But sometimes designers turn snooty and defensive at his critique. One lady snapped when Jim said that her military-style dress looked like it belonged to a drum majorette, and she made the shoulder pads bigger out of spite. She lost the challenge and was booted out.

Three, be a team player: One girl was swiping pattern pieces when others weren't looking. Then there was a group challenge using materials from a hardware store, and her job was to hot glue little metal washers all over this 1920s style ball gown. When the washers fell off and scattered across the runway, the other designers had no problem pointing their fingers at her. She was kicked out.

Four, when you do get kicked out, be gracious. The ousted designers almost never turn bitter. They always say something like, "Thanks for the amazing opportunity." Then they tearfully hug ex-supermodel/show-host Hilaire Kay as she bids them "au revoir."

I know I'll have trouble with that. My exit out of *The Holdout* was anything but smooth. I guess I've never been good at accepting defeat. So I'm mulling this over, resolving to change, when a draft of cool air accosts me, making me shiver even though I'm wrapped in a blanket on the couch. Andrea has opened the front door and she enters in a flood of stuff—the heavy book bag that's weighing her shoulders down, a dripping rain poncho, and in her arms, a mysterious package.

"So you don't have orchestra today?" I ask. "Or study group, or Key Club, or Young Farmers of America?"

"You know I'm not in Young Farmers of America." Indignation tings her voice as she drops her bag and sheds her rain gear.

"Right, right." I watch her wring out her soggy ponytail; the water drips onto the little piece of carpet that's underneath our little mail table, in the entryway that's right by the little living room. "What's with the package?"

She picks it back up and brings it over to me. "It's for you. The mailman left it outside."

I make an annoyed grunt. "He could have rung the doorbell. I've been here all day. Now whatever is in here is wet."

"Were you expecting something?" Andrea sits next to me.

"No." I look at the return address, and instantly I know. "It's from *The Standout*." I rip open the package, which isn't hard to do, since the cardboard is softened by rainwater. Inside I find two yards of muslin and an instruction sheet, which thankfully had been wrapped in plastic. *You must create a piece using only the material provided. It should represent who you are as a designer. You will show your look before the first day of filming. The two contestants whose looks are judged with the lowest score will be immediately eliminated.*

Andrea reads over my shoulder and gasps. "You mean you might not be on the show after all? After postponing your wedding and your honeymoon, they could kick you off before filming even begins!"

"I guess so." I run my hand over the coarse fabric, already imagining what I might design.

"They could have told you that before you agreed to hijack your life." Andrea doesn't grow indignant on my behalf very often, but I love it when she does. I place a soothing hand on her knee.

"That's not how reality television works. Signing on to do a show is like saying, 'No, please hijack my life, and throw in some massive road construction too.' All I can do now is start working." I turn off the television, get up, and prepare to go downstairs.

"Wait, don't forget about this." Andrea holds up an envelope. "It was sitting on top of the box outside."

She hands me the soggy piece of paper, and the only writing on the envelope is my name, ROBIN, in big block letters. "Somebody must have dropped this off," I say, "I don't think it's from the show."

"Well, aren't you going to open it?" Andrea looks up at me from the couch, her eyes big and expectant as she waits. But I just stuff the envelope in my fist and move away. "Later," I tell her. "I want to get to work."

But as soon as I get downstairs I tear open the soft, wet paper, and my nerves are already dancing around my gut. One glance inside confirms my suspicions; it's from my crazy hater-fan.

Yes, I know where you live. I'm starting to think you aren't taking me seriously. Well, you ought to, because I'm not about to stop.

Chapter Ten

A couple of hours later, Nick comes home. "You wouldn't believe the day I had!" Nick is practically radiating light, he looks so happy. He finds me in the kitchen, where I am heating up some leftover Asian takeout, and kisses me firmly on the mouth.

"What happened?" I ask.

"I got not one, but two big commissions today. And I got an A on my curriculum project." He wanders over to the piano, which sits in the only space in our house where it'll fit: between the "foyer" and the living room. I follow and plop down next to him, and watch as his fingers skim the keys, like they often do when he's in a good mood.

"I think things are going our way, Rocky." He smiles, gleeful. "You're going to be a big star in the fashion world, I'm finally making some money, and pretty soon we'll have the careers we both want. Everything is good right now. I can feel it."

I stroke his cheek, taking a moment to revel in his happiness and to admire the curve of his strong chin. "I'm sure you're right, but I'm starving. Let's eat dinner." I pull him up and towards the kitchen.

Later, after we've eaten and I've told him all about the new *Standout* challenge, Nick finds me in our dank little basement, where I have a sewing machine and a cutting-table set up. I'm sketching, playing with the fabric, and studying an art book of shadowy silhouettes. I hear the thump of Nick's feet, first on the ceiling above me and then descending the steps to where I am. I become aware of the time; it's almost midnight. "Hey," I mumble, clenching a pencil between my teeth, "I'm coming to bed soon."

He runs his fingers through his hair and it occurs to me that he's been wearing his stress-hair look a lot lately. "Shouldn't you wait until tomorrow to get started," he asks, "when you can be at your studio with the proper space and lighting?"

"I know, but I can't help myself. The moment I got this package my mind starting racing and I had to begin."

Nick comes and peers over my shoulder, shifting his gaze from my sketch pad to the book I have propped open. "What's this?" he asks, pointing to the book.

"They're fashion illustrations by Mats Gustafson. My mother really loved his work. She even had a first-run print by him."

Nick looks at the page that my book is open to. Like most of Mats Gustafson's work, this illustration is about shadow and light, and it's almost as if the page itself is illuminated. The model's face is impossible to make out; she's all contours and strategically placed smudges, but her body is dynamic yet relaxed, draped in billowy fabric that curves into a little black dress with a v-shaped neckline and a cinched waist. Behind her there's a feathery bustle that's as airy as a cloud. She's perfection.

"How are you going to make this dress out of two yards of muslin?" Nick asks.

"I'm not going make this dress," I say, pointing to the page. "I couldn't even if I wanted to. That would be fashion plagiarism. But I'm supposed to create something that represents who I am as a designer, and if I have to name one thing that's influenced me, it would be these illustrations." I leaf through the book. "This book was mom's before she died, and when I was a kid I'd grab a stool and pull it from our highest bookshelf, and stare at the pages, over and over. Something about them just mesmerized me. Finally, when I was around twelve, my dad said, 'keep the book, your mother would want you to,' and on rainy Saturdays I'd hole up in my bedroom, pouring over it, trying to make similar sketches of my own."

Nick runs his fingers over the page, as if he could feel some texture rather than the flat, glossy paper that's dulled with age. "Was it because you knew your mother loved these pictures?" He looks up and meets my eyes. "I mean, they're beautiful. But was the fascination with them because of her?"

"Maybe." I examine a sketch of a woman's face, simple in its construction. The lines of her hair, mouth, eyebrows, and chin are slanted with very little curve, but they're all emphasized with beautiful blemishes. "Every woman in here is so mysterious, like they're standing behind a sheer curtain, just out of reach. But they're all so striking too."

"Like how you imagined your mom to be?" Nick's voice is gentle.

I shrug. "Sure, if you want to get all Freudian on me." I snap the book shut, resigned to thinking about something else.

"Hey, I have to show you something, but please try not to overreact." I reach for the note, which earlier I'd shoved out of sight, into a drawer. I hand it to him and he reads, his eyebrows tensing and his jaw clenched.

"Did it just come today?"

"Yes." I scratch absently at my wrist and then I just start rubbing. I can tell that Nick's blood pressure has already spiked. This is just one more reason for Nick to be stressed, rather than happy, like he was when he came home this evening. Impulsively, I grab the note from his hands, tear it up and throw it away. Now it's nothing more than lonely shreds of paper in a metal wastebasket.

"I can't believe you just did that," Nick says.

"Forget about it, okay? It's stupid to even worry about."

Color creeps into Nick's cheeks, which I've learned is a warning sign of angry words to come. I'm bracing myself, but there rapid are footsteps coming down the stairs. "Nick!" Andrea's voice sounds throttled with tears and she's holding out her phone. "Nick, I just got the worst text ever from Dad. I didn't even know he knew *how* to text! Look!"

Nick shudders in confusion. He's trying to shake off one drama so there's room for another. "Let me see."

Andrea shows him her phone. "How can he be so mean?" Then she starts sobbing.

Nick wraps his arms around her, makes shooshing noises, and leads her upstairs. For a moment I consider following, but what would be the point? I'd rather feel useful, so I pick up my pencil and sketch pad and get back to work.

Chapter Eleven

The last time I saw my old sex-buddy Robert was years ago, when he ran from Clara's tree house, but this morning he texts me with a picture attached. He's sprawled on his bed, wearing nothing but a suggestive pose and a cowboy hat. What's even more horrifying is the message: *I've been thinking about you too.*

Never mind how uncanny the timing of his text is. No. My first reaction is repulsion; how could I ever have slept with a guy who'd send a picture like this? The hat is so tacky! But after I get over his poor taste in accessories, I realize there are multiple reasons to be disturbed. The feathered cowboy hat is just the tip of the pornographic iceberg.

What if Nick had been around when I'd gotten that text? How could I possibly explain it away? And why did Robert decide to text me now, with everything else that's been going on? It has to be more than a coincidence.

So I text him back. *Can we talk? Today?*

Sure, he responds, and sends me his work address.

His single-story office building is on the edge of downtown and I wait outside during lunch hour. At 11:52 I spot Mr. Tall, Dark, and Handsome walking out and heading straight for the Jimmy Johns. I step into his path.

"Hi, Robert."

His face has aged little in the last few years. Unlike Clara's mother, Robert seems virtually unchanged by tragedy.

"Robin." He smiles like he can picture me in nothing but a lacy thong. "Hey, how are you?"

"I'm fine, good actually. I'm getting married." I dig my heels into the sidewalk and hug my arms to my chest. The wind whips through me but I'll make it clear: I do *not* want him warming me up. "I've never been happier and I can't imagine EVER doing ANYTHING to jeopardize that."

"Congratulations." He tugs at his tie and the realization that I'm not going to sleep with him skips across his face. "Look, it's great seeing you but I'm pressed for time—"

"This won't take long. I'm sorry to hear about Clara."

Robert's finely chiseled jaw goes rigid. "Thanks. But we separated years ago, pretty much right after she found out about you and me. I mean, it's terrible that she's missing, but—"

"Missing? Her mother said she'd died."

"She's presumed dead." Robert's nostrils flare but his shoulders sag. "Clara was traveling in Greece and there was a bus accident. Lots of bodies were burned. It was pretty gruesome. But they looked at dental records and her body was never found."

"Oh." Images flood my mind: a bus tumbling down a cliff and erupting into flames, Clara's beautiful face melting in the ashes, or perhaps, Clara getting up and walking away?

Robert raises his hand as if to pat my shoulder but then he changes his mind. "Sorry, Robin. I really do need to go. Good luck with your marriage; I'm sure you'll need it."

He's almost become a blur on the sidewalk before his comment sinks in.

What a jackass.

"Hold on," I shout, and he stops. I've also caught the attention of several other passersby. "Why would you say that?" I jump to where he is. "I never even asked for an apology, so spare me the snide comments."

Robert's mouth twists in disgust. "Why would I *ever* apologize to you? You destroyed my marriage!"

"If that's how you feel, then why did you send me that picture?"

He does a double take. "Gosh, because I was looking to get laid? I mean, after you sexted me today —"

"What?" I yell, too angry to care if other people can hear. "I didn't sext you!"

He takes out his phone and scrolls down. "Then what's this?"

I read the crazy, dirty message, things I would never, ever say (to anyone but Nick), yet it's from my phone number. "I didn't send you this," I tell him. "I'm engaged!"

Robert barks out a sardonic laugh. "Okay, fine, rewrite history. I don't have time for this!"

"What are you talking about? I'm not rewriting anything!"

He had turned away again, but once more he circles back, this time stepping dangerously into my personal bubble. His voice is a fierce whisper. "You pretended like you didn't know about Clara the entire time we screwed around. You played the innocent very well, but it was always just a game."

I shake my head, stuttering. "No. No! I wasn't playing any games."

"You were BFFs with my wife! The signs were everywhere." Robert starts walking away, backwards down the street, and big guy that he is, people step to the side and make room for him. "So good luck, Robin! If you want to stay married, you'll need to work on the honesty thing. You can start by being honest with yourself."

Chapter Twelve

I call my cell phone company and they tell me to call the FCC. The FCC says they'll look into it, but I should contact whoever is getting spoofed calls from my number, and have them report it too. I know that Robert will be the opposite of helpful, so I send a text to all my contacts: *Hey, I have reason to believe that someone is spoofing my phone. If you get any weird, out of character texts that look like they're from my number, please let me know ASAP!*

I get a gleefully sarcastic response from my brother Ian, a concerned response from my dad, and confusion from my friends. That's it.

The more I think about it, the more I know that Nick was right to be annoyed last night. I never should have ripped up that note and destroyed the evidence. What compelled me to be so impetuous and self-destructive in that moment? Probably whatever compels me to be impetuous and self-destructive in every other moment, but enough. As soon as I get home I head directly to the basement. I plan to find that ripped up note, tape it back together, and show it to the police. I can report the texting and the email too, and maybe they'll actually help.

But the wastebasket is empty.

Anxiety attacks aren't really my thing, but I'm pacing around my living room, wringing my hands and breathing shallowly.

Calm down, I tell myself. *Redirect your energy. Things will be okay. You just need something to do.*

I know. I'll get a head start on my packing.

Soon I'm sorting through my dresser and I find all sorts of mismatched socks and worn-out pairs of underwear. I guess it's been too long since my last drawer-cleanse. No wonder I feel dirty.

I convince myself that this urge to clean is all about frayed undergarments and not about my lying-by-withholding the truth to Nick. But when I imagine telling him about Robert, all I can do is picture an avalanche, where I'm trying to catch one rock but get pummeled by a million more. I shove a mateless green knee sock into a garbage bag that's already almost filled and try to decide what I should take with me to New York.

Nick gets home, strolls into our bedroom, and takes it all in: the pulled-out dresser drawers, the pieces of clothing strewn everywhere, the large trash bag of irredeemable items, and an open suitcase with nothing in it.

"What's going on? And what was with that text you sent earlier?"

I spin towards him. "Did you empty the trash downstairs?"

He steps over a pair of woolen black tights that I haven't worn in years. "No. Why?"

"I was going to tape that note back together, but I went to look for it and it's gone. Do you think maybe Andrea took it?"

Nick laughs. "Andrea doesn't even empty the trash in her own room."

I rub my forehead, trying to massage away the tension that's pressing against my skull. "I need to get this cyber stalker thing settled before I leave town. Once I'm there I won't be allowed to use my phone or the internet and then I'll really be helpless."

"I'll help," Nick states simply. "Seriously, let me help you so you can just worry about doing the show."

I sigh in response, surveying the clothes strewn haphazardly around our bedroom and I'm more overwhelmed than ever.

"Have you even bought your ticket yet?" Nick asks. His raised eyebrows are his only comment on my mess.

"No. I still can't find a flight to New York that's not outrageously expensive." I pull out some lacy black panties that I bought from Victoria's Secret last month. Looking at them shouldn't make me feel guilty but I curl them up into a ball, which I shove to back of my drawer.

"You should fly into Philadelphia." Nick leans against the bed post. "I bet Philadelphia's cheaper. Plus, that way you could see Ted."

"Ted wasn't even planning on coming to our wedding. He and I couldn't be less close."

Nick comes over, places his hands on my tense shoulders and begins to knead. "All the more reason for you two to spend some time together."

"Easy for you to say," I grumble, but later I look into ticket prices for Philadelphia, and discover that of course, Nick is right.

Chapter Thirteen

The evening before I leave I'm packing my suitcase again, this time more productively, and I can't find my favorite long-sleeved black T-shirt. I look in the laundry room but there's only a fuzzy brown sweater that was flattened, left to dry, and forgotten about. On a hunch I go into Andrea's room, because she's picked through my closet before. As usual she's not home and the intrusion feels slightly criminal. Still, I switch on the light, and after searching through her laundry basket, under her bed, and finally in her dresser, I find my shirt.

I also find something else.

In between the folds of one of her blouses is an envelope with my name on it and it's just like the other one: same handwriting, same stationary, but no postmark or return address. It's already open so I slide out the sheet of paper and read:

Robin:

I've never known anyone more entitled than you. Women like you don't deserve nice guys, so leave Nick. If you don't, I'll make sure that he leaves you. Get ready.

"What are you doing in here?"

I'm startled by Andrea's voice and I whip my head around, not quite ready to face her but forced to do so, nonetheless.

"I was looking for my shirt," I hold it up, "and I also found this." I wave the letter with my other hand. "*Why* do you have this? And where is the other one?"

Andrea shrugs and slides onto her bed, taking out her phone in the process. "I dunno," she mumbles, and then makes herself comfortable and starts texting.

"Answer me, Andrea! Have you been writing these letters?"

She smirks and glances up, but barely for a moment. "Don't be mental. Why would I write you letters? We live in the same house."

"Maybe you don't want me to know they're from you."

She keeps texting, ignoring my presence. "Look at me!" I'm shaking with anger.

Andrea does as ordered and I'm shocked by the contempt in her eyes. "I found the letter on the front porch the other night when I came home," she says. "I was curious so I opened it, which I shouldn't have done, so sorry. But I decided it would be better not to show it to you. I figured you'd be too upset."

Umm, yeah. "That seems awfully, convenient, Andrea."

"Meaning?" she spits out.

"Meaning, this is the second letter you've found. What's with that?"

We hear the front door open and Andrea bolts toward our entryway. Nick doesn't even have a chance to take off his jacket before his sister flies at him. "Robin just accused me of stalking her!"

I follow close behind, and Nick throws his shoulders back, clearly feeling cornered, clearly wishing he could bolt. I'm practically pressed up against the piano and Andrea's directly in front of the coat rack. Nick struggles out of his jacket but he can't move enough to hang it up.

"I did not accuse her of stalking me!" I declare. "But she had another one of those letters in her room, opened and with my name on it."

Andrea spins toward me, her cheeks bright red. "Why would I open it if I had written it? Have you asked yourself that? And have you asked yourself why I would write something so awful in the first place? God! I was trying to protect you!"

I refuse to cave. "You should have let me see it! It's not your place to protect me!"

"Fine! Next time I won't!" Then Andrea bursts into tears, runs off, and slams the door to her bedroom shut.

Meanwhile, Nick looks like someone sucker punched him. "What the hell was that?" He finally hangs up his jacket, but with pained, migraine-like movements.

I hand him the note. "I found it in her dresser when I was looking for my shirt. She walked in, and yes, I asked her if she wrote it, but I wasn't trying to upset her."

"Well, you did upset her." Nick's voice is tight like a rubber band. "She obviously feels accused. I mean, how could you think, even for a minute, that Andrea would write something like this?"

I snatch the letter back. "Fine, take her side, Nick."

I head briskly towards our bedroom. Once there I fling open the lid to my suitcase and resume packing, though I'm too angry to do more than squish up pairs of underwear to make room for more shirts.

When Nick comes in he doesn't seem ready to apologize. He says nothing, crosses his arms over his chest and stares.

"I'm not sorry," I say. "Somebody has to be behind all this. Why not Andrea? It would make sense. If we get married she has the most to lose."

Nick's tone is soft when he answers, but it's a scary soft, a petting a ferret kind of soft. "Andrea's not capable of that sort of duplicity."

"Okay. If it's not her, then who is it?"

"Maybe the same person as who did this." Nick hands me his phone, and it's on Facebook. "Dave texted me earlier, to make sure I saw this." There's a photo, supposedly posted by me. It shows Robert and me together, it's time-stamped from the other day, and it captures the moment when Robert was looming over me and whispering insults. But the looks on our faces could be misinterpreted as desire. Underneath the photo is an update: "A lunchtime rendezvous with my married ex-lover. I love to be naughty!"

I sink to the edge of the bed, letting my shoulders slump in shock. "I didn't post this. Someone must have hacked into my Facebook account."

"That doesn't explain the photo."

My stomach rolls. "I met with him because I got this weird text and it turned out someone was spoofing my number, texting him with lewd messages..." I let my words trail as I take in the stoniness of Nick's face. He's not buying it. "Someone must have followed me, snapped the photo, and posted it. But who?"

"I don't know," Nick answers, "but it's not my sister."

I drop the phone so it's next to me on the bed. "Well good. I guess there's nothing else to worry about."

"I didn't say that." Nick ignores my sarcasm, picks up his phone, and puts it in my face, compelling me to look at that photo of Robert and me again. "Why didn't you tell me you met with him?" I bite my lip, trying to form an answer through my bottled up guilt. But Nick is impatient for a response. "It is him, right? That's Robert, the married guy?"

I look down at our worn shag carpet that was once sea green. If I was weaker I'd release a torrent of tears and they'd fall onto the now faded, now brownish clumps of yarn in a wet, salty mess. I want to grab Nick by the collar of his Oxford shirt and pull him close enough to feel his body heat seep through the fabric; I want to tell him that I need him to believe in me as much as I need his help.

But all I say is, "I just wanted to find out what happened to Clara. He said she was in a bus accident overseas and her body was never found. He didn't mention suicide."

"And you didn't think to tell me any of this?"

"I couldn't. I didn't know how."

Nick nods yes even though his face is screaming no. "I thought we were done with secrets."

"That's what you're worried about? It's okay if some wacko sends me threatening notes, follows me, takes photos and hacks into my Facebook account, but how dare I go behind your back or implicate your sister?"

A subtle shade of scarlet spreads across Nick's cheeks. "No, it's not okay, but at least I always gave you the benefit of the doubt! I never thought for a second that it was actually you who posted this on Facebook, but here you are, jumping to conclusions and being judgmental!"

"That's not fair!"

"You're not being fair when you keep things from me!" I think Nick is going to say more but he clamps his mouth shut, and then he runs his hand through his hair so that it's sticking straight up. "I should go talk to Andrea," he says. "See if she's calmed down."

"Fine. I should finish packing."

Nick opens his mouth again but no words come out. He just leaves our bedroom, shutting the door behind him.

Chapter Fourteen

In the empty bed with a laptop that's hell-bent on betraying me, I feel like a blank space, a vacancy. I don't know much about this sort of thing, but I contact Facebook, reset my password yet again, do a Google search on my name, and look at my settings. Nothing seems amiss, but I know that can't be true.

I call the police station and explain the situation to an officer. "You can certainly come in and make a statement," he says, yawning as he speaks. "But unless you know who's behind it there's not much we can do. There are too many people in real danger for us to worry about pranks."

"Thanks," I tell him, and then I hang up.

Our window is open and the curtains billow from a breeze, which brings a delicate scent of springtime. It makes me think about that feeling as a child, when school is about to get out for the summer. It promises swim lessons, sleep-overs, or if you're me, spending time alone.

I have always valued my independence, maybe a little too much, because months ago I had to learn to trust Nick or face losing him. But have I gone too far in the other direction? Do I rely on him so much that I've fallen into that needy-girl trap? I think of all my previous relationships, of all my superficial couplings after I lost my first true love. How, whenever a new guy was in danger of loving me, I'd find a way to sour things, self-destructing my way through serial monogamy. Then I met Nick. No more pushing him away. No more heart-wrenching loneliness in the fading light of a cold Sunday afternoon.

Unless I'm destined to always screw things up.

After spending over an hour in Andrea's room, their voices a low murmur, Nick comes back to our bedroom and sits down next to me on our mattress. I'm scouring my laptop, looking for some visible indication that it's been hacked. "Have you found anything new?" Nick asks.

"No." I literally give him the cold shoulder and edge away. "I called the police and they said I can make a statement if I want, but it sounds like a waste of time."

"Don't worry, okay?" He rubs my neck halfheartedly. "It's just some deranged nut job with an axe to grind."

I glare at him. "How can I not worry? That deranged nut job has it out for me, and now, apparently, for you too."

Nick raises one eyebrow at me and crooks his mouth, which he knows I find endearing. His hair is sticking out in multiple directions and the collar of his shirt is stretched out, and that just makes him look cute.

And that just makes me mad.

"Forget it," I tell him. "You're obviously not taking this seriously."

"I am too." He picks up my hand and kisses my palm. "You contacted Facebook and changed your password again?"

"Yeah."

"Good. I'll take that note to the police, first chance I get. And I'll keep an eye on your account activity. Leave a list of all your passwords, okay? That way, if there are any more hacking attempts, I can be on top of it." He squeezes my fingers, almost too hard. "It will be okay. I promise."

"So you're not mad at me?"

He shrugs. "Life's too short to stay mad." He gets up and moves my laptop, so it sits opposite us, on the dresser. "Besides, you're leaving tomorrow." Nick rejoins me on the bed and sits, leaning in. "We're not going to see each other for so long."

"Too long," I reply.

He cups my cheek in his hand and kisses me with such rawness that my heart could break. I kiss him back, even though I can't let go of my anger as easily as he can. I close my eyes, and as he lowers me down, pressing his weight against me, I feel him playfully tug on my earlobe. "Look at me," Nick says.

I do as requested, sure that in this moment we're both telepathic and he knows all my deepest wishes and darkest desires. Nick releases a labored breath, full of anxiety that's almost tangible enough to touch. His arms tighten around me and our bodies move to the same rhythm as we hold each other's gaze.

He tenderly removes my blouse, jeans, bra and everything else, so I'm exposed and vulnerable in his arms. "Now you," I murmur, tugging on his shirt, which, with my help, he quickly pulls up and over his head. Soon we're skin against skin, just a tangle of limbs, tongues and pounding hearts. We're coupled, moving in a passionate tempo and not looking away from each other, not until that moment of release, when his eyelids pull down, his head tilts back, and his entire body shudders with pleasure. I put my hand against his pounding chest, waiting for his heart rate to slow before I ask the question that's creating pressure inside my skull.

"Do you agree with that note?" I ask, now unable to meet his eyes.

"What?"

"Does a woman like me not deserve a guy like you?"

There's an interminable pause, where Nick stares at the ceiling and I feel like I've lost him. "Why would you ask that?" he breathes out.

"That's not an answer." I sit up. "I hate it when people answer a question with another question." I start gathering my clothing, desperate to cover myself. "It's like the worst avoidance technique, ever."

"I asked you to marry me! I tell you how I feel every day! I'm not avoiding anything; I just really don't get how you could be so insecure."

"Insecure?" I pull on my shirt and underwear and slide into my jeans. "Wow. I guess I didn't realize." My words are like spitballs as I stand over him and Nick nearly flinches at their impact. "Next are you going to call me clingy, or how about needy? Needy is a good one."

"Stop it, Rocky."

"You stop it."

He stands and faces me, naked as the day he was born. "No."

I turn away, but he steps in front of me, refusing to permit my escape. "Now who's avoiding?"

There are a million things I could say if I only had the words. However, Nick still has the power of speech and he's not letting this go. "Tell me what's going through your head. Be totally honest."

"No."

He winces, but I'd rather offer him nothing than tell him a lie. I can't admit to my biggest fear, that lies are all I know how to give him and that though I love him and make love to him with all my heart, I fear we are nothing more than strangers, because how can we, or anyone, be anything but?

"Come on Robin," Nick whispers. "Don't do this. Tell me what you're thinking."

I meet his eyes and in those brown flecks I see the Nick I know, the person I trust, the guy I'd do anything for. "That note just freaked me out," I admit. "She keeps saying that I'm a whore who doesn't deserve you, and I know it's crazy but if you hear something enough times, you start to think that it's true..."

"Robin, of course it's not true. Please don't ever doubt how much I love you. I need you to promise me that."

"I promise," I say, but already I'm wondering if it's a promise I can keep.

He hugs me and we hold each other, him stroking my back and me swallowing down tears.

Later, to calm the waters I apologize to Andrea and we all carry on like things aren't totally, bat shit crazy right now. Still, I don't sleep well and the next day I feel like one big flesh wound. Nick drives me to the airport and when he drops me off at curbside check-in, I grab him in a hug and refuse to let go. How can I possibly live without the spicy scent of his hair for two months? "Maybe I shouldn't go," I mumble into the side of his head.

Nick places his hands on my hips and gently pushes me away. "Rocky, you'll be fine." He attempts a smile, though I can tell it's hard for him. "I'm the one who will be a mess without you."

"Then I'll stay!"

"Don't say that unless you mean it." Nick looks down at his feet, scratching at his temple, while the smell of exhaust accosts my nose. "If I asked you to stay you'd be pissed. You'd feel smothered and you'd tell me this is something you have to do, for yourself and your career."

Cars are lining up, trying to find a place to park along the curb, and an airport traffic cop is circling, ready to enforce the three-minute parking rule.

"You don't know that for sure."

Nick sighs. "So you seriously don't want to go?"

I wonder if this is a moment I'll look back upon one day, and pontificate, *if only I'd chosen differently, would everything have changed? Would everything be better?*

"I'm sorry," I tell him. "You're right. I should go."

Nick rolls his eyes heavenward as his chest heaves. "Good! I promise I'll be here when you get back." He gives me a crooked smile that almost says I still own his heart. I kiss him, hard, sniffing as I pull away.

"You'd better get going, before you get towed." I tell him.

"Go get em', Rocky." Nick belts out the movie's theme song as I walk away, and I shake my head, laughing and crying at the same time.

"I love you!" I call out, suddenly aware I hadn't said it yet, and that this will be the last chance I have for two months, unless you count saying it on the phone while being filmed.

Nick doesn't hear me. The traffic has drowned out the sound of my voice, and his song is over anyway. He's gotten back in his car and he's ready to drive away.

Chapter Fifteen

Ted is waiting for me in baggage claim when my flight gets in. He looks as impeccable as ever; even when he wears jeans and a sweatshirt it's hard to imagine him eating a sloppy joe or trimming his toenails. His face is a little more lined than I remember, but he's athletic and trim, and with his blondish hair and confident gait, several women give him a second glance.

When I reach him we don't hug. "Hey, good to see you," he says, patting me on the shoulder.

"Thanks for picking me up."

"Sure." His nod is firm, and then we've run out of things to say. Luckily I have only carry-on luggage, so we make it to his car pretty quick. Once we're on the highway, driving toward his home in Buck County, I ask him about work, Tina, and the kids. His answers are all perfunctory and brief. When I can't come up with any more polite questions, Ted takes his turn.

"So, what's with that weird Facebook post?"

I wince. "You saw that?"

He shrugs as he hangs a left. "I got a notice that you posted a photo." The muscles that surround Ted's high cheek bones barely move as he speaks, and I wonder for the umpteenth time how it is that we're related. "It's a good thing, too. I never know when a coworker will bring up my famous little sister, so I like to be up to date."

I tug at the seatbelt, which is cutting into my shoulder. "I'm not famous. I mean, sure, I had my fifteen minutes, but that was a long time ago."

Ted laughs sardonically. "Says the girl who's about to do another reality TV show."

Ted will always think of me as a twelve-year-old, so I ignore being called a girl and heave a sigh. "No, you're right. But I didn't post that photo on Facebook. Someone hates me, Ted, and honestly, I'm sort of freaked out."

He raises his eyebrows but keeps his gaze on the road. "Why? Tell me what's going on."

It's rare for Ted to be solicitous; usually, if he listens to me at all, it's with half an ear and a fraction of patience. But right now I get the feeling that he actually wants to hear about my problems, so I tell him everything: about Clara and Robert and the notes and the texts, about accusing Andrea and her subsequent freak-out, about Nick's seeming lack of concern over any of it except Andrea's hurt feelings.

When I'm done I wait for Ted to respond, and when he doesn't I realize I'm holding my breath. Right as I exhale, he finally speaks. "Big things happen to you, don't they?"

"What's that supposed to mean?"

"Exactly what I said: you lead a dramatic life. Maybe Nick isn't unconcerned as much as he's overwhelmed." Ted raises one corner of his upper lip as if to smile, but settles on a smirk instead.

"That's kind of mean, Ted."

"I'm not trying to be mean. I'm just giving you my opinion." He pulls into his driveway and turns off the ignition. "And you have to admit that you're a drama-magnet."

And you have to admit that you're a schmuck. "Sure," I concede, though I'd love to give him a tongue-lashing.

Instead, we get out of the car and I follow Ted inside.

"You have a big day tomorrow," he tells me, as we walk through their shiny kitchen, towards the staircase to the second floor. "So unless you need anything, I'll show you to the guest room."

"Are Tina and the kids asleep?" I ask.

"Yeah, but you can see them in the morning at breakfast."

"Okay." I follow Ted upstairs, for he's already carrying my little suitcase. He leads me down the hall, right past a bathroom illuminated by a nightlight. When we walk into the guest room he flicks on a lamp, and I see there's a double bed with a navy blue spread pulled tight, and a nightstand with a digital alarm clock.

But those things are nothing, inconsequential at best, because my eyes are instantly drawn to what's hanging on the wall. I gasp. "It's the Mats Gustafson!" I walk closer, reaching out my hand though I know I'd never touch it. "She's so beautiful."

I stand there, revering the shadowy lady, hands in her pockets, clothes billowing behind her as she walks. Her chin is tilted down and she's wearing a large-brimmed hat, making her face indistinguishable. She's the epitome of casual grace and just looking at her makes me catch my breath. "I can't believe you have this hanging in the guest room. If it was mine, I'd put it where I could see it every day."

"Well, it's not yours," Ted snaps. "You got the jewelry, and you're lucky, because Ian didn't get anything at all. Quit mooching."

Stung, I turn towards Ted, away from the painting. "You know that's not what I meant."

Ted taps his feet like he has somewhere to be. "Sure, sorry." He shakes his head. "Tina spent a long time decorating our house and it was her decision to hang the painting here. I left it all to her, so

I couldn't exactly argue about this one little thing, you know?" He hangs his head and the blond highlights in his hair are illuminated. "You'll understand soon, now that you're getting married."

"Yeah..." I fish for more of a response but the words stick in my throat

"Well, if you're sure there's nothing you need, good night." Ted flicks some invisible lint off his polo sweater, straightens himself, and walks past me, closing the door behind him.

"Good night," I say to an empty room. Then I turn back around, and stare at the picture until my eyes are too tired to stay open.

Chapter Sixteen

The next morning, after breakfast with Tina and the kids, Ted drives me to the station and he even gets out, carries my bag, and walks me to the train. "You know which stop to take?" he asks.

His brotherly concern is so unexpected that I don't even laugh at the ridiculousness of it. "Yeah," I tell him. "Besides, there will be camera crews waiting, so my stop is sort of hard to miss."

"Right." He leans in and gives me an awkward hug, unsure of where his arms are supposed to go. "Well, good luck," he says as he pulls away. "I hope they like your outfit."

I glance down at what I'm wearing; it's another one of my upcycled creations. The fabric is from a man's spring sport coat: silvery, textured, and surprisingly easy to drape. I made it into a sleeveless tunic with little ruffles over the shoulders, a drop waist, purple stitching around the collar and hems, and tiny purple buttons running vertically. It's short and slightly longer on the sides than it is in the front and back, so I thought it would be perfect to go over a pair of worn Levi's 501s that I dyed a deep indigo and rolled up. The rip in the knee is totally organic.

"Thanks," I say, louder than is warranted. My bravado is coming out in a big, fake burst. "I'm totally ready for this."

Ted nods and looks at his watch, which reminds me of Nick, because other than Ted, Nick is the only guy I know who still wears a watch. "I should get going. I have a meeting at ten."

"Go ahead," I tell him. "I'll be fine, waiting here on my own."

"Of course you will. You're always fine, right?"

The question is without irony, and as Ted meets my eyes, he and I share a brief moment of connection. Ted and I don't have much in common, but I've always felt that if there was a zombie apocalypse, or a super flu epidemic, or a mass hysteria due to the evils of technology, Ted and I would somehow hang on while everybody else perished. It's just what we do.

"Right," I say with half a laugh.

"Yeah..." Ted blinks and looks over his shoulder, towards his parked car. "I should go. Call me after you get kicked off. You can stay with us for however long you need."

"Thanks, Ted."

He nods and walks toward the parking lot. Although his direction is clear, his steps are tentative. An unexpected surge of nerves makes my feet wobble against the sidewalk. I should just run and capture him in a reckless hug. We should just return to those days when we cared about each other.

Then he pauses before he gets into his car.

"Robin!" Ted calls, jiggling his keys as he stands by his Lexus. "Don't worry about your cyber stalker. I'm going to look into it for you. I know how to take care of stuff like this and it's going to be okay."

Stunned, I hear myself say, "Great, thank you."

He gives me a genuine smile, and for a moment my big brother looks like the shaggy-haired, late 80s teen he used to be, so long ago. My heart twists with nostalgia.

The train pulls in and I board. At first it's fairly empty, and I stare out a window as the scenery rushes by. But with each stop, more and more people board, and soon the space becomes tight. I take my copy of *Vogue* from my bag, flip through the pages and study the fashions, trying to incorporate all the latest, hippest trends into my mind before I'm in a high-pressure design situation. I'm analyzing how big the cuffs are, and how every blouse seems to be white chiffon or beige satin, and how they're all fitted with big lapels. Then I feel a set of eyes on me.

I glance around. The train pulls to a stop and several people stand. One of them is a woman in her early-thirties, with reddish brown hair secured in a low bun. She's wearing dark rimmed, square-framed glasses and she's pretty without being remarkable, like the best-kept mom at playgroup. But there's something familiar about her.

She shifts her gaze. Her eyes had been on her shoes, or the opposite wall, or on the door which was about to slide open, but now she looks squarely at me and my stomach drops straight into the earth's molten core.

It's Clara.

My body temperature skyrockets, blood rushes to my face, and I'm torn between saying hello and bolting out of sight. But bolting is impossible, and anyway the train doors open and she gets off before I can think of what to say. When the train pulls away I see her standing on the platform, watching me, and for a crazy, irrational moment I fear she'll lunge forward, jump back onto the moving train and track me down.

But it can't really be her. I'm nervous and emotional and my mind is playing on tricks on me. *Get a grip*, I tell myself. *Now is not the time to fall apart.*

Chapter Seventeen

Getting ready for the first *Standout* fashion show is a flurry of activity and over-stimulation. I should feel awed, star-struck, and intensely competitive. And I do. But every so often the image of Clara, with her silent accusations scorching me on our morning commute, disorients me all over again.

"I love the dress," says my model, Zelda. She reminds me of Andrea and she looks just as young. Her huge, doe-like eyes make her seem innocent, and unlike all the other models here, her brown hair is in a pixie cut.

"Thanks." I inhale, breathing in the scent of steamed fabric and deodorant. "Why are all the other girls wearing their hair back, in buns?" I ask.

"Didn't they tell you?" Zelda arches her eyebrows at me.

"Tell me what?"

"The entire season is a ballet-theme. Most of the models here are actually ballet dancers."

"Oh." I look around the room; all the designers seem self-assured as they fit their models into dresses that look like something from the extra-expensive section of Bloomingdales. Does everyone here know more than me? "What do you mean: a ballet theme?"

"You know, like all the challenges will be based off of famous ballets, with their themes of *passion and betrayal...*" She keeps talking, but passion and betrayal reverberates in my head. "...and we're supposed to really move in the outfits you design. Maybe even dance in them."

"Oh." I'm trying to tighten a seam so it's more closely fitted to Zelda's waist, but my fingers feel like they're covered with cotton and so does my brain. "Well, at least now I understand why you're so graceful."

Zelda blushes at my compliment but I'm being sincere. Her limbs don't simply move; they levitate. She stands up straight and I drape the halter dress over her body.

I dyed the muslin a charcoal grey, to mirror the shadows in a Mats Gustafson drawing from my Mom's book. I also took a portion of the fabric and beat it, stretched it, washed it a dozen times, and then beat it and stretched it some more. I dyed it a lighter shade of grey, so it would look transparent, like an extra layer floating over the base of the dress. That extra layer also crisscrosses in front, and turns into a knee length train in back.

I step back to assess it.

"It's gorgeous," Zelda says.

"Really? You think so?"

Zelda nods fervently. "I've never liked anything I've put on so much. Of course, I mostly wear leotards, sweatpants, or tutus, but I totally think you'll win."

"Okay, designers!" Jim Giles' sudden entrance into the workroom is punctuated by his officious, well-projected voice. "It's time. Line your models up."

I gulp and let my hands flit, because they're unsure if they ought to be adjusting the dress or clawing their way to safety. I settle on stretching, reaching up and out, so I can almost skim the fluorescent light beams that hang from the ceiling. "Thank you," I say to Zelda, and I try not to puke all over the workroom floor or into the camera lens that's pointed at us. "You're going to be a great model."

Zelda takes a steadying sigh, and we walk together, past the workroom's purple walls and towards the bottleneck of models and designers trying to get through the doorway. "I've actually never modeled before," she says. "I'm sort of nervous. All those cameras, and standing up there in front of Hilaire Kay..."

"Be brave, Zelda." I myself am melting with fear so I'm not cool enough to manage her pangs of doubt. I will pretend I am someone else, someone who has studied in New York, someone who knows the difference between Cashin and Cassini, someone who didn't have to postpone her wedding and risk so much, just to be here.

I will not get sent home before the show even begins.

I will be a winner.

Chapter Eighteen

Zelda enters the runway and my dress floats exactly as I wanted it to. She's the beautiful woman behind a sheer curtain, just like the Mats Gustafson picture: the essence of light and beauty without corruption.

Then Zelda's toe snags against the floor and she falls: ripping my dress, my hard work, and my aspirations, all with a gut-wrenching shred. There's a collective gasp followed by a moment of stunned silence and the music is turned off. "Are you okay?" Hilaire asks her.

"Fine," Zelda mutters as she stands back up. "But I ripped the dress." She cups her hand over her eyes, trying to find me in the audience against the glare of the stage lights. "I'm so sorry, Robin."

"Robin!" Hilaire demands. "Get on stage and look at the dress. Is it too damaged to be judged?"

I shuffle from my seat and onto the walkway. I imagine my dress as a roadkill squirrel that I just ran over with my car. I don't want to see but I must.

"The straps are torn," I tell Hilaire, "and there's a rip in the back. The train is all messed up."

"So you're saying it is destroyed?" Hilaire asks.

"Umm..."I falter. "I don't want to forfeit, if that's what you're asking."

"But we can't judge a ripped dress." Hilaire crosses her arms over her chest like she's been insulted.

It is hard to be a winner with a ripped dress. With a ripped dress, I am just me, posing as a designer in my purple jeans and thrift-store tunic. With a ripped dress I am still from Des Moines and I never went to fashion school and I'm nearly old enough to be the mother of the youngest contestant here, had I been a teen, no a tween, mom. With a ripped dress I am waylaid in defending myself because I have momentarily lost my voice.

But Zelda surprises me by speaking. "It's not Robin's fault! Fire me if you want, but you can't hold this against her. That isn't fair."

Hilaire looks at Zelda like she's the roadkill. "You are a model. Models do not talk." Now Hilaire addresses me. "Your dress should be strong enough to endure a fall."

Suddenly my voice returns and it's chauffeured by my temper. "But it's made from muslin!"

"Still, if your stitching was strong, this would not happen."

"I disagree." I tilt my chin. "I want ten minutes to repair the damage, and then you can judge me however you want." I square my shoulders and using false bravado, stare down at Hilaire and at the other two other judges.

Hilaire narrows her almond shaped eyes. "You give me permission to do what I am already able to do, whenever I wish." But she then turns her head, lowers her voice, and confers with the other judges.

"Fine." Hilaire says. "We will take a ten minute break. You can use that time to mend the dress, and afterwards, your model will walk down the runway again."

"Thank you," I say, doing my best to sound reticent. I grab Zelda's hand and pull her to the workroom. Within an instant I am assessing the damage, sticking pins in my mouth and then into Zelda.

"Okay, take this off," I tell her. "I need to use a machine."

"I really am sorry," Zelda murmurs.

I shake my head and the words just fall out. "This morning my brother was like, 'call me after you get kicked off.' He was trying to be nice, but after I thought about it, I'm annoyed that he thinks so little of my chances." I lower the dress straps from her shoulders and then I'm tugging it all the way off her. Zelda crosses her arms over her chest in modesty. "And I almost didn't come at all, because my life is like a Lifetime movie lately, and my fiancé is all, 'you'd be pissed if I told you to stay,' so of course I came even though I'm paranoid that a dead woman is following me. And now Hilaire hates me and I postponed my wedding. So I can't get kicked off first. I just can't."

"I get it." Zelda says. I take my eyes off the stitching for a second and look at her face instead. "I mean," she wavers, "I get what it's like to feel pressure, to not know if you're making the right choice, like everyone is judging you and everything is at stake. So I won't mess up again. I promise I'll make your dress float down the runway exactly how it's supposed to."

"Thanks," I tell her, but I'm more grateful that she listened to my tirade than I am for her promise. "Come on, let's put this back on you. There's not much time left."

I refit Zelda into the dress and practically push her back onto the runway. She makes it down and back, and both my dress and my model survive without falling apart.

After every designer's piece has been seen, Hilaire and the judges tally the scores. Then they call all the models onto the stage, turn up the house lights, and tell the designers to stand next to their models.

"You did great," I say to Zelda, patting her hand.

"If I call your name, please step forward," Hilaire says. "Amos. Simon. Casey. Nadia. Elliot. Tara." Half of the designers have now stepped forward, and the other half, including me, are still in the back. Hilaire pauses and suspense drips from the air. "If I called your name, congratulations. Your score was high enough to qualify you to be a contestant on this season of *The Standout*."

The chosen six let out a whoosh of relief and they are excused back to the workroom.

Once they're gone, Hilaire addresses those who are left. "The rest of you represent the highest and the lowest scores. One of you will win this challenge, and two of you will be out."

Chapter Nineteen

tanding up there, waiting for Hilaire to declare my fate, is like
ingesting an acid that eats away at my soul. I can speak from experience on this, because once I had food poisoning, and the stomach
cramps that followed made me want to die.

But anyway, I don't get kicked out.

Only because the judges decided that two other designers were
more of a disaster than me. One couldn't seem to muster the enthusiasm required for the show. He shrugged when Hilaire asked him why
he made a shapeless sundress as his signature look, and his garment
swathed him in defeat. The other designer had "taste issues." Her
ensemble barely covered her model's crotch and she had actually tie
dyed her muslin. Hilaire said it was part Grateful Dead, part "I Wish I
Was Dead."

So, hooray, I'm officially on the show! But I sort of wish I could
go home, curl up into a ball, and mumble all my woes into the curve
of Nick's neck. I'd tell him that I was put on the bottom, because
the "crafting" of my dress was "poor", how Thomas Craig, one of
the judges, joked that my dress looked like the apron for a sexy maid
costume, and the other judge, Evie Messina, said the execution was
stiff. Meanwhile, Hilaire questioned my vision, implying that I don't
have one.

And I wasn't allowed to defend myself or tell them my dress looked a million times better before it was ripped, because that would be making excuses while I'm supposed to be grateful for their critique.

Now I'm in the apartment that I share with three other contestants: Nadia, Casey, and Tara. Everything is shiny, like living in an Ikea showroom, with white walls and furniture and red accents. There are no televisions or computers allowed, and the bedrooms have two single beds each. I'm bunking with Casey, who is twenty-five and from LA. She strikes me as the bohemian, granola type.

Casey unpacks her bag, which is full of soft, flowing blouses with cords that have little bells tied at the end, and skirts that will touch the floor when she wears them, because they're long and her legs are short. "Where did you go to design school?" she asks in a husky, musical sort of voice that reminds me of an oboe.

I try to make myself comfortable and recline on the bed but the mattress is stiff, and there's only one thin pillow. "I went to Hoyt College, in Iowa, where I majored in theater. I worked in the costume shop all through school. But basically, when it comes to design, I'm self-taught."

"Ahh, that's awesome." Casey hangs a paisley blouse in her closet. "Good for you."

Gabe, the cameraman, is in the corner of our small little bedroom, probably looking for some conflict that can be blown out of propor-tion through clever editing. I smile. "What about you, Casey? Where did you study?"

"California College of Arts, in San Francisco."

"Wow, I bet that was great."

"Yeah, you know." The musicality of her voice turns nasally. "It was the right move for me, learning design theory. I want my work to have a strong foundation before I venture off into my own style." She's done unpacking, so she sits on the bed and a smile teases the corners of her mouth. "I know that's not for everyone. Some people are better off, just doing their own thing. But we can't all be celebrities, right?"

It takes me a moment to catch her drift. I'm the celebrity here, which supposedly affords me the option of ignoring fashion fundamentals. And while my first instinct is to get annoyed, Casey has a point.

I wouldn't be here if it wasn't for my reality-show past.

"Well, I almost got kicked off today, and I'm really not much of a celebrity, so I wouldn't worry about me having any sort of advantage."

"Oh! No, I wasn't." She laughs.

Should I turn snarky? My reality-show past tells me no. No snarkiness allowed.

I get up to use the bathroom. After I splash my face with cold water and rub some of Casey's stress-relieving essential oil on my temples, I come back out. Gabe has lowered his camera and he and Casey are laughing about something. They turn and their faces fall when they hear me enter the room.

Clearly their joke isn't intended for me. I'm only surprised at how quickly and completely I feel like an outsider.

The next morning our call is at 6:30 AM. Jim and Hilaire meet us at the Metropolitan Ballet, where there is a special, ten minute performance for us of *Swan Lake*.

A beautiful ballerina in a white tutu dances mournfully while a misty background hangs behind her. She twirls and stretches, defying normal human movement, and a guy in black tights and a white satin tunic comes out and joins her. He lifts her over his shoulder, so her back is pressed against him and her arms are toward the ceiling. They spin like figure skaters, only the ice is merely in our imagination. But the longing they communicate is also icy, like they want each other but know it's impossible.

Or at least, I think that's it. I could really use some coffee.

The whole thing is being filmed of course, but the cameras are focused as much on us, sitting in the audience, as they are on the dancers. When the pas de deux is over, the prima ballerina curtsies and we jump to our feet in a standing ovation. Then Jim Giles, who is dressed in an impeccably tailored light grey suit, and Hilaire, who is wearing a black tutu dress (which she can totally pull off) enter the stage.

"Bonjour à tous!" she cries, "Good morning, designers! And congratulations! You have all survived the initial challenge and we officially welcome you to the show." She gestures toward Jim. "Jim, would you like to tell them why this will be such a special season?"

"Thank you, Hilaire. I would love to." When he speaks I'm reminded of my middle school science teacher, Mr. Monroe, who was known for his ability to say *Uranus*, patiently and repeatedly, without ever cracking a smile. "This season, *The Standout* is doing something special. Every challenge will be centered on a famous ballet, like *Giselle*, *Swan Lake*, or *The Firebird*, just to name a few."

"Hold on!" Hilaire shouts to the cameramen and they all poke their heads out from behind their heavy equipment. "I don't think the designers look amazed enough." Now her focus plows into us. "Designers! This is incredible news. Respond to it! Ah! D'accord! Okay!"

We're all packed into the first two rows of the audience, and Gabe the cameraman comes and shoves his lens within spitting distance of my mouth. But I don't spit; I smile like I've just been told that we're skipping winter this year.

"All of the garments you construct must be practical for a dancer to move in," Jim says. "Your model should be able to stretch, or even fall, and the garment will withstand it." He looks over at me and I laugh as if we're sharing an inside joke.

But on the inside, I'm breathing fire.

"Your first challenge will have a *Sleeping Beauty* theme," Jim continues. "We don't mean the Disney version, but the classical ballet. You all have your Samsung tablets, and we're giving you thirty minutes to research and sketch. Then we will go fabric shopping at Metaphor. Any questions?"

"Jim?" Casey raises her hand. "So we're supposed to pick a character from *Sleeping Beauty* and design a gown they can dance in? I'm not sure I understand."

Jim weaves his fingers together, unflinching in his absolute composure, just like Droopy Dog. "You are letting yourself be inspired by the ballet."

Casey cocks her head in question. "I don't understand."

"Well, we can't spell it out for you Casey." Hilaire's tone is not as patient as Jim's. "You must think abstractly, comprendre?"

"Umm, I guess?" Casey's voice lilts and I'm guessing she doesn't understand.

But I do. And I can't wait to get to work.

Chapter Twenty

It's late in the evening and I feel like the exclamation point at the end of a panicked sentence. It's just a dress, I tell myself. It's not your future; it's just a dress.

"Robin, how are you?" Jim approaches my work station. His salt-n-pepper hair is slicked back and today's suit is navy pinstripes with wide lapels and a dark purple tie. I wish I'd designed his outfit instead of this garment, which is half nightgown, half cocktail dress.

"I'm okay," I answer.

"What have we got going on here?" Jim points to the dress dummy that is wearing my *Sleeping Beauty* look.

"Well," I say, projecting false confidence, "I was thinking about how Aurora is woken up by the prince's kiss, and that's what I'm going for with this look: an awakening."

"Uh huh." Jim fingers the midnight blue satin that's the base of the strapless bodice, but over it is a long-sleeved teal chiffon blouse, with wing-like draping. There's also teal chiffon as the lower layer of the skirt. "I like the teal," he says, "it's very subtle. And the fit is lovely: the combination of tight and loose is a great aesthetic." He looks up at me and tilts his chin. "Robin, I totally think this works."

"Oh my God, thank you!" I'm so relieved that I almost start to cry. "I've been so scared, after the last challenge..."

Jim waves one hand dismissively. "Oh, please. That whole thing was ridiculous. Your dress was lovely. It's not your fault your model tripped and fell. And what muslin dress is going to survive that?"

I feel like I'm swallowing air. "Really?"

Jim leans in and whispers in my ear. "You didn't hear this from me, but Hilaire was against your being added to the show. She said she wants designers, not reality TV stars. I said you are a designer, but she can be... well..." Jim straightens up, steps away, and speaks at his normal, nasally pitch. "Well, hang in there, Robin. And good work with your dress! You can do this!" He pats me on the arm to be reassuring, but suddenly there's a pound of gravel in my stomach and I don't even know why.

I need a break.

I leave the workroom and go outside, to the rooftop terrace. The air is crisp and the evening skyscape is millions of tiny lights. Although I'm not up very high I still feel small and unsteady, and just gazing at the stars gives me the sensation that I could fall. But I imagine that Nick is standing in our backyard right now and he's looking up at the same sky. I hope that he's missing me and I hope that he isn't. He should be both happy and miserable, just like me.

I think about how I was here in New York many years ago, with a different love, dreaming of a future with him in this very city. And for years I believed I would never recover from the loss of him or from the loss of that dream. But I did, and if I can do that, I can go a few weeks without Nick. I can trust that he'll take care of my cyber-stalker for me while I'm gone, that I can focus on winning while I'm here, and that once I get back we'll figure out everything else.

I go back inside, resolved to finish the straps of my dress before it's time to go. But as I approach my work station I see that someone has been messing with my Samsung tablet, which all the contestants were provided with as a perk for doing the show. Mine had been put away in my desk drawer but now it's sitting out and the power is on.

The internet has been accessed. That's totally against the rules and I'm about to exit out before I get caught, but too soon I'm hit with a sickening realization: my tablet is on something called *The Rotten Robin Website*. There are multiple unflattering photos of me and my cheeks sting as I read the descriptions:

Robin is an adulteress: She slept with a married man and now she's cheating on her fiancé.

Robin is a whore: Do you know how long her "list" is? It's well into the double digits and I can give you the names to prove it!

Robin is a cheater: She cheated on *The Holdout* and she's cheating right now, while filming *The Standout*.

Robin is a liar: She lied about her past, she's lied about her present, and she's lying about her future. Does this girl ever tell the truth?

Then there's this tirade of made up accusations, but made up or not, shame blisters my lungs as I try to breathe.

And that's not even the worst of it. At the bottom there's some video footage.

I don't want to press play but my finger acts independently of my brain, and it touches that little arrow. I see a montage of carefully selected moments: me on *The Holdout*, saying "I'll do anything to get ahead." Me, making out with Grant (who I actually trusted) on the beach. Me, on a talk show, saying, "I did what I had to do. Cheating and lying were just part of the game."

After that there are clips from plays I've been in, some dating all the way back to college. Who had access to my computer so they could post these? There's me as Karen in *Speed the Plow*, admitting I only had sex with a guy so he'd green-light a movie; me, taking off my blouse and making out with the guy; me in more clips from more plays.

I never realized how slutty my characters were.

But they were just roles I stepped into. Maybe it was typecasting, but I have been misrepresented and I don't know who to blame. I could blame Clara, or Andrea—hell; I could blame Nick for not taking care of things like he said he would. I could even blame the Internet or anyone who uses the Internet for more than reading NPR's headlines or Skyping with their grandchildren.

That reminds me of my dad. God, what if he sees this?

The way it's put together, it all looks real and I look like a terrible person. And then there's the grand finale photo montage: me in a bathing suit, me in just a T-shirt, me with my hair all mussed and my lips pursed—a selfie that I sent to Nick one evening when I was anxious for him to get home.

"Robin, what are you watching?" Amos, the designer whose work station is next to mine, startles me out of my trance. I close out the screen and slap my tablet's cover shut.

"Nothing!" I lean against the work table and pretend my insides don't feel pulverized. "Hey, did you see anyone come over and mess with my tablet?"

He shakes his head no. "But you should be careful. If they catch you on the internet you could be in big trouble. I'm surprised you were even able to access it."

"Yeah, well, I didn't. Somebody else did!" Amos flinches at my indignation but the smile never leaves his face. He gently tugs at the tape measure draped around his neck as he responds. "Okay... I swear I didn't see anyone come over."

Meanwhile, Gabe the cameraman has approached and now we're being filmed.

I remember myself and paste on a smile. "Okay. I guess it's just a mystery."

I need to think this through. I need to come up with a plausible explanation for how someone who is neither Nick nor Andrea got access to these photos and videos. They're the only two people who would be able to access them, but I can't think that it's Andrea. And it certainly can't be Nick.

So until I have a workable theory, I can't mention a word, not to anyone, not unless I want to walk away from the show right now.

With trembling hands, I get back to work. Even as images of Clara flash through my head I shake them off. *Clara is dead*, I tell myself. *Some bully is trying to get to you.* But that still doesn't explain who, or why, or how.

I'm not allowed to call Nick. I'm not allowed to call anyone, or use the internet, or investigate this stupid website. So I work on my dress, even though every time I look at the straps, all I see is a noose.

The next day we're picking models. All the designers sit in their stadium seats in the runway room and the models are made to stand on the stage. They all look so cold, dressed in their identical black slips, even as the bright stage lights shine on them from every direction.

Hilaire picks a designer's name from a bag and then the designer gets to choose her model. It's like waiting to get picked for teams in gym class, only a million times worse. Zelda's chest caves a little more each time a designer doesn't choose her, because two models will get the boot today.

When Hilaire reads my name, I don't hesitate. "I'll stick with Zelda."

I give Zelda a wink but I doubt she can see it. She walks off stage, going out of her way to sit with another one of the chosen models who looks about her age. Zelda goes in for a fist bump and the other girl returns the gesture, but with a plastic smile. As soon as Zelda looks away, the other girl shares an eye roll with the model sitting on her opposite side.

After all the models have been chosen and the two rejected girls walk gloomily off stage, we're released into the workroom, where we can fit our models into their dresses. I'd already fit my dress to Zelda anyway, which motivated me all the more to choose her. And the dress conforms to her body like a fantasy.

"Okay," I tell Zelda. "Do a pirouette or something. You're supposed to be able to dance in this, so let's test it out."

Zelda chews on the corner of her mouth for a moment. "Are you sure you want to risk it? What if I fall and rip it again?"

"You won't."

"But what if I do?" She wraps a short lock of hair around her finger. "I can't believe you even chose me. I'd have picked someone else."

"Don't be silly. I want a model who is on my side, who will make my dresses look fabulous. That's you. Now do a pirouette."

Right now the workroom is packed with designers and models/dancers, running around like their lives depend upon a garment, but Zelda claims a spot and does a perfect pirouette, twirling around four times before her raised foot meets the floor. She stretches her arms out and over her head, and the chiffon flaps like a butterfly wing, which is exactly the effect I wanted.

"That was perfect!" I cry. "How does it feel?"

"Awesome," she answers, "like I could fly." She's smiling so hard I could squeeze her cheeks. Zelda looks across the room, sees that girl she was sitting next to before, and gives her a broad wave. The girl waves back but with about a fifth of Zelda's enthusiasm.

"So you know her?" I ask.

"That's Julie, my best friend. We auditioned for the show so we could do it together."

"Oh. Cool." But if that girl is Zelda's best friend then Zelda must be some ballet version of Charlie Brown, always letting Lucy pull the football, or toe shoe, away.

"Okay, designers!" Jim Giles enters the room and calls out. "It's time for the runway. Let's go. You all can do this!"

This time I am chosen as one of the possible winners of the challenge. However, Thomas Craig and Evie Messina like my dress better than Hilaire does.

"It is pretty, yes, but I do not see a vision." Her French accent makes this, and everything she says, sound like it's from an art film.

"Well, my vision was an awakening. *Sleeping Beauty* is awakened by love, and the colors and the shape are supposed to represent going from darkness to light, from paralysis to movement."

"Oui, I get that," says Hilaire, and her voice softens in a nuanced way. "What I do not see from you is a unified vision. I do not look at your garments and understand why you are here." She waves her hands expressively as she speaks. I can understand why people respond to her; everything she says and does is passionate.

"But this is only the second thing you have seen from me."

"Two garments should be enough!" Hilaire's perfectly proportioned face twists with commitment. "I do not know, so you must tell me. Robin, what is your goal here?"

"I..." I could tell her that I'm content to run my online business of upcycled clothing from Des Moines for the rest of my life. Maybe I'll start my own fashion blog; maybe I'll start a side-business of wedding and prom dresses. I could admit that I just want visibility so I can stay comfortable in my own little corner of the world.

But every other contestant here is dying to show at New York Fashion Week, dying to network with famous designers, dying to start their own line that will be featured in *Vogue*. "I'm here to learn and grow,"

I finally tell her. "I never went to design school but I love fashion and I want to be as good as possible. So when this opportunity came up I couldn't turn it down."

"Ah yes," answers Hilaire. "You want to learn. That is not a bad goal. But *The Standout* is not design school, Ma Cherie. If you want your work to truly stand out, you must decide on your real goal and you must show it in your work."

I nod as if I understand how to do that. "Thank you."

Then Hilaire turns her attention towards Casey, whose score was on the bottom. Apparently her white dress looks like a dance recital reject and Casey's chin quivers as she tries not to cry. But in the end, the winner is not me and the loser is not Casey, and we both exit the runway, relieved to see another day.

I grab Zelda before she disappears out the door. "Thanks for today," I tell her. "You were great."

Zelda beams. "I really did like your dress and the whole concept of being awakened by love. I mean..." she drifts off for a second, gazing ahead like she can see more in the distance than just a row of sewing machines, "it's just a dress, but I could feel all that when I wore it. And maybe that's your purpose, you know? To make people feel."

"Yeah, maybe it is." Indulgently I reach to hug her. "Thanks again, Zelda."

She squeezes me, hard, and I get the feeling this girl has needed a good hug for a while. "I'll see you in a couple of days."

"Right. Sounds good."

She walks off toward outside, and even though I hardly know her and I'll see her again soon, I already miss the one person here I can trust, the only one sure to be on my side.

Chapter Twenty-One

Today's challenge is based off the ballet *Ondine*.

I'd never heard of it until now, but apparently Ondine is a water nymph who falls in love with a human named Palemon, but he's engaged to a woman named Berta. Palemon leaves Berta for Ondine, and then there's a storm and Palemon thinks Ondine is dead, so he marries Berta anyway. Of course, Ondine is still alive and heartbroken, so she finds Palemon and gives him a deadly kiss. Then she goes back into the sea and loses all memory of him forever.

Love, betrayal, revenge: this challenge should be right up my alley.

But we don't get to go shopping at Metaphor. Instead, we are randomly given boxes of fabric and that's what we get to use. When I lift the lid off my fabric box I find bolts of red, but nothing silky and no chiffon. No, it's bright red linen, which is difficult because it wrinkles so easily. I also got a yard of delicate pink cotton printed with tiny white flowers.

"What did you get?" I ask Casey. She shows me the contents of her box. There's some sea-green taffeta, which looks way more appropriate than what I got for a challenge about a water nymph.

"Nice taffeta," I say. "I'm sure you can do something great."

"Yeah, but there's not enough to make anything long and flowy, and my other fabric is awful." She holds up a yard of mustard-colored oxford cloth. "What the heck am I supposed to do with this?"

I take the fabric and gently pull with two fingers, examining its weave. "Do you want to trade? My pink cotton for this?"

Casey raises her eyebrows so high they nearly bump into her hairline. "Seriously?"

I shrug. "Sure."

She grabs my pink cotton before I can change my mind.

Now I'm putting together my dress, keeping in mind that my goal is to make people feel. I've decided to focus on poor Berta, who couldn't compete with a water nymph for her boyfriend's love. She must have felt so spurned. She must have felt like inviting Ondine up to her tree house just so she could push her to the ground.

Berta is lit up with hurt and anger, like a fireball of resentment, so I design a tight fitting top out of the mustard-colored oxford cloth, with long sleeves and a straight, horizontal neckline. But it's cut right below her bust line, and I'm draping the red linen so it forms a long skirt that's hangs in triangular shapes around her calves, like flames. It's not as easy as I thought it would be, to construct something that even resembles what I imagined. I'm running out of time, and when the production assistant beckons me to do a filmed testimonial, my frustration threatens to overflow.

"Does it have to be now?" I bark, aware that she's only doing her job.

"Didn't you hear?" she asks. "We're filming Skype sessions with everyone's loved ones today. Your fiancé is waiting for you."

I jolt up and move urgently past her. I get to hear his voice. I get to see his crooked smile. The production assistant points me in the right direction and I practically jump into that computer. "Nick?"

He's sitting at our dining room table, where his laptop usually is. He grins as soon as he sees me and then laughs in this joyful sort of way.

"Hi, Rocky! How are you?"

"I'm okay. I didn't know until just now that I get to talk to you."

"Really? Because some producer called me and arranged it several days ago."

"Umm…" the production assistant, who is standing off to the side, breaks in. "You guys only have a couple of minutes, so you need to talk about your lives and not the details of this show."

"Oh, okay." I turn back to Nick's beautiful face. I wish more than anything that I could reach through the computer screen and touch him, to brush his hair that's grown kind of long off his forehead, to give him a kiss. "So what's new?"

"Well, I have great news." Nick's gravelly voice turns down a notch, like it always does when he feels humble. "Two pieces of great news, actually."

"Tell me!" I demand with a smile.

"I got a long-term sub job at East High, because the band director is going on maternity leave. And I guess they're looking to expand their music program, because the principal said they hope to have another full-time position the following year."

"That's amazing! And you'll have an in, right?"

Nick shrugs. "Yeah, maybe." His smile fades just a little and he grows thoughtful. "I'll have to take extra courses this summer if I want my teaching license by then. But they said that I can count the subbing as my student teaching, so that's really, really good. I didn't know how I was going to afford teaching full time without getting paid, you know?"

"Yeah. That's wonderful, Nick. I'm so happy for you." But would a public school be so keen to hire him if they knew he was engaged to a notorious internet whore like me? My stomach sways at the idea. I should really say something, figure out a code to warn him...

The productions assistant clears her throat and taps her watch, and I swallow back an exasperated sigh.

"So," Nick continues, "the other great news is that Andrea got a scholarship to Drake. Almost a full ride."

"Wow! This is quite the month for the Davies siblings," I say. "Drake was her first choice, wasn't it?"

Nick nods. "Yeah, she's pretty excited. But not everything is covered. She'll, um..." Nick's eyes dart around nervously. "...she'll have to keep living with us if she wants to afford it."

Deep down, I knew this was coming. Realistically, there was never any way that Nick and I would get to live alone, just the two of us, during our first year of marriage. And I can see the regret mixed with anxiety in his face. He wants me to be okay with Andrea living with us, so he can be okay with it too.

"Well, that's not a problem" I try to sound extra flippant to mask my true feelings. "Once she has her fancy degree, she'll thank us by taking us out to eat at some expensive restaurants."

Nick laughs in relief. "You haven't told me anything about you! Are you doing okay? Winning every challenge?"

He raises his eyebrows expectantly and his face is just this blank slate, ready to be filled with good news. For a brief, irrational moment I'm annoyed. He has no idea of the pressure I'm under and he's not interested in hearing the rough parts. But he must detect some flicker of irritation because he leans forward and lowers his voice, like he would if we were alone. "Hey?" he breathes. "Tell me how it's going."

"It's fine." I execute a smile through a vat of anxiety and longing, and the P.A. is tapping her watch again. "I guess I need more of a vision. I need to show them what I want, through my clothes."

"How do you do that?"

"I don't know. I guess I need to figure out what I want, first." I run both of my hands through my hair, wishing it is his hair my fingers are coursing through.

He grins but there's that line between his eyebrows when something stresses him out. "I thought you already know what you want, Rocky."

"No, I do. Of course, but career-wise, I have things—"

"Okay! Time's up!" The production assistant steps in front of me. "You have ten seconds to say goodbye and then it just automatically shuts off." She steps out so Nick and I can see each other again. "Ten seconds, starting now."

"Bye, Nick. I love you." It's like a switch has been flipped, my tear switch, and now I'm bawling. I wipe my face with my sleeve. "I think about you all the time, okay?"

"I love you too. And don't worry about—"

The screen goes blank.

****

My outfit is ugly. What was I thinking? It's like spilled ketchup and mustard with a neckline. All it needs now is some dead meat, which is what I'll be if I show this later today. And if I wasn't sure of that before, I am now that Jim Giles is standing before me, assessing the dress as if it's my fourth grade science project.

"Robin," he slowly drawls, taking a breath of procrastination, "I'm sorry, but I just don't get it. It looks like a picnic gone wrong. I mean, the color combination is unfortunate, and the lines of the dress resemble an apron or a table cloth."

I gasp. "So it's even worse than I thought!" I throw my hands up in the air. "I've used up all my fabric, Jim. Everything I have is cut. What do I do?"

He spins the dress form around 180 degrees. "That's for you to figure out, Robin. But you'd better do something. I don't want you to be out for this."

I bite my lip, trying not to hyperventilate.

"Robin..." Jim's voice is firm, like a warm, dry handshake. "You can do this."

"I sort of have to, don't I?"

"Yes, you do. You'll figure it out. I believe in you, okay?"

I nod my trembling chin in thanks, and Jim moves on to the next designer. I run my hands up and down the dress form, hoping that just by touching the fabric I'll be divinely inspired with a game-changing idea.

I close my eyes and think. Berta thought she was marrying Palemon and once he left her, she was wounded. My eyes reopen with a jolt. So there's my inspiration. It's so easy that I'm ashamed I hadn't thought of it sooner.

Two hours later Zelda shows up and I fit her into my Ace bandage dress. I've recut the fabric so it now looks like horizontal strips of Ace bandages, which are wrapped around her to form a tight, strapless bodice. It starts out red at the top but turns into yellow about halfway down, and all over is blood-red stitching in small diamonds that overlap one another. The skirt fits snugly around her hips and rests at her ankles, but I made a slit on the side so she could move easily. The result is very flame-like, to represent the fire that's within her.

"Well," I say, "if I go home for this, at least it wasn't because I didn't take a chance."

My words seem to reach Zelda and she pulls herself out of whatever deep thought she was in the middle of.

"You think you'll go home for this? But it's so cool." Zelda spins and the fabric holds its shape beautifully.

"Ooh... could you spin like that on the runway?"

"Sure. Is there anything else you'd like me to do? Like, a jump or something?" Zelda takes a timid little leap in the limited space of the workroom. Then she frowns, which is unlike the Zelda I've witnessed so far. Every other time I've seen her dance I've also seen her smile.

"Are you okay?"

"I had a long night and some weird stuff happened."

I now notice her eyes; they're puffy, with dark circles underneath and the whites are a little pinkish. Maybe it's allergies or maybe she's been crying.

Zelda juts out her chin and it's like she's continuing aloud a conversation she was having with herself. "I mean, I'm such an idiot, getting involved with a guy who will take off and let me get arrested! God knows what else he's capable of! Julie is right, there's something weird about him. If he calls, I'm telling him that we're done."

I fumble for a reply. "You got arrested?"

"Yeah, and my mother is going to kill me once she finds out." Zelda does a teenage-girl-sigh and looks at the clock. "I think we should head over to styling. Maybe I should have slicked back hair with blood red lips, to match the outfit? That could be cool."

"Um, yeah. Maybe."

I'm glad Zelda can focus on what might be cool, because I feel overheated.

Soon I'm headed toward the runway, where I might be eviscerated, shredded and torn like a discarded piece of fabric. Have I focused on what matters? Does my dress make people feel? I wonder where this might lead me and if I even know where I want to go.

Whatever. It's time to face those stage lights that are brighter than the sun, to pretend that I can see.

Chapter Twenty-Two

"Robin, tell us about your look."

I'm squinting against the glare of the stage lights. My outfit has either gotten one of the highest or the lowest scores. I wish I could steady my shaking hands which dart around while I talk, but I am powerless to do anything but blab, so I answer Hilaire's question. "I was inspired by Berta's betrayal, and I wanted people to feel that in this dress. So I thought of flames, and Ace bandages, because you know, she was wounded."

"So, Robin," Hilaire asks, "do you think you're in the bottom, or the top?"

My hands travel toward each other and my fingers scratch at my left wrist. "Umm..." I laugh. "I don't know, but I'd have put me in the top."

There is an eternal, excruciating moment, when Hilaire and the other judges gaze at me with blank faces. "Well, Robin," Hilaire finally says, "I loved your look. You are on the top."

You know how when it doesn't rain for a while and our primitive animal instincts can sense the tension? And when the gathered storm clouds finally release the rain, there's this carnal break in the atmosphere? That's what this moment is like.

I gush out a thank you and devour the praise. The stitching, the cut, the vision: they say it all came together perfectly and it's wholly original and lovely. But best of all, the guest judge, Martice Van Patten, whose clothes I buy whenever I have the money, tells me that I can work for her, any time.

That is huge.

Of course, I could never take her up on it. I'd have to move to New York and that's just not possible. Nick is tied to Des Moines and to Andrea, and I'm tied to Nick.

The other designers are picked apart, and then we are sent off into the other room while they decide who wins and who is out. We're all instructed to sit on a couch in the green room, and several cameras record our interaction.

"So, who was on the bottom and who was on the top?" Kyla, one of the designers, asks. Her dress was scored in the middle, so she's been sitting on this couch for a while. "No, wait, let me guess." She raises her dark eyebrows, scoops her long brunette hair back over her shoulders, and then points a finger at each person who just stood before the judges. "Top, bottom, bottom, top, top…" and when she gets to me her smile broadens, "bottom."

I should be pleased, right? Because it's better to have people underestimate you. "I was on the top, actually."

Kyla's smirk offers no apology. "Really?" She pushes up the sleeves of the lightweight men's blazer that she's wearing over her faded black AC/DC T-shirt. "They *liked* the Ace bandage dress? I guess the network executives have more power than we thought."

Casey, who is sitting next to Kyla, pushes her shoulder teasingly and grins. "Don't be mean, Kyla."

"Oh, no, that's okay," I sit up straight, ready to stare Kyla down. "Explain what you mean by that."

Kyla just laughs. "It's nothing to get upset about, Robin. Obviously the network wants you on the show for ratings, so they've pressured the judges into liking your stuff." She gives an annoying little shrug. "You should be flattered."

"I should be flattered that you're insulting me?"

Her face hardens. "Whatever. This isn't about you, okay? It's about network politics and I wasn't insulting *you*. I was insulting your dress and the way the executives run the show. So calm down."

I look around at the other designers, scanning their faces for a sign of support. Of course it's occurred to me that one of them found that *Rotten Robin* website and left it on my tablet. Was it Kyla, or is she just the most open about not wanting me here?

"I liked the Ace bandage dress," says Amos, whose design also scored high.

"See!" Kyla waves her hand, gesturing broadly as if to make an easy point to a very dim student. "Amos liked your dress. Stop acting like everyone is against you."

"I wasn't acting like everyone is against me. But if you refuse to censor yourself, don't expect me to follow some script on how to respond."

"Oh, don't worry. We all know how spontaneous you are, Robin." Kyla chortles. "We'd never expect you to be anything but uninhibited."

My body temperature skyrockets. She must be referring to the *Rotten Robin* video montage.

"Thank you," I say, as if her compliment was genuine. If Kyla insists on playing mind games with me, fine. I'll be a worthy competitor. So a few minutes later, when I'm told that I won the challenge, she's the first person I go to hug. The cameras are rolling, and Kyla can't afford to look petty by turning away from my squeals of enthusiasm.

Later, after we're all shuttled back to our apartments, I'm jumpy. The building where we're staying has a little exercise room in the basement, and I go there, prepared to work up a sweat. I'm not used to getting so little physical activity and I'm a bundle of mismatched wires—sparks are coming out at dangerous times and inappropriate places. I'm sure I'll feel much better if I can run off a little bit of adrenaline.

Thankfully, the windowless, beige room is empty and I can work out on my own. A fluorescent lamp flickers over the treadmill as I climb on and hit the start button. I wish I could run outside but I'm not allowed, so this will have to do.

I power on my iPod and soon my feet slap against the moving belt in rhythm to the music I'm listening to. I'm keeping pace and my heart rate is rapid but even. But everything inside me is still unsettled.

Then I notice a shadow behind me.

Is it because of that sputtering lamp over my head, like something from a horror movie? I attempt to turn around but that's not easy to do on a treadmill; you have to either slow the thing down, or jump off of it, or move both feet to the edges. I'm disoriented, trying to figure out which option to take, but it doesn't matter because I'm sure there are hands against my back, shoving me down.

Or am I just imagining things again? I don't know, but I do know that I fall and land on my butt, which I suppose is the best of all landing options, yet I hit my head in the process. That's when things get really freaky.

I'm lying on the floor, my body twisted around the treadmill, a low buzz reverberating from its moving belt. Above me the fluorescent light still flickers and when I try to sit up I see that my iPod fell from my grasp. It's in the corner of the room. I move to get it, marveling that

I don't feel any pain from my fall, when a foot clad in a Gucci platform heel steps right up into my face.

I reel back, look up, and discover that the foot belongs to Clara. "Oh hi," I say, as if no time, emotional distance, or life-ending events have elapsed since we last spoke. "I like your shoes. Very 1970s."

"They were my gramma's."

"Neat." She just stands over me, which is kind of intimidating, but I don't have it in me to get up. "Did you just push me?"

"Of course not. I'm dead, remember?"

"You're missing."

She sighs. "Robin, you really think I'm going to walk away from an explosive bus crash, just so I can torment you and push you off a treadmill? Please. Bobby wasn't worth the effort and neither are you." She sits down on the edge of the treadmill so I can see her face. It's still beautiful, but there's an angry red scar along her chin. "You need to find out who's doing this to you, though. Don't take it lying down."

Then everything turns white, like I'm unable to shut my eyes against the sun. I don't know how much time passes, but it could be an entire night where I've slept until 10:00 AM. "Robin!" Someone is shaking my shoulder. I blink several times and see the flickering fluorescent light once more. "Robin, are you okay?"

Now I focus on who's in front of me. It's Gabe the cameraman.

I mean to tell him I'm fine, but I grunt out something that sounds more like "Ergg..."

"Should I call an ambulance?"

"Won't you lose your job? Shouldn't you be filming me instead?"

He laughs and, placing his hand beneath my shoulder, hoists me up to sitting position. "I guess you are okay, after all."

I rub my head as Gabe goes over to the water cooler, fills up one of those thin paper cups, and brings it to me "Here," he says, "you should drink." I don't disagree, and as I swallow down my water he looks at me, eyebrows arched quizzically. "How did you fall?" he asks.

"I'm not sure. Maybe somebody pushed me."

Gabe's round face distorts in surprise. "Who would do that?"

"I don't know. Did you see anyone leaving as you came in?"

Gabe shakes his head no. "The place was empty, except of course, for you. But I should hit record. This sort of thing is gold." Gabe picks up his camera and points it at me. "Now tell me again everything that happened, and don't worry if you cry a little. Viewers will love that."

Chapter Twenty-Three

The next day is a brand new challenge and my head hurts like a bad breakup. I'm convinced that one of the designers snuck up behind me last night, and now, as we're shopping at Metaphor, I should be careful. Maybe Kyla will blindside me with a bolt of fabric or Casey will attack me with a set of industrial-strength scissors. Amos is several feet away, kneeling down and examining some burnt sienna brocade. I look at his large hands. Were they the ones that shoved me off that treadmill?

Aware of being watched, he glances up. "What?" he asks, referring to his fabric choice. "Is it too much? I'm thinking avant-garde and exotic."

The fabric is amazing and I wish I had his eye. I realize that Amos is way too talented to feel threatened by me. "I'm sure whatever you do will look great," I tell him, and his cheeks lift with a smile that's even shinier than his bald head.

"Are you feeling blocked?" Amos asks, genuinely concerned. I am just standing here in a daze when we only have a half an hour to shop. Probably twelve minutes have gone by already.

I struggle for an adequate answer and it comes out in a snivel. "I don't want to fall into that curse, you know? One week you're the winner, and the next week you're on the bottom. It seems like it happens all the time. Not to you, obviously, but to other contestants from other seasons."

"But you have immunity," reminds Amos, who is now standing upright, clutching his bolt of golden fabric. He reaches out a warm, chubby hand and pats me on the shoulder.

I flinch.

"Sorry," I mumble. "I'm just jumpy."

"You need to keep your head in the game, Robin." Amos's chastisement is gentle and warranted. "Don't flake out now. I want to be up against you at Fashion Week, not someone who shouldn't be there. That way, when I win, it will be well-deserved."

I laugh and nod. "Point taken."

Amos carries his fabric off to the cutting table. Gabe, who has caught my conversation with Amos, stays with me and lowers his camera. "You should tell someone, you know. What if you have a brain injury?"

"I really don't think I have a brain injury, Gabe."

"I'm just saying..."

"I'm fine," I hiss. "Stop pressuring me! I know you only want to capture some dramatic footage." I feel a pang of guilt as I turn my back on Gabe and start searching for the perfect fabric, but the last thing I need is to fall apart. This splitting headache is going to disappear. I'll spirit it away through strength of will and in addition, I'll catch whoever is out to get to me.

****

It's funny how even the ballets with happy endings, like *Scheherazade*, are pretty twisted. A sultan has the nasty habit of always killing those who serve him, until Scheherazade tells him stories of love, betrayal, and adventure. Then, after 1001 nights, her survival no longer depends on her ability to spin a good yarn.

She just has to marry the sultan.

At least my relationships aren't that unhealthy. Still, if I have to compare my life to the plots of ballets just to feel good about myself, then I'm in more trouble than I thought.

Jim has come to assess my work and his finger is resting against his chin. There's that moment of undying suspense as I wait for him to speak. "I just wonder if it looks too ready-to-wear?" Jim cocks his head, studying my dress. "But then I wonder if it's bordering on costume-y, and I start to worry that it's like something from an upscale children's Halloween catalog."

"Well..." I laugh self-deprecatingly, "at least you said 'upscale'."

Jim frowns but pats me on the shoulder. "Figure out how to fix it, Robin. You can do this."

I don't let out the angst that's building in my ribcage. I just grab my tape measure and start measuring the navy blue organza I selected at Metaphor. It has large white flower petals printed all over and I'm constructing a simply lined dress with sleeves that flare, hopefully creating a sense of mystery. The dress itself will be kimono-like; I thought that would be exotic without being too literal about the *Scheherazade* theme.

Maybe if I shorten the dress, and have the skirt flare like the sleeves do? Or would that make it even more costume meets ready-to-wear?

I feel a tap on my shoulder. Nadia, one of the few designers who's older than me, is by my side. "Hey, Nadia. What's up?"

"Umm..." Her voice is always whisper soft. "Robin," she breathes. "I'm having an issue? My fabric isn't working and I don't have enough?" Her big brown eyes pool with tears. "I don't know what I'm going to do!"

My head still hurts and I'm on the verge of tears myself, mostly over my own misguided ensemble. But I have immunity and Nadia is a wreck, so I stop what I'm doing and search for a way to help.

I consider giving her a yard of my black chiffon, but I might still use it for a camisole. "Couldn't you make the dress sleeveless, and add the extra fabric where you need it?"

"But I'm not sure how to do that," Nadia whispers. "You're so good at reworking things. Would you mind, just for a minute, showing me how?"

I shrug with resignation and walk with Nadia towards her work table. "I feel so out of place here," Nadia confesses.

"We all feel that way," I reply. But we pass Kyla, who couldn't look more comfortable if she were wearing a pair of jammies and slippers. What's more, Kyla has no problem letting everyone know that she is the best designer to ever appear on *The Standout*. Maybe that's why she sticks out her foot just as I step in front of her. I stumble forward and fall, hitting my knees on the hard linoleum workroom floor.

"Oh my God," Kyla cries, rushing toward me. "I am so, so sorry. I wasn't paying attention to what I was doing. Are you okay?"

Two falls in twenty-four hours: No, I don't feel super-okay. But I'm not going to give Kyla the satisfaction of seeing me suffer or go crazy with accusations. "I'm fine!" I chirp as I stand and brush myself off. "No worries." I can hear how hollow I sound, how full of fake cheer, but there's nothing to do about it. If I'm going to catch Kyla in the act of true duplicity, she can't feel accused over a benign tripping incident. "Come on, Nadia. Let's look at your sleeves."

We walk away, and I swear I see an evil smile spread across Kyla's face. When we reach Nadia's station she steps in close and speaks in even more of a whisper. "Be careful, Robin. I think Kyla has it out for you."

"What did I ever do to her?"

"Nothing. You're just confident so she feels threatened. Anyway, I'd watch your step around her. Literally, right?" Nadia laughs at her own little joke and I smile in appreciation.

"Okay, we don't have much time, so we'd better get moving." I spin Nadia's dress form so I can see all 360 degrees of her outfit. It sort of reminds of early Carol Brady: a super short baby-doll mini-dress with bell sleeves and a square shaped, lacy collar. But the skirt is too short; it will be riding her model's butt cheeks. "Yeah, I would just get rid of the sleeves and make a pleat on the skirt. You don't want to be accused of having taste issues."

"But how do I do that?"

I go through it with Nadia, step by step, of how I'd use the sleeves for the skirt even though this is basic stuff. She seems distracted, eyes darting around the room, and at one point I turn, thinking I'll see someone communicating with her behind me. But there's no one. "You got it?" I ask.

She grabs my hand and gives it a squeeze. "Thank you so much, Robin. You're an angel."

I head back to my work station, walking in the middle of the aisle, away from Kyla's feet or from anyone else who might trip me. But the wind is knocked out of me nonetheless. Somebody has dumped water all over my kimono dress.

"Who did this?!" I yell. Every cameraman in the room, including Gabe, rushes towards me. "This is sabotage! Who did this?"

Amos comes over. "What happened?"

"You must have seen, Amos! Someone ruined all my work!" I circle the room with my eyes but nobody will even look at me. "Who did this?"

"I... I don't know." Amos is either a really good liar or the confusion on his face is real. "I went to get a snack. I only came back a second ago."

I turn to Gabe and the other cameramen. "One of you must have seen it happen! Who has it on film?"

Gabe shakes his head and frowns. The cameraman MO is that they're an invisible, silent presence in the room.

"Where's Jim?" I ask, to nobody in particular. "I have to talk to Jim about this."

Amos stands next to me and inspects my sodden dress. "Robin, is it possible that somebody was walking with a water bottle, stumbled and spilled accidentally?"

I let out a harsh laugh. "I don't know. Did they stumble because Kyla tripped them?"

Kyla's head snaps up and she makes a dry response. "Watch yourself, Robin. You're acting crazy."

Amos examines the fabric. "Well, nothing is destroyed. I mean, it isn't torn or shredded or anything. It can be fixed by a run in the dryer."

I try to steady my breathing and become aware that all the cameras are focused on me, as is every set of eyes in the room, and even Nadia is pretending like she doesn't know me. I've become the chimpanzee at the zoo, rattling the bars of my cage, hooting and hollering, while everyone silently observes how primal I am.

"You're right," I chirp. "In fact, I was probably just given a favor. I need to rework that dress anyway. Now I can start fresh, but I'd better get going because I have a lot to do."

I throw all the charm and pluck I have directly into the dark abyss of the camera lens and then I get to work, removing pins so I can give my dress a run in the dryer. I should know better than to lose my temper or let my emotions show. If I can remain calm and unshaken then I will win this game of cat and mouse, even if I don't know who my cat is.

Chapter Twenty-Four

The judges hate my kimono dress. They say it's too gimmicky and that the construction is poor. They're right. My organza shrank in the dryer and I couldn't drape it correctly afterwards. Plus, I lost time, having to re-pin everything. This is one of the worst dresses I've ever made, including the prom dress I put together in high school, after watching *Pretty in Pink*. "You're lucky you have immunity," Hilaire tells me.

Kyla, whose dress is on top, glows.

When the other dismissed designers and I get backstage, I mumble something about needing the bathroom, and I take a surreptitious route into the workroom. This is the perfect time to sort through Kyla's stuff. Maybe there will be some tell-tale clue, like the password to the *Rotten Robin* website, scribbled on a scrap of paper. Or maybe she'll have left behind her membership card to the official "I Hate Robin Club." I suppose that's as likely as anything else.

I pull open her desk drawer. There's a notepad, but there are only sketches with no writing. I flip the latch to her sewing box, which is perfectly organized with spools of thread, scissors, and multi-sized pins. But it's her Samsung tablet that will hold the answers, if there are answers to be held. I take it out, praying that there's no password to access it, when I hear footsteps.

Shit. I know the booted contestant always has to come up after getting kicked out, to be filmed cleaning out his or her workspace. But it's too soon for that. So who is coming?

I hastily put all of Kyla's belongings back where they belong, and I'm praying they're in the right spot. Then I bolt over to my own work station, knowing that whoever is coming will find me out of breath, in the dark, and making some lame excuse for what I'm up to. I am so totally busted.

"Robin?"

A whoosh of relief: It's just Zelda.

"Hey," I squeak. "What are you doing up here?"

"I think I left my phone on your table." She flicks on the lights and walks over, instantly finding a phone in a shiny pink case. She swipes and as it lights up, she winces. "My head is pounding," she says.

"Tell me about it," I reply. Zelda is already scrolling through her missed correspondence, completely unconcerned with my awkward situation. That gives me an idea. "Zelda," I say, and her eyes meet mine. "Can you keep a secret?"

I go to bed that night knowing I can trust Zelda one hundred percent. But my sleep is restless and disturbed. I dream that I am standing outside my bedroom door, but the handle will not turn and the hinges are rusted shut. I know that Nick is on the other side, his smile wide and his arms extended, ready to hold and accept me. But not only are we separated, I feel sure that danger is lurking: invisible, like a poison gas.

I have to get to him.

All our lights are off, and the shadows play tricks with my mind. I stand there, rattling the door and calling out to him, when I feel the foundation of our house slip away, as if we are growing and diminishing at the same time. The floor beneath my feet sprouts into a skyscraper, high and unstable, so beautiful, so full of potential, but so vulnerable as well. I am numb with terror.

I look up and see the moon and stars; somehow the roof has disappeared and the sky is within reach, but that means the ground is far, far below.

I am about to fall.

When I wake, breathless with a racing heart, it takes me a moment to remember where I am. Heck, it takes me a moment to remember *who* I am.

Oh yeah. I'm posing as a fashion designer on another reality show. That's my identity right now.

****

At 9:00 AM I'm standing at my work table, trying to construct a tutu out of an old prom dress and a red plaid flannel shirt. I have to win *The Firebird* challenge, because as the other designers all made sure to point out, it's geared towards me. Jim Giles would never admit it, but when he announced that we'd be shopping for fabric at a thrift store, the ball was officially thrown into my court.

I keep sticking my thumbs with pins, because folding and pleating together tulle and flannel is like cooking with hot butter and ice cream. But what's worse is I can't decide if this design is genius or hideously ugly. At any moment Jim could come by, assess my work, and furrow his brow for that awful, silent moment before he says something fatal, like, "Robin, I'm worried this looks like a drag queen's kilt."

I feel someone standing near me, so I look up and am met with Kyla's fierce glare. "What?" I ask.

"Somebody messed with my work station last night," she says venomously.

"That's terrible!" I widen my eyes in hyperbolic concern. "You must feel so violated, like somebody tripped you or sabotaged your design."

Kyla's mouth hardens like concrete. "So it was you."

"I didn't mess with your stuff."

She steps in closer while raising her voice, which is super annoying. "You disappeared last night while everyone else was being filmed in the green room. I *know* it was you, Robin, and I'm telling Jim."

Mercifully, a production assistant chooses that moment to come right up to me. "Robin," she says softly. "You have a phone call."

"I'm allowed to get phone calls?"

She nervously tugs on the hem of her shirt. "I guess it's an emergency?"

I feel the blood drain from my face and my body goes cold. Nick. Something happened to Nick. That's what my dream was about. I was being warned and I ignored it and now it's too late.

These thoughts whirl through my mind in the space of a second, as I hurry past a bewildered Kyla and follow the PA out into the office area, where I can get my call. My mouth is completely dry as I pick up the receiver and attempt a "Hello?"

"It's Ted."

Ted. If Ted is calling me, then it's not Nick who is in trouble. It must be my father, which is also terrible. "What's wrong?" I ask. "Is it Dad? Is he okay?"

"Yeah, Dad's fine. I'm calling about this *Rotten Robin* website. I don't know if you've seen it, but Robin..."

I stamp my foot against the linoleum floor. "I've seen it, Ted and I watched that montage. Look, I need to hang up. If they catch me on the phone—"

His voice is loud and urgent as he interjects. "There's more, Robin. A sex tape with you and Nick was posted. And on the same day there was stuff about a bribe, which seemed to be all talk, but now—well, I wanted you to know before it's too late."

"Huh?" Something in my brain explodes and I literally see flashing lights in my peripheral vision. "God, Ted! What are you talking about?"

He coughs in his self-important way. "Look, Robin, this is truly an emergency and I think I know who is behind it. I will tell you everything, but you're really not going to like it."

Part II: Ted

Chapter Twenty-Five

The sun is setting and I'm sweeping off the helicopter seeds that fell from the Maple tree to our deck below. I wonder why I bother. The deck will just be covered in more of them tomorrow. When I was a kid I loved this time of day, sunset, when the sky turned orange over the plains, and I'd sit on our patio in West Des Moines, enjoying a cherry Popsicle and dreaming of all the places I could travel, the thousands of paths my life might take.

I could blame it all on my mom. No.

I could blame it all on the truck driver who rammed into my mom late one afternoon, killing her just two weeks after my fourteenth birthday. But that's so cliché. Maybe her untimely death has nothing to do with my unpleasant personality or my sense of hopelessness. Maybe I'm just a dick. End of story.

Still, she saw the beauty in everything. She saw the beauty in me.

Dad was aware of this, and he liked to give her beautiful things. When I was born he gave her a teardrop pearl necklace, which she wore every time they hired a babysitter and went out to a nice restaurant. When my younger brother Ian was born, Dad gave her pearl stud earrings to match.

When my baby sister Robin arrived, Dad got creative. He found a first run print by her favorite artist, Mats Gustafson. It's a watercolor of a woman, her face in shadow while she walks toward light. She's slouched yet graceful, dynamic yet still, perfect in her ignorance of all those admiring eyes.

Sometimes my love for that picture and my love for my mother became intermixed, like the blurred lines that formed the beautiful lady's silhouette, like the fading memories I still cling to, like the sense of possibility I know I have lost.

Chapter Twenty-Six

When Robin was a toddler she loved playing peek-a-boo with Mom and me, and she was convinced that when she closed her eyes, she actually disappeared. "Where did Robin go?" Mom would cry, and Robin would giggle, her smile huge as her sticky hands covered her face. I'd join in the search, always being loud and outlandish, because that tickled Robin even more. "I can't find her anywhere! Is she behind the couch? Under the pillows?" And because I knew Robin was peeking between the cracks of her fingers, I would make a show of looking underneath our worn, brown couch cushions.

Mom thought my charade was almost as funny as Robin did, and her goofy laugh still echoes in my ears.

I was a lonely kid at thirteen-years-old; even then something was missing for me. I never had the "fun" gene that my younger siblings seemed to inherit. For me, life has always been serious, but when I played with Mom and Robin, the weight of my heavy personality lessened a bit. Suddenly Robin would drop her hands from her face, and squeal, "Here I am!" only it sounded like "Hey A MMM!" and we'd all laugh and I'd hug her, telling her how happy I was that she wasn't lost forever.

I have photographs of my mother and one of the last ones comes from the early 80s. She's wearing a down parka vest over a lavender ski sweater and corduroy pants; her hair is up and pale lipstick is her only makeup. She squints at the sun and smiles at the camera, unaware that this will be one of the last moments that's ever captured of her.

She's beautiful and I try to feel her when I stare at that fading Polaroid, conscious that every day, the chemicals in the photo paper break down a little more, distorting her truth. Maybe photographs aren't the most accurate representations of who we are, or were. They change even as we cling to the memories they represent.

I'm a businessman, but if you ask me, that's the purpose of art. It captures truth, and even through a million different interpretations, the truth doesn't change.

Chapter Twenty-Seven

Last night I woke from a dream where I was being smothered and it took me a moment to find my breath. I stared at the darkness, listening to Tina breathe steadily as she slept next to me, and I remembered that in a few hours I have a meeting, where if one thing goes wrong, I will be destroyed. But there's no pressure.

I have one of those jobs that nobody really understands. I rarely try to explain it because people aren't interested, unless that person is a client, and then they're only interested because it's their money I'm messing with. But in a nutshell, I give financial advice to major corporations and the decisions I make can cost millions of dollars.

My meeting is with a client from Singapore, and we'll be discussing his assets. Now I take the elevator up a skyscraper in downtown Philadelphia, to my client's office, and when the door opens I am greeted by a huge picture window that gives view to the city below. I take a moment to enjoy it, appreciating the cityscape: all the angles and shadows that the buildings create. There was a time, before Harvard business school, that I thought about becoming an architect, about building and creating. But I'm no Howard Roark.

I work within people's expectations but I never defy them.

I make my way towards the reception desk, where I announce myself to the young woman sitting there. "Ted Bricker to see Mr. Chew Choon."

The receptionist, whom I've encountered before, smiles and waves her finger at me. "I know who you are," she tells me in a lilting voice. "Your sister is Robin, from *The Holdout*! Am I right?"

I feel heat gather behind my cheeks and under my arms. "That's right." I try to smile.

"She was incredible! I just watched the whole season on Hulu, and I was totally rooting for her. You must be so proud that she's such a survivor."

"More proud than you'll ever know." I mumble. "Now can you announce me to Mr. Chew Choon? He's expecting me."

She picks up her phone, speaks into it, and places it back in the receiver. "You can go on in," she tells me, then lowers her voice. "Good luck," she whispers. "He's sort of in a mood today."

I feel my breath catch the way it did last night, in my dream. I wish I was back at that window, staring at those buildings, looking down but protected by glass. And as I walk in to face Mr. Chew Choon, I think that next to me, Robin knows nothing about survival, but the world will never know, never understand.

Mr. Chew Choon rattles on about investments and I nod my head like I care. I assure him that everything is under control, that he should trust me, that I would never let him down. But I am actually thinking about the video I found online the other day. Some guy was singing, playing the piano, and proposing to my sister. It happened a while ago but I only just found out, like I'm some fan of hers and not the guy who taught her to drive.

Mr. Chew Choon finishes his spiel and makes me promise that he won't be disappointed. "Of course you won't be," I tell him. But even I don't believe what I'm saying, so why should he?

When I get home from work, Tina is upstairs in our bedroom, trying on outfits. I loosen my tie as I walk in, looking forward to changing into jeans and a sweatshirt, even as she's draped in a cocktail dress.

"What's going on?" I ask, gesturing with my eyes towards the strapless, red sequined gown she's adjusting over her breasts. It keeps slipping down.

"I need to figure out what I'm wearing to the auto show gala." Tina keeps her eyes on her reflection. Her light brown hair falls loosely at her shoulders so she scoops it up, but that action makes her dress fall down even more.

"You probably need to get that taken in. It's falling off you." I grin and stand by her, placing my hands on her warm, bare shoulders. "You and your dieting... I know I give you a hard time about not eating more, but God, you're in great shape." I kiss her neck and she steps away from me.

"Not now, Ted."

Stung, I walk towards my closet, where I remove my work clothes and put on something more comfortable. "What's for dinner?" I ask, thinking I was wrong to compliment her, to encourage her at all. If she's cooked anything, she won't eat it.

"There's salad and some chicken breasts you can sauté for the boys. I'm not very hungry."

"Okay." I turn back towards her. She's taken off the red dress and has put on a midnight blue, strappy thing with beaded flowers. It's also way too loose on her. "Hey," I say, trying to sound warm, "why don't you get a new dress for the gala? Wouldn't you rather have something from this season?"

Tina rolls her eyes. "Aren't you the one who said we should be cutting back? Miles and Mason's tuition has just gone up, and we're renovating the patio, and I'd really like to get these done." She grabs her breasts and squeezes. "They've gotten so droopy."

"That's because you've lost so much weight."

She spins toward me like she's that girl in *The Exorcist*. "So you agree that my boobs are sagging? What about my face? Or my neck? Are they okay, Ted? Or should I just have work done everywhere?"

Tina is practically spitting out fire and I back away. "You know I think you're beautiful," I tell her. "I just want you to feel good, happy about yourself..."

"Whatever!" she huffs.

I try to apologize, to say something that won't get me in more trouble, but my cell phone rings. I pull it out, thinking it's work and my stomach contracts at the mere idea. Today's meeting didn't go well.

But it's not work; it's Robin. My finger is poised, ready to swipe "ignore," but Tina slams a door, locking herself in the bathroom. There's nothing productive I can say to Tina right now so I go ahead and take the call.

"What?" I realize I sound like a dick, but at the moment I don't care.

There's a moment's pause as my sister finds her voice. "Ted?"

"Yeah, it's Ted. Who else would be answering my phone?"

"Sorry... you just sound stressed. Is this a bad time?"

Well, I just got home from a hellish day of work, I need to make dinner, and my wife hates me almost as much as she hates herself, but other than that, sure, it's a great time. What's up, Sis?

"It's fine," I gripe. "But I need to get dinner going. Did you need something?" I move downstairs, grasping the heavy maple railing, my feet shuffling down the thick carpeted steps. Every one of our decorating choices was carefully researched by Tina, from the skylights to the molding along the floorboards.

And it's never felt like home.

"I, um, well, I just wanted to let you know that I'm getting married."

I grunt-laugh. "Good luck!"

At first she doesn't respond and I busy myself, looking for the chicken breasts in our stainless steel refrigerator, and then for a frying pan to cook them in. "Okay, thanks, I guess," Robin mumbles. "Don't you want to know the details?"

"I already know. It's all online. You're marrying that one guy, right? Rick?"

"His name is Nick, actually, but yeah. And we're getting married in a few weeks. The wedding is at Monty's house, so hopefully you can come."

I drop the frying pan onto an unlit burner. "Wait. A few weeks from *now*, at *Monty's* house?" Suddenly I care about this conversation. If the wedding is so soon, that means she's been planning it for a while. And if my cousin Monty, who I've always resented, is once again stepping in to be the family's savior, and for *my* little sister, well –

Well, what?

"You could have told me sooner!" I snap. "As it is, Robin, I have a life. There's no way I can come if the wedding is so soon."

"Never mind then," she replies, voice terse.

"I'm sure you'll have a good time without me there."

"Yeah, I'm sure we will."

"Fine."

"Fine."

I press end and drop my phone onto the kitchen counter like it's burning metal. But the real heat is gathering behind my eyes as tears form. "God dammit," I mumble, and I swipe my face with the sleeve of my ratty Harvard sweatshirt. I sniff, chastising myself for being such a crybaby.

Robin is the dynamic one. My brother, Ian, is funny. And I'm the douche-bag-crybaby who barely gets invited to his own sister's wedding, whose wife won't let him touch her, who doesn't feel like he belongs in his own house.

How did I get here?

Chapter Twenty-Eight

It was my junior year of college.

I was on a spring break trip to Miami when I was tossed together with the most alluring creature I'd ever seen: a blond goddess in sandals and a swimsuit. She was playing beach volleyball and when she used her strong, sinewy arms to spike that serve, I was speechless, in love. Anyone could see me gaping, already drowning in a quicksand of emotion. As the tide came in and the waves tickled at her toes, she turned, saw me, and smiled.

I was so happy and so panicked that I wished to fade into nothing, to become a white light underneath the shining sun.

Instead I summoned the nerve to talk to Tina, and ever since I've been desperate not to let go.

Except lately, it's become more and more difficult to maintain a grasp on my marriage. Every day, Tina slips further and further away from me, and I slip closer towards disappearing into that white light. Only this time it wouldn't be pleasant, it would just be a ceasing to exist. Nobody would care, few would remember, and life would go on like it always does for everybody, except me.

Mr. Chew Choon calls, wondering why one of his international stock funds has been cashed in at a loss. I tell him it's a temporary measure, meant to guard against a decline in market value. He's also worried that other stock shares, ones I sold for profit, will be too severely taxed, but I urge him to be happy with a gain.

He's not convinced, and eventually he hangs up on me. I'm sure he'll complain to my superiors, I'll hear about it, and there will be repercussions.

I take a swig from the bottle of Pepto-Bismol I keep hidden in my desk, and stare out my window, at the Philadelphia skyline. Everything will be okay, I tell myself, but I don't believe it. So I call Tina.

"Don't tell me you can't pick up the boys tonight," she barks into the phone the moment she picks up: no prelude, no warm hello.

"Umm..." I hesitate, trying to remember what it is I'm supposed to be picking them up from.

"Ted?" Her tone is demanding, a contrast to my stuttering silence. "You know I have a board meeting for the Banard Foundation tonight. This is important to me. If I'm not there, I'll never get elected to the senior council."

"Right, no, of course." Tina is on a dozen different boards of a dozen different charity or non-profit groups. Most of them have to do with the arts, horticulture, or curing childhood cancer. I'm pretty sure the Banard Foundation focuses on all three. "You won't have to miss your meeting. That's not why I'm calling."

"Oh." The annoyance in her tone outweighs the relief. "Then, what?"

I squeeze my eyes shut and rub my temple. There was a time, long ago, when just hearing Tina's voice could be an antidote for whatever was ailing me. But what would she say now, if I told her how scared I am? That I could lose my job; that our way of life, our house, and our sons' educations are all at risk? I doubt she would console me in soothing tones.

"Nothing." I clear my throat. "Sorry. I was flipping through the contacts on my phone, and I accidentally called you." I force out a staccato laugh. "How's your day, though?"

"Um, it's fine. I went to the gym and Nancy Adams was there. I guess she was in the hospital! Turns out she caught hepatitis. She thinks she got it from an apple that she didn't wash."

"Which type?"

"What? How would I know? Granny Smith? Golden Delicious? Who cares?"

"No, what type of hepatitis?" The lights on my phone flash, which means I have a call on another line. It's probably important; all my calls are.

"Oh. I don't know. I didn't ask. Anyway, it sounds like she was really sick. I think they sell something at Whole Foods that you can spray on your fruits and vegetables to protect from stuff like that. I always thought it was a waste of money, but now I'm thinking—"

"Tina, I have to go. Sorry."

"Okay, you're the one who called me, you know."

"I know. I just have another call and—"

She clicks her goodbye before I can finish my apology. And as I answer this other call, I long for the time when Tina and I hated to say goodbye, when all I had to do to make her smile was just be myself.

Several hours later I'm still at my desk, reviewing figures that can't be right. If these numbers reflected on the page are real, I'm a dead man. Then Tina calls, I look at the clock, and realize I'm already a dead man.

I answer my phone. "I'm so sorry, Tina. I'm on my way right now."

"You said you'd pick them up!" she screeches. "The school called me. Miles and Mason were waiting for an hour by the curb after baseball practice."

My blood goes cold, even colder than my bed has been lately. "Tina, I'm so sorry. I lost track of time."

"You are such a bastard. Now there's no way I can make the board meeting tonight. By the time you get home it will be practically over."

"No, I'll leave right away, and—"

"No!" Tina's voice is strangled with tears. "Forget it, okay?"

"Tina, come on. I'm sorry. It's just that work has been really diffi-cult and I got caught up."

"That's always your excuse, Ted. Nothing comes before work: not your kids and definitely not me."

There's a tug of anger in the pit of my stomach. "That's not fair. Everything I do, I do for you."

"Please!" She takes a series of shallow breaths. "You only ever think of yourself. You are the most selfish person I know."

Then it just slips out. "Well, if that's the case, you don't know yourself at all."

There's a long pause, where I know I should start groveling and offer up lame justifications for why I'd say something like that. The words run through my mind but my lips stay clamped shut.

"Fuck you." Tina finally says. Then she hangs up on me, again.

I let my head drop so that my chin is pressed against the smooth wood of my desk and all I can see is dark. The fact that today hasn't gone much differently than any other day doesn't make me feel worse, doesn't make me feel better.

I turn back to my computer. Tina just said I shouldn't rush home, and if I do, she'll probably be even more pissed. It's better to stay here, so it will seem like I had a real work emergency. But I can't go over these figures one more time, so I start surfing. On one of the sites I visit, an ad pops up: "Looking for a change of career? We have online courses in over thirty topics! Start your new life today!"

The idea that it's possible to start a new life is what makes me click on the link. I know it's silly, but sometimes just considering the options can help. I scroll down: accounting, cosmetology, early education, funeral services. No, no, no, and no.

But then I get to private investigation.

I do feel like I'm always the last one to know things. Wouldn't it be nice to change that? I could lurk in dark corners and do stakeouts. I'd start wearing dark jeans and crew necks and I wouldn't have to shave every day. People would respect me, maybe even fear me a little. And perhaps I would finally understand what's going on.

I read about the course. It's nine hundred dollars but if I enroll now I get three hundred dollars off. *What the hell?* I think.

I sign up.

Chapter Twenty-Nine

Most days blend into the background of our memories but a few stand out, and they will always be high definition, bold print shapes in our mind. I wish we could select which days those would be, but of course we can't. My graduation from Harvard, my wedding day, the days my sons were born... those days are still pretty vivid. Less extraordinary days stay with me too, like when Tina and I walked to this Mexican restaurant and she laughed at my lame jokes and the sunlight bounced off her hair. But certain moments are lost, victims to the happiness, excitement or boredom I was feeling at the time.

Others are on an endless loop inside my head, moments that seem to capture certain life-long themes, for better or for worse.

The summer before my senior in year in college I was home, stuck driving Robin from one summer camp to another, and she hung out with a mean girl named Gwen. They were only eleven but Gwen was already a teenager, wearing makeup and earbuds from the CD Walkman she always had with her. Gwen was addicted to *New Kids on the Block*.

And Robin wanted to be like Gwen, so when Gwen invited her for a sleepover, she begged to go. "No way," I stated flatly.

"You're not my father!" Robin insisted, and she ran to Dad, imploring him to be nicer than me.

"I don't see why not," Dad said.

"Did she tell you about their plan to sneak out?" I asked. "Did she tell you they're inviting boys over after Gwen's parents go to sleep? And that they're going to try cigarettes and alcohol?"

"That's a lie!" Robin insisted.

Maybe it was, but I could imagine such duplicity from Gwen. More importantly, I'd overheard her making fun of Robin while I sat in my car, waiting for her after her swim lessons got out. Gwen had emerged first, laughing and drinking a Slurpee. "Robin's such a loser!" Gwen had said as she looped arms with another girl. "I only pretend to like her because her brother is cute."

Gwen was talking about Ian, who was eighteen, still in the closet, and irresistible to all the girls.

So I lied to keep Robin from going to that slumber party, because I'd heard the stories of how cruel girls can be, playing pranks and setting each other up for torment. I couldn't tell Robin the truth without hurting her feelings, so I did everything I could to keep her as far away from Gwen as possible.

She hated me for it. "You're the worst brother in the world!" she cried, her face streaked with tears and her voice choked with rage. "You don't have any friends so you don't want me to have any either!" Those were the last complete sentences she'd said to me all summer, and in the years since, she hasn't said much more.

And I found my place in life; I'm the guy who makes the hard choices that nobody likes, and thus, nobody likes me either.

Robin wants to stay with me before she goes off to do another reality show. I say sure, and I even pick her up at the airport. We talk on the drive home and the conversation actually goes well.

In the morning I make French toast and sausage, place some halved grapefruits in dishes and sprinkle them with sugar, make coffee, and pour glasses of orange juice for Miles and Mason. They are the first ones downstairs, and their excitement at finding such an elaborate breakfast, on a weekday no less, gratifies me. They sit down and dig in.

"Where's Aunt Robin?" Miles asks. His nine-year-old rooster hair is sticking up and he already has a smear of syrup on his face. I feel a rush of parental protectiveness. I can't send him off to school like this, not unless I want the other kids to pick on him. I grab a paper towel, wet it, and use it to wipe his face, and then I smooth his unruly curls.

"She's upstairs getting ready," I tell him. "Robin has a big day ahead of her. She's going to be on TV."

"God, what smells so good?"

As if on cue, Robin enters the kitchen, and Miles and Mason jump up, ready to give her sticky syrup hugs. She returns the affection, somehow managing to keep their fingers off her weird, grayish purple outfit. All of Robin's outfits are eccentric, but this one is especially so.

"You're not wearing that for the first day of filming, are you?" I ask.

Robin's face, which had been lit by a bright smile, turns blank and wounded.

'I have to make a statement, Ted." Her mouth turns down. "Anyway, we can't all wear Ralph Lauren, all the time."

"I like what you're wearing,' says Mason, who is the more fabulous of my two sons. "You remind me of a girl dinosaur."

I burst out laughing, which doesn't help. But Robin quickly recovers from Mason's compliment. "Thank you, Mason. 'Girl dinosaur' is totally what I was going for."

Tina enters, her hair pulled back and her makeup on. I almost never see her disheveled, not even first thing in the morning or last thing at night. And unlike Robin, she's wearing neutral colors, with a shirt tucked into trim pants. She looks even skinnier than usual.

"Hey, good morning," I say. "There's grapefruit, French toast, and sausage."

She frowns. "Just the grapefruit and coffee, thanks." But when she reaches for a dish she rolls her eyes. "Ted, did you sprinkle sugar on this?"

"Yeah, only a little. Grapefruit is so bitter otherwise."

Tina drops the grapefruit in the garbage. "Just coffee, then," she mumbles.

Robin can sense the tension, I'm sure of it, but she pretends that she can't. "Hi, Tina!" She goes to hug her, and Tina half-heatedly returns the embrace. "It's good to see you."

Tina pastes on a smile. "It's good to see you too! How exciting, that you're doing another reality show! I guess you're the success story in your family."

"Or the laughing stock," Robin replies.

"Oh, no. Not you!" Tina sounds so fake that my neck grows warm. It's okay for me to condescend to my sister, but other people are not allowed.

"Robin, do you want coffee?" I ask, trying to distract from my wife's rudeness.

"Sure. Thanks." I pour her a cup, and we all sit down to eat. Thank God for my sons, because they chit-chat with Robin, asking her questions about *The Standout*, so that the awkwardness isn't unbearable.

I give Tina a sideways glance, and think to myself, *what's happened to us?*

Chapter Thirty

This evening, I consider the options with my wife. Should I tell her the truth about my job? Should I convince Tina that she's better than the latest diet she is on? Should I ask her to get some Mexican food with me, so we can drink Margaritas and laugh at stupid stuff?

I want to, but I know she'd shoot me down.

But when the kids are in bed I find Tina downstairs in the rec room. She's staring at our widescreen TV, watching one of those movies where the big-city-single-girl has a lot of clothes and a lot of boyfriends, but she needs to find herself. I know this from glimpsing at it for two seconds and I want to turn it off.

"Hey, are you attached to this movie? I was thinking we could watch *Breaking Bad.*" Tina and I are on the fourth season, and I want to find out what happens with Gus.

I expect Tina to throw a mini-tantrum. *Why didn't you mention this before I started watching something? Really, Ted, you can be so inconsiderate. Don't you care at all about what I want?* But she just picks up the slim, silver Apple TV remote, and without a word, switches off her movie and turns on *Breaking Bad.*

"Thanks," I say, a little too shocked to believe my luck. "Are you going to watch with me?"

"Of course." She pats the cushion next to her and I sit. There's no rhyme or reason to her mood swings, but right now I don't care. I have my Tina back, the one who looks at me like I'm a guy worth knowing.

Chapter Thirty-One

My boss wants me in his office. I tell myself that this isn't good; this can't be good. And it's not. It's *we want to work with you, Ted. We want to keep you here, but this sort of thing can't happen again. Complaints like these, over mistakes like yours, aren't acceptable. A chain is only as strong as it weakest link. You understand, right?*

I understand that we can't lose Mr. Chew Choon's business. But I hate that stupid chain-link cliché. And I hate my boss' stupid, shiny bald head and the raspy sound of his laugh, like he's a used car salesman and not a high-powered executive

"So am I fired?" I ask, half-hoping that the answer is yes.

But no, I get a second chance. My last chance. And I'm supposed to be relieved. But that night at dinner, all I can think about is how unhappy I am, how I wish I had more to give Miles and Mason, how one day they will look at their father and realize he is an empty shell. And I want to tell Tina, but the words freeze in my throat, so I do the dishes, wishing the hot tap water would melt the ice that's inside me.

After that I hide in our office. Both Tina and I have computers in here and I use mine now. They've already sent me the first lesson of my P.I. course and I'm eager to get started, eager to crack Robin's case. But it's slow going and I have a lot to learn.

Later, I go to bed and fall into a restless sleep. In my dream I am standing on a high ledge. I don't question why, because it's so freeing up here, like I have wings. I'm invincible and I realize that I haven't felt this way in so long, maybe ever, but this, I am sure, is my natural state of being. It is how I am meant to feel: financial reports, tedious meetings, tension headaches, and family responsibility seem as far away as the tiny lights of the city below me.

Then I hear her crying and I fall back into reality with a thud. I reach toward Tina but her side of the bed is just smooth, cold sheets. I get up, put my feet against our thick, plush carpet, and walk into our double-sink, shiny chrome bathroom that sparkles brighter than day. This sort of bathroom ought to make her happy. Our life ought to make her happy, but obviously it doesn't. My wife is curled up in a ball by the toilet, sobbing so hard that she doesn't even hear me enter.

"Tina, honey, what's wrong?" I kneel down and tentatively reach for her. Again, I'm reminded of my dream, where my movements were so confident, so opposite of how I really am. My hands shouldn't hesitate to touch my wife, but they're shy, timid, barely remembering the feel of her. When my fingers make contact, her skin is cold and clammy.

She jerks her head up, out of the cradle her arms had made against the toilet, and she spins toward me. "What are you doing in here?"

"I heard you crying. I wasn't just going to ignore you."

"Well, I wish you would!" She shrugs me away, stands, and goes to the sink to splash cold water on her face.

I stand too, so I'm behind her and speaking to our reflection in the mirror. "Tina, tell me why you were crying."

She drops her gaze and appears to be studying the still-running water as it flows down the drain. "You'll think it's stupid," she murmurs.

"I promise I won't."

"My dress doesn't fit right, okay?"

For the first time I notice a dress, one of the possible evening gowns for the auto show gala, lying on the floor by her feet. "It's too loose?"

"No, Ted, it's too tight across the stomach!" She grabs her non-existent belly and tries unsuccessfully to jiggle it. "It makes me look fat, seriously fat, and okay: I know there are people with worse problems. But all the work I do, trying to keep fit, trying to be disciplined, what it's all for, if I can't fit into a stupid dress? What's the point if my aging hormones are just going to fuck everything up?"

I pick up the dress and examine it. It's black with horizontal white stripes, and I remember it now. She bought it years ago, before Miles and Mason were born, when it was just her and me and we went out all the time. The first time she wore that dress I gave her a wolf whistle and she'd laughed in pleasure. I'd pulled her to me and my hands roamed up and down her firm body, resting on her flat stomach, where the fabric was pulled taut. "You look amazing," I'd told her. "I want to rip this dress right off you."

"You'll do no such thing," she'd said. "Not many women could pull this dress off. Someday I won't be able to pull it off. So I'm wearing it while I still can."

Now, so many years later, the dress is just fabric lying limp in my hands. Meanwhile Tina stands next to me, defeated, wearing flannel pajama pants and a stretched out T-shirt.

"It's just a dress," I tell her. "You're still beautiful."

She doesn't look at me, but at her reflection in the mirror instead. "No, I'm not. I'm getting old, Ted. And there's nothing I can do about it."

I nod because I don't know what else to say. The fact that I think she's beautiful isn't enough for her, no matter how much I wish that it was. My heart starts beating a little faster, like I'm up on that building again, but no. I'm stuck in this bathroom, my feet planted firmly on the ground. How nice it would be, to be up high, looking down, with the option of letting go.

I'd be unafraid. I would just jump and let fate decide where I land.

"Aren't you going to say anything?" Tina demands.

"It's just a dress," I repeat. "You're still beautiful."

Only this time, when I say it, I believe it a little less.

Chapter Thirty-Two

It's lunch hour. I find a park bench, sit down, and I tilt my head up, so I can let the daylight warm my face. I probably look like some yoga-meditation type of guy, one I would make fun of if I were in a different sort of mood. But I don't care who sees me. And, thinking about the afternoon I have waiting for me back at the office, I discover that I don't care about any of it.

Not even a little.

I usually eat lunch at my desk: an orange, a bottle of water, and a sandwich from the stand downstairs. But today the sun is that desired party guest who's finally stopped pouting and come to socialize. Maybe summer will actually happen this year.

Summer has always been my favorite season. I love the smell of chlorine and burning charcoal, and that feeling that the day is stretched out in front of you, even if it isn't. Even if you have a million meetings and a million problems to fix, summer can still feel like it's full of lazy possibilities.

So I lose track of time as I sit here, thinking about Tina and Miles and Mason, and our house that I sort of hate and the fact that my own family doesn't really know who I am. How could they? I don't know who I am.

It's time to get up, to walk back to work, and I stand and stretch my legs. But when I cross the street I go towards a construction site, not towards my office. They're building a new arts center, and the plans are posted so anyone can come over and take a look. I could get lost in that, checking out the progress, trying to identify what has been built and imagining the rest.

Eventually my phone rings. Then a text, from my secretary. *Where are you?*

I don't respond.

Later, I'm standing in line at a food truck to buy fresh squeezed lemonade, which was one of my favorite treats as a boy. This time when my cell phone rings I see that it's Stan, my boss. I could avoid his call or I could do the brave thing and get this interaction over with. So I press answer.

"Hey," I say casually, as if he could be anyone.

"Where are you?" His voice burns through my phone. "We talked about this, Ted. We agreed you had one more chance, and then you go MIA on me—"

That's so like him, to ask a question but refuse to let me answer. So I interrupt. "I had an emergency. It's extremely personal, and I can't go into detail, but it's best if I don't come into work for a while. Sorry Stan, but I need to go on leave, indefinitely."

There's some shocked but controlled breathing on the other end of the line. "You understand that it will be unpaid leave?"

What a prick. For all he knows, my emergency is real. He could have a little more sympathy.

"I get it." It's almost my turn in the lemonade line. I need to get off the phone. "Just don't give away my office. I'll be in touch soon. Gotta go, Stan."

I press end and hand the lemonade girl six dollars because I'm paying extra for some cherry juice. When she gives it to me, I take a deep, satisfying sip. It's amazing how easy life can be if you're open to the possibilities.

When I get home Tina seems normal, for her at least, and she actually asks me how my day was. I let out a beleaguered sigh. "You wouldn't believe it," I say.

"What?"

"My latest account has gone crazy. I need to go to L.A. tomorrow."

Tina tilts her head quizzically, like she's trying to figure out the answer to a riddle. "Why?"

I swat at the air in answer. "It's not worth going into: big meeting, lots of jackasses laying blame...you know...same old, same old."

"How long will you be gone?"

"I'll be back Monday."

She doesn't ask why I have to stay for the weekend. She must not care. Maybe she's relieved at the idea of my absence. I know I'm relieved that she's not questioning it. If I told her the truth, that I'm flying home to Des Moines so I can investigate who is harassing my sister, she'd mock me, but only after she yelled about how I can't just blow off work whenever I feel like it.

So I use our computer to buy a ticket to Des Moines, which would be super easy to trace. But Tina doesn't believe I'm worth the effort.

Chapter Thirty-Three

I remember every detail even though it happened over thirty years ago.

It was sleeting outside. Dad came home at 5:18 and I ran up to him the moment he walked through the door. "Mom's not back yet." This was unusual. She liked to pick Robin up from daycare and be home to greet Ian and me when we got off the bus. Dad's skin went sort of pale, matching the beige trench coat he wore.

He called Mom's work. No answer. He called Robin's day care. "I'm going to pick up your sister," he said. "You're in charge, Ted." I nodded and sat on the edge of the couch. After a moment Ian came out and asked what was going on. I didn't want to worry him, so I said, "Let's watch TV." Ian turned on *Power Rangers*, which I hated, but I let him watch it anyway.

Dad got home with Robin and he made grilled cheese sandwiches, but he didn't eat one. Instead, he called some of Mom's friends, asking if they'd heard from her. None had.

Ian figured out that something wasn't right. "Why isn't mom back yet?" He kept asking this, over and over, even though Dad couldn't give him a good answer.

"Shut up!" I finally told him. It was the seventh time he'd blurted out the same question. "Dad doesn't know why Mom isn't back yet. Nobody does."

Robin gnawed on her sandwich. "More milk?" she asked. Dad didn't hear her, so I got up and refilled her Elmo cup.

We were in the dining room and Dad was in the kitchen, staring out the window, when the phone rang. And with that shrill sound, life as I knew it was over.

Dad came in from the kitchen, slowly enough that the phone rang two more times.

"Hello." His hands were trembling and he closed his eyes when he spoke again. "Yes." His voice was like a dying animal. "Yes, I understand." Then he hung up.

"I have to go out," he said.

"What! Why? Where's Mom?" Ian demanded.

"I'll be back soon," Dad answered, as if Ian had said nothing at all. "You're in charge, Ted."

I let Ian play video games while Robin and I crept into Mom and Dad's bedroom and lay against their pillows, Mom's sandalwood scent wafting around us. I read Robin *Sleeping Beauty*, and even if she was too young to understand the story, Robin liked the picture of the beautiful Lilac Fairy. Across from us, Mom's Mats Gustafson print hung on the wall, over her dresser. I was never completely sure if the lady in that print was walking towards something or if she was walking away.

But that night, as I waited for Dad to come home and tell us the horrific news that would scald my ears, I became sure.

She was definitely walking away.

****

The house is asleep but I'm awake, my muscles and my mind far more alert than I'd like them to be at this late hour. Lying in bed is an exercise in futility, so I get up and sit for a while out on the deck, staring at the stars. But I grow cold and a little bored. I'm not in the mood for television, so I wander the house until I arrive at our guestroom, where my mother's favorite painting hangs. I study it like I've never seen it before. The frame is worn and scratched, but the lady inside is beautiful as always, a walking shadow of light. I run my hands along the edges, softly, so not to damage anything.

Then this really weird thing happens.

A piece of notebook paper falls to my feet, as if it had been lodged between the back of the frame and the wall. I reach down and pick it up; it's the kind of paper I had in high school, torn from a spiral notebook, with frayed edges and thin light blue lines. I swear it's from my old Trapper Keeper, because Miles and Mason haven't yet graduated to narrow-ruled paper.

Get yourself together, don't be afraid, and jump.

The letters that flow along the page were obviously written by a gentle hand. It's definitely not my own messy scrawl, and it's neither neat nor blocky enough to be Tina's. No. I've seen this writing before, plenty of times... The fourteen birthday cards I have, saved in a shoebox, with their yearly messages about how much I've grown, how proud she is, and how much she loves me: they're all the same.

I'd know my mother's handwriting anywhere.

Chapter Thirty-Four

The next afternoon my brother Ian picks me up at the Des Moines airport. "I wish we'd known you were coming sooner," he says. "Eddie and I are remodeling the downstairs so the water in the second bathroom is turned off."

Ian is a contractor and he and his husband Eddie are constantly remodeling their house. "That's okay," I reply. "I don't mind."

"You'll mind when the toilet doesn't work at three AM. Besides, it's just a mess down there." Ian grips the steering wheel, his smile not meeting his eyes. "You really don't want to stay with us."

I rub the back of my neck and think. "Dad is out of town?"

"Yeah, he and Catherine are in South America. I think they're trying to hit every continent before he turns eighty."

"Oh." I look out the window, at the flat landscape and the expansiveness of everything. Compared to Philadelphia, Des Moines is so spread out and undeveloped. "Well, I guess I could stay at a hotel."

"Why? Monty has plenty of room, and they've already invited everyone over for beer and foosball. Just stay with him."

A headache is creeping in. That's so like Monty, to hold an unasked for, unwanted get-together in my honor. Now, if I don't stay with him, I really am the family prick. "What about Jack?" I ask. I prefer my younger cousin to my older one.

Ian shakes his head ruefully. "I don't know; apparently the bathroom at his condo is haunted. I think it's just an excuse for him to shack up with Isobel."

"Isobel is his new girlfriend?" I ask and Ian nods. "And let me guess, her place is really small?"

Those dimples in Ian's rosy cheeks appear. Maybe if I'd gotten dimples like Ian's, people would like me more and I'd be a better person. "Yup," Ian answers. "It's small with thin walls, and Jack and Isobel are still in their honeymoon stage. I'm telling you, Ted. Stay with Monty."

I know when a cause is lost so I let him drive me there. By the time we arrive it's practically dinner hour. We go downstairs, to a cavernous rec room that's like the common area in a family hotel. But this is Des Moines so I bet Monty only paid around $500,000 for it. Location, location, location.

Soon Jack and Isobel show up, and Ian drives home to retrieve Eddie and their children, and then everyone is too consumed with beer, pizza, and foosball to be super-annoying. I only have to explain why I'm here a half dozen times. Nobody buys that I simply had a few days off and was feeling nostalgic for the place where I grew up. I mean, why not wait until Dad is in town? Why not bring my family along? It must show that I'm on the brink of a midlife crisis, because everyone is treating me with kid gloves.

"So you have a haunted bathroom?" I ask Jack, and there's an eruption of laughter.

Jack glares at Lucy, who is both his sister-in-law and his good friend. "Thanks again for blabbing about that," he says to her.

"I can't help it if he overheard!" Lucy cries, gesturing toward Monty, who laughs, slings his arm over her shoulders, and plants a kiss on top of her curly head of hair.

"She can't keep secrets from me," Monty boasts.

"And you can't keep secrets from anyone else," Jack retorts. "Seriously, you have the biggest mouth of anyone I know."

They've been playing a half-hearted game of foosball but now Monty removes his arm from around Lucy's shoulder so he can use both hands to rotate the knobs. "Yes!" he cries when he sinks a goal. Then he gives Ian a high five.

When Jack, Monty, Ian and I are together, we always have competitions and we're always looking for new ways to divide into teams. This time it's the shorter siblings versus the taller ones.

Jack stands at his full, impressive height, which is a couple inches higher than me, and frowns. "Sorry I lost," he says to me. "But yeah, my bathroom is haunted. You'd understand if you stayed there a night or two."

I think about last night and that piece of paper I found. I swear that my mother wrote me that message. But how could that be? Maybe Tina wrote it and hid it behind my mom's picture, but Tina is neither perceptive nor solicitous enough to think up a stunt like that.

"How can you tell it's haunted?" I ask. "I mean, did you ever think that you're just going crazy?"

He grins. "All the time. But then Isobel witnessed it: this white, pasty stuff that formed in quick clumps, the puddles on the floor when no water was running, and the sound of footsteps when no one was there. And one night the lights just started flickering for no reason."

I gesture toward the other side of the room, where Isobel is sitting with Eddie and all the kids, watching a Disney movie and eating pizza. "Well, it's working out for you, though."

"Yeah, it is." Jack bounces on his toes a couple of times before he walks to Isobel, sits down, and gives her a sideways squeeze, his blond head tilting toward her as she sinks into him. It's about time that Jack is lucky in love.

At family gatherings it's easy to forget that we're adults because we all automatically slip into the roles we played while growing up. It doesn't matter how much time goes by; Monty will always be the leader, Ian the jokester, Jack the nice guy, and I'm the asshole.

"Okay, so it's you and me, Ted," Ian says, stepping closer to the foosball table. "You have a chance to redeem the taller siblings, but I doubt you'll succeed." He flexes his fingers, crouches a little, and grabs the knobs on the side of the table.

"Hey!"

I turn toward the voice at the end of the room and see that it belongs to a young man with wavy brown hair and a crooked smile. "Sorry it took me so long to get here. Class went late. Is there still room in the foosball competition?"

"Sure, Nick," Monty states. "You can join the short team."

Nick comes over, sees me, and extends a hand. "Hi!" he says. "You must be Ted. It's nice to finally meet you. I'm—"

I cut him off. "I know who you are. You're the guy who wants to marry my sister."

Chapter Thirty-Five

I make Nick promise to have lunch with me tomorrow. Unfortunately, Monty invites himself along, and we're going to eat at Jack's restaurant. Two extra family members will make figuring Nick out more difficult. At least Ian can't be there. As it is, I don't know how I'm supposed to interrogate Nick with Jack and Monty around.

Right now Monty leads me to the guestroom. It's spacious, like everything else in their house, with brown walls and a low, square-shaped bed that looks like a waterbed but the mattress is firm.

"I hope you'll be comfortable," Monty says. "Let me know if you need anything."

"It's perfect. Thanks for letting me stay."

"Of course. You're welcome any time, Ted." He taps his fingers against his thigh, as if his mind is racing with unasked questions. I put my suitcase on a low table and unzip it, to signal that I'm about to unpack. Maybe now he'll leave me alone.

Nope. Monty clears his throat. "So, is everything okay?"

"Yeah. Of course." I can hear the tightness in my voice but can't be bothered to loosen it. "Do you have a Wi-Fi password? I need to catch up on some work emails."

"Yeah. I'll write it down for you." Monty grabs a pen and a slip of paper from a basket on the dresser and scrolls down the information. "Here you go." He hands it to me.

"Thanks." I try to make my smile genuine but I can imagine how stressed my face must look.

"So, Tina is okay? You and Tina are okay?"

Is it because he's a lawyer that he'll ask anyone anything, no matter how personal the question? I take out my laptop and I plop it onto the bed. "She's fine. We're... you know. Marriage is hard." Shit. I shouldn't have said that. I wasn't planning to but the words just trekked out.

"You don't have to tell me."

Please. The way Lucy looks at him is like how Tina used to look at me, but that light left her eyes years ago. Besides, Monty is used to adoration because he's lived with it his entire life. "You haven't been married for as long as Tina and me," I tell him. "Just wait, it gets worse." I know that if I sound too negative he'll cross-examine me more, so I pump some air into my words. "Still, Tina and I are fine. I'm just here to meet Nick. I didn't want Robin's wedding to be the first time we were introduced."

"I thought you weren't coming to the wedding."

I pause, caught in a lie. "Robin told you that?"

Monty looks at me, unblinking. "She and Lucy have grown close. It was Lucy who offered to host the wedding at our place, and they went shopping for dishes and stuff together. They tell each other things, and then Lucy tells me..." Monty shrugs like it's no big deal that he's more of a big brother to Robin than I am. "Anyway, it's great that you want to get to know Nick. He's a good guy. I'm sure you'll agree."

"I don't remember asking your opinion."

Monty raises his dark eyebrows and smirks. "Still got the same old charm, huh Ted?" He slaps the wall and heads for the door. "Good night."

He leaves. What a douche.

Never mind; now I can work on my second P.I. lesson. I power up my computer and log on. Luckily, today's tutorial is on investigative observation skills. It quotes Sherlock Holmes, where he says an investigator should be seen but not observed. There's no way Nick won't observe me tomorrow, but I can at least let him drive the conversation. I also need to awaken that primal hunter within me, the one who doesn't miss even the smallest details, because it could be a clue that will make or break the case.

The next day Monty and I are crammed into one side of a wooden booth and a pale-faced Nick is on the other. Jack has been in and out, at times dealing with restaurant business but mostly sitting with us, like he's doing now, casually cozied up to Nick as if they're best buddies. "So you got to skype with Robin?" Jack asks Nick. "How did she seem? Isobel is worried about her."

"Why is Isobel worried about Robin? Do they even know each other?" I ask.

Jack scrunches one side of his face at me. "They've been best friends since college. That's how she and I met. Robin introduced us."

"Oh. I guess I miss a lot, not living in the area."

Nick wipes his brow even though it's breezy in here. He looks like he has food poisoning, or maybe the plague. "Yeah, I know Robin wishes she saw you more."

I have to bite my lip not to laugh.

"Anyway," Nick throatily continues, "I only got to talk to Robin once and there was a production person standing off to the side the whole time, tapping her watch and giving us directions. Robin seemed...stressed. Honestly, I'm worried about her too."

"I wouldn't be too concerned," Monty says, tapping his fingers in that way I hate. "She's pretty tough."

"Yeah, she is tough. But with everything that's going on, you know, with the website and the, um..." he rocks slightly in place as his cheeks grow pink. "...the sex-tape. I think she feels powerless."

Monty sits up straight. "Sex-tape?"

"You haven't seen it." Nick shakes his head. "Thank God." Then the words spill out, like the vomit he must be holding back. "At first it was just this weird photo montage, you know, clips of her from TV and plays she's done, but I checked the website again this morning and there's..." Nick struggles to swallow as he hyperventilates through his nose. "Well, it's of the two of us. I'm blocked out, but you can see a lot of Robin, and..." He lets his head drop into his hands. "That video is from the night before she left! I didn't even know we were being filmed and I doubt she did either. Robin would never..." He raises his eyes, suddenly mortified by who his audience is. "I mean," he stammers, "she's just not like that. And I called the webhost but all I got was a load of bull. I have to do something! I promised Robin I'd take care of things while she's gone, and now, I mean... I am so completely fucked!"

There's a moment of the most awkward silence ever, as we all squirm in our seats and wish the world would end. Nick takes a deep breath. "I meant that metaphorically, obviously...I am metaphorically fucked, because Robin is.. I mean, she's obviously my number one concern, and..."

"Can I see it?" Monty asks, and I swivel towards him as much as the cramped space will allow.

"No you can't see it!" I answer. "What the hell is wrong with you? Nobody should watch it! We need to get it taken down!"

"Exactly!" Monty retorts, his cheeks flushing underneath his tan skin. "And I will write the scariest, most threatening legalese letter ever to the web hosts, or I'll call them, but first, unfortunately, I need to see the video so I have something to base my threats on."

"Forget that! Go to the police!" I tell Nick.

"I already have," he tells me. "But the police just said they'd look into it. Meanwhile I can't even trace who started the website which means I can't contact the coward myself."

"I'm sorry Nick, but can I please see the video?" Monty asks again. Nick takes out his smartphone, calls up the website, and hands it over. While the video plays, Monty squints and holds the phone away from him, like it's infectious. I try not to watch while Jack looks uncomfortable and winces at the sounds. After a few of seconds of grunts and groans, Monty mercifully presses stop.

"It's, um..." Monty's fingers listlessly go limp against the table. Even he can't think of the appropriate thing to say in this situation. "It's pretty dark. You're, um, sure this is the two of you, in your bedroom?"

"Yeah," Nick replies. "Of course I'm sure."

"Well, you're the expert!" Jack states jovially, but his words fall flat when no one cracks a smile. "You know," he continues, "there are all sorts of stuff you can download now, programs like Spyware that will film you without your knowing about it."

"But who would have access to Robin's computer to do such a thing?" Nick asks. "Can it be installed by hacking in from a remote site?"

"You need to think outside the box," I say. "Whoever's doing this is very creative. We need to get creative too."

Monty scrolls the website down. "What's this about her sending money to one of the judges on *The Standout*?" he asks.

"What?" Nick urgently reaches for his phone and he holds it close, scanning a blurb and reading it aloud. "It has been confirmed that as a guarantee for her success on *The Standout*, Robin has transferred $40,000 into the account of judge Evie Messina." Nick's face is blank. "That's crazy. Robin doesn't have that kind of money."

"May I see it again?" Monty asks, reaching for the phone. "This is definitely slander," he says after he's taken a look. "We'll have it taken down too."

"But what about the $40,000? What if someone accessed her bank account?" Nick looks to each of us, his eyes wide.

"Can you log onto her account and see? Do you have her password?" Monty asks.

"It's written down at home." Nick runs his hand through his hair, making it stick out in varied directions.

"Don't worry, Nick," Monty says, in a lawyer-voice that I wish he would reserve for clients. "We can find out who's doing this and we'll make it stop."

Once again, Monty is trying to swoop in to save the day. But not this time. This time I'm going to be the hero.

The lunch is strained after that and Nick isn't in the mood for chit chat. He and Monty are anxious to contact the webhost and get the tape taken down, but personally, I'm more concerned with busting whoever is behind the tape so it can never be posted again. I decide that it's definitely time to take this investigation to the next level. I tell Monty that I'm spending the evening over at Ian's. Then I borrow Monty's car and drive to Nick and Robin's house.

Nick had mentioned that he's playing piano at some restaurant tonight so his place is dark when I get there. I get out of the car and stroll around to the back, careful not to trip over stray twigs or sprinkler systems. Their house is on a quiet street and it's the smallest one on the block. I need to make sure that the next-door neighbors, with their expansive Ranch-style home, lit up windows, and the "We Watch, We Report," yard sign don't see me.

So I stealthily move through the shadows. I don't have a real plan; if I can't get inside, I suppose I'll just sort through their garbage or do some surveillance from Monty's parked car. Once Nick gets back I'll knock on the door and find a way to snoop while he's home. But hot damn! There's a spare key in the nozzle of their garden hose in the backyard. I'd bet my favorite tie that Robin was the one who hid it. We had a very similar hiding spot for our spare key at our childhood home.

Their house is tiny. In the corner of the room, underneath the table that holds their mail, I see a file box. I crouch down, turn on my cell phone's flashlight app, and start digging. This has to be Nick's work because there's no way Robin has suddenly become so organized. He has neatly labeled folders for everything: tax records, tuition bills, home equity, medical information, and on and on. The files aren't alphabetized, which surprises me, but towards the back there's actually a folder labeled "passwords."

Okay, so he's organized, but not very bright. Hasn't he ever heard of intruders?

The file contains one sheet of paper, which I lay on the floor and I take a picture of with my phone. After I check to make sure that my flash worked well enough for the photo to be readable, I put the file box back as it was, and start going through their mail. Mostly it's a lot of bills.

I'm heading for what I think is the bedroom when I hear footsteps and voices. Suddenly my pulse is pounding in my ears. I dart out the back but I don't have time to close the door all the way behind me. So I hug the side of the house, hoping I can creep back to the car before they notice the intrusion. Nervous sweat drips from my forehead as I struggle not to breathe too loud.

"Thanks for dinner, Dad." The voice is female, and only now do I remember that Nick's younger sister lives here too. She flicks the lights on and I hear them walk inside.

"It was my pleasure." He sounds stiff and formal, like he's trying too hard. "I'm glad we had our talk."

"Me too."

There have been no further footsteps, so I figure that the sister is still in the entryway, facing away from the backdoor, and the dad is focused on her so he hasn't looked up yet. I should use this opportunity to make my get-away, but she says something that makes me stay and listen.

"You understand why I'm so concerned about Nick?"

"Of course," he answers.

"I really hope he knows what he's doing."

"I know, Sweetheart. And you've had to make some difficult choices."

"Yeah, but—" she cuts herself off. "What is it, Dad?"

"Did you leave your back door open?"

Crap! I bolt, running across the yard and nearly slipping on the wet grass. But I make it to Monty's fuel-efficient family sized vehicle, which is also my get-away car. I have no idea if they've seen me or not as I get in and drive off.

Chapter Thirty-Six

The rest of my trip is uneventful; Monty is the big hero when he gets the sex tape taken down. So I'm anxious to get home, but when I do, Miles and Mason are at their baseball game, which Tina has taken them to. They don't get home until late, and then it's like they'd forgotten I was ever gone.

A few days later, Tina is silent in the passenger seat as I drive us to the auto show gala. She's barely spoken to me since I turned my back on her the night she was crying and I haven't known what to say since. I glance at her while we're stopped at a red light. Her dress is blue. The top is loose but the bottom is tight across her butt, and there's a long slit that shows off her leg.

"You look amazing," I tell her. "Everyone will think I'm the luckiest guy in the world."

She just huffs, crosses her arms over her chest, and turns toward the window, away from me. The light turns green but I don't press my foot against the gas petal. We just sit, until the cars behind us honk.

"Ted, what are you doing? Go!"

I do, but I turn left instead of going straight, so we're no longer headed in the right direction for the gala.

"Ted, you're going the wrong way! Have you gone crazy?"

The squeal of the tires is my only answer as the car accelerates. I don't even know where we're headed, but I do know that we've been on the wrong path. Besides, some of my co-workers will be at the gala, which means Tina would for sure find out about my unpaid leave. That can't happen, so I turn down random streets and alleys while Tina white knuckles the dashboard, too surprised at my behavior to protest.

After a few minutes I see a Mexican restaurant, the type we used to eat at when we were in college. It looks small and dark, and I bet the menus all have salsa stains, and the margaritas come in huge, plastic glasses full of tequila and limeade, and all the food is covered in brown sauce and cheese. I pull up and park along the curb.

"What the hell, Ted?"

I unfasten my seat belt, so I can lean in and touch her bare arm. "Tina, let's forget about the gala. Please, for one night, can't we just talk like we used to? Remember when we used to get a little drunk and laugh at stupid jokes? Let's do that again."

I brush my fingers along her shoulder and by some miracle she doesn't pull away. I can see her thinking. She's blinking rapidly and biting the corner of her mouth, probably calculating how many calories are in a taquito.

"Sugar, you're so lovely." I whisper, because all of a sudden I'm kind of choked up. "Please believe that."

Tina's eyes wander for a moment but then she looks back at me, and the moment feels honest, like we're naked in front of each other. "You stopped calling me 'sugar' about five years ago."

Is that true? Surely not, but I think back, trying to remember our moments of affection. There was a time when Tina was the only sweetness in my life, the only sweetness I'd ever really felt, and when I held her in my arms all I wanted was to protect her, to make her happy.

But have I become so engrossed with losing myself that I've cut her off as well?

"I'm sorry, Sugar. I guess I've just been distracted."

And then it's like sun breaking through the clouds, because Tina smiles.

Chapter
Thirty-Seven

Tina moans and tightens her grip around me, her nails digging into my back. I can taste the fiesta salad and Margarita she had earlier as I plunge my tongue through her lips. I kiss her with enough passion to make up for the all kissing we haven't done for months. She's like this little lightening rod. Her body has gotten so small; there are fewer soft spots than before, but I am so grateful to have her in my arms that joy is my one, overreaching emotion. The gala dress she so carefully put herself into is lying in a careless heap by my office chair and we're actually on top of my desk. I'm taking her in the way you always see hot couples in movies do, the way I've always wished she'd someday agree to.

After we're done my body feels like warm, oozy lava. I collapse into my chair and Tina lunges for her dress to cover herself. It's not that she doesn't want me to see her naked, I decide, but that she's worried somebody will walk in.

"My office door is locked. We're safe." My voice is soft. Tina's back is to me, and if she hears me she doesn't acknowledge it. "Come here." I'm a little louder now, but I make sure not to sound demanding. I just want to sound like the guy who desires his wife, who needs her like he needs water and sunlight.

She turns, and hot damn, there's another smile. I pat my knee in a "come hither" gesture and she actually complies. "You have a lock on your office door?" She betrays a hint of laughter as she descends into my lap. "Why do you need a lock, Ted? You'd better not be having assignations with any other women on your desk."

She's wrapped up into me. My arms are around her legs, her arms are around my shoulders, and her head is tucked up against my chest, directly below my chin. Possible jokes come to mind, like all my assignations are on the floor or against the wall; or the lock is to keep me in, not to keep others out, but the words just wilt on my lips. All I can manage is, "You know there's only you, Tina."

If she's startled by my sincerity, she doesn't show it. We just sit there for a while, feeling our hearts beating. After a while she says, "I suppose we should get back. I told the babysitter we'd be home by eleven."

She climbs off my lap and begins dressing. I watch her, marveling at her beauty. The way that the shadows play across her profile makes me think of the Mats Gustafson watercolor.

"Hey, can I ask you a weird question?"

Tina looks at me as she straightens the dress strap over her left shoulder. "What?"

"Did you ever write me a note in my mother's handwriting and hide it behind that painting in the guestroom?"

She squints and puckers her lips. "Why would I do something like that?"

"I don't know. But I found the weirdest thing the other day. There was this sheet of paper in my mom's handwriting with the message: *Get yourself together, don't be afraid, and jump.*"

"What's your point, Ted?" Tina's arms are crossed over her chest in a defensive pose.

"Never mind. I was just asking." I reach down for my pants and suddenly I'm nicked in the forehead by something heavy and blunt. I realize that Tina's thrown a paperweight at me.

"Are you crazy?" I yell. "You could have killed me!"

"Don't be so dramatic!" It's like flames are shooting from Tina's eyes. "And don't call me crazy! You're the crazy one! Are you seriously letting a note from your dead mother trigger your midlife crisis?"

"What are you talking about?"

She counts on her fingers. "Your trip to Des Moines; your unpaid leave; your private investigator course!" Tina walks toward me and puts her face in mine. "You didn't even try to hide any of it. Instead you just lied! How stupid do you think I am?"

"I don't think you're stupid." I'm flailing, grasping for words I don't have. "I just didn't know how to tell you."

"Obviously." Her breath comes out in short, angry puffs. "I ran into Stan's wife at the club and she told me you've stopped going to work. I pretended like I knew. All it took was one look at our account activity to figure out the rest."

"Why didn't you say anything until now?"

"Because it wasn't worth my time." She straightens out her dress and grabs my car keys, which were lying on my desk. "It's a good thing you still have your office," she says. "Because you're not sleeping at home tonight."

And with that, she storms away, slamming the door on her way out. I don't chase after her. I just let myself drown in the waves of defeat that wash over me. What hurts the most is that tonight was just an act.

She was just biding her time until the right moment came to confront me.

She's right to be angry. But, bad as I feel, I don't believe I'm the crazy one. She threw a paper-weight at my head. What was that about?

My hand creeps over to my computer and I flick it on, though I hadn't thought consciously to do so. I have access to all sorts of data bases here that I don't have at home.

If I can't figure out my own life, maybe I can fix Robin's.

Part III: Robin

Chapter Thirty-Eight

"**S**low down, Ted." He is usually so calm and composed that I don't even recognize this half-crazed voice at the other end of the line. Besides, his "emergency phone call" to the production team at *The Standout* is also out of character. I look at the caller ID screen and see that it's neither his home number nor his cell. "Where are you?"

"At my office."

"But it's Sunday morning! Why are you—"

"Never mind about that! I have to warn you. The sex tape was awful but we got it taken down. Even still, I think Nick did something bad. Or maybe it was his sister, but I doubt she'd know how. Several days ago, that *Rotten Robin* website claimed that you bribed one of the judges on *The Standout*. There was no evidence of it in your bank account. Well, today there is. There's a transfer of $40,000, only it's from Nick's account and in your name."

"What? How do you even know all this?"

I hear him start to answer, but suddenly the phone is snatched from my grasp. I turn and see that Jim Giles is the one who did the snatching. Kyla is standing behind him, chin down, sneering triumphantly. Jim places the phone back in its receiver like it weighs 100 pounds.

"I was talking to my brother!"

"Well, we'll add that to the list of rules you've broken!" He literally waves his finger at me. "We have to talk. Now!"

The cameras follow the three of us to a private space, but "private space" is an oxymoron on any reality TV show. Once we're behind closed doors, with several cameras pointed at our faces, Jim confronts me for real. "Kyla says you invaded her work station and stole her best pair of fabric sheers."

"What? No I didn't!"

Jim lifts the shears for me to see. "We found these with your stuff, Robin."

"Kyla is lying! She framed me!"

Jim shakes his head. "You're the one who disappeared during filming last night, so I'm afraid I can't give you the benefit of the doubt." Jim's face is pink with strain as he turns to Kyla, giving her back her shears. "Kyla, I need you to step out now."

Kyla, poser that she is, nods gravely. "Of course," she says, giving me a snaky grin as she shuts the door behind her. Then Jim speaks again. "Evie Messina got a text from you this morning."

"Um...Uh," I stutter, "I haven't been using my phone. It's against the rules. And you guys have it anyway."

"I don't know how you managed but we have proof." Jim gives me my phone. Sure enough, there's a text from me to Evie Messina. *Check your bank account. I've just given you another reason to take me to the top.*

"Robin," Jim drawls, "if this text was all it was, I'd believe that you're being framed. But $40,000 has been transferred into Evie's bank account in your name."

"I knew nothing about this!" I say. "I mean, not until just now when my brother called to warn me. But someone has been messing with my phone and my computer. I can even show you the website!"

"So you're saying that your fiancé acted independently of you?" Jim purses his lips and I wonder if he's actually listening to me.

"What? No! Nick would never do that. Besides, he doesn't even have that kind of money. We're both being framed."

Jim shakes his head, deeply disappointed. "I can assure you, Robin, he has the money because it came from his account. I'm sorry, but, given the circumstances, I have to ask you to leave."

I can't let this happen. I'll be the Tanya Harding of the fashion world.

"Jim, I swear I'm innocent. Don't I even get a chance to defend myself?"

"This is your chance!" He places his hands on his hips. "Can you give me some details about how this happened? I mean..." his eyes roll toward the ceiling, "if it's not you, can you tell me who *is* responsible?"

Chastised, I scratch at my wrist. "Someone has been messing with me. I think I was pushed while I was on the treadmill, and yesterday someone dumped water on all my fabric..." saying it out loud sounds so lame, just schoolyard crimes.

"And you didn't report it because...?" Jim asks.

"Because I was worried I was just being paranoid."

Jim strokes his chin slowly, deep in thought. "I wish you had reported it. Maybe you'd have a leg to stand on now."

"Talk to Gabe." I gesture towards him, as he's holding a camera in my face. "He came in right after I fell and he got it on film. And he also caught my freak out after I found water on my dress."

Jim glances at Gabe but he doesn't actually say anything to him. That would be taboo. You don't talk to cameramen, not while you're being filmed. Meanwhile, Gabe stays silent; he's merely the eyes and ears but definitely not the voice, and no matter how much I implore him, that's not going to change.

Jim sighs. "Unfortunately, that's just not enough." He sighs. "Robin, I really want to believe you're innocent, but there's too much evidence stacked up against you. I hate to say it, but I need you to go clean out your work station."

"Fine." Angry tears threaten to burst like a broken dam, so I rush out of our "private space" towards the workroom. I'd rather just get out of here fast. At least now I'll have use of my cell phone. I can talk to Nick and we can figure out what's going on.

Everybody's looking at me while I pack up my stuff and the room goes silent. I keep my head down because if I meet anyone's eyes, I'll bawl, and it will be ugly crying, with oozing snot and possibly drool. I'm throwing sketchpads, pincushions, tape measures and spools of thread haphazardly into my box when the models come in. Zelda must have heard the news because she's wiping away tears as she rushes over.

"But you're innocent," she cries, as if we'd already been arguing about my dismissal.

"I'm sorry," I tell her, trying not to let my voice shake. Gabe is capturing all of this. "I know this totally screws you over too."

Zelda shakes her head. "Don't worry about me. Amos's model has mono, so I'm not out. They're shifting me over to him."

"Well, good. Amos is a great designer, so that should work out."

"But I want to work with you." Zelda is wearing a black sweatshirt and her short hair is slicked back. It makes her appear even more waif-like than usual, and her big brown eyes grow so large, she reminds me of a tearful, saucer-eyed tot from a kitschy 1970s painting. "I'm going to figure out who's behind this," she says. "Don't worry, Robin. I'll do some snooping, and I'll catch the person and then they'll bring you back."

I'm sorting through stuff, disoriented, when my phone dings with a text. What the heck, I may as well look at it. What are they going to do, kick me out twice?

It's from an unknown number. *Now do you believe me? Break up with Nick or this torment will never end.*

I look back at my only friend here. "Don't snoop around, Zelda. We don't know what this person is capable of. I don't want you getting hurt."

"Somebody pushed you. Somebody dumped water on your fabric. And I'm finding out who!" Zelda yells this last part and she looks around the room, deliberately letting her eyes land on Kyla. Then she breaks her gaze and gives me a hug. "Don't worry, Robin. This isn't goodbye."

I hug her back, speechless. If I had the words, I would thank her for being the one person who believes me without question. But as it is, I just give her a trembling smile, pick up my stuff, and walk out through the workroom door.

I don't even say goodbye.

Part IV: Zelda

Chapter Thirty-Nine

I'll start at the beginning.

Around eighteen years ago my mom and dad temporarily fell in love and had me. As I grew, people said I was sort of graceful, relatively smart, and not completely unattractive. But I was timid, afraid to take my share. Until one day I met Julie, who knew how to fight for what she wanted. Sometimes I even believed she could use magic to help her cause.

I met her on my first day of dance class, where the other girls pointed and snickered at me. Everyone else's leotard was black but mine was pink. The teacher looked at me and nodded, but it was a dismissive nod, a "what are you doing here" nod.

I was ten years old. I was following in my mother's footsteps. I was making a big mistake and I was sniffing, trying not to cry, until the girl in front of me turned, and her whisper floated to my ears.

"Don't worry. Everyone here has a bad first day."

Her smile was better than hot chocolate with marshmallows. Then the music stopped while the teacher chatted briefly with the piano player. There was just enough time to thank this short girl in a black leotard, black tights, and pink ballet skirt. "Cool skirt." I whispered. "I still like pink."

"Me too." She winked at me. "I'm Julie."

I marveled that someone so nice could also be so good.

Julie learned to dance before she learned to walk. When she's in the midst of a pas de duex, twirling and jumping into her partner's arms, her body stretches like a swan's neck and she defies the laws of gravity.

And I see something in her that I don't have.

Chapter Forty

I can tell you a story, she says. *I can tell it with the flex of my foot and the arch of my back. I can spin tales of love and betrayal through arabesques and grande jetes.*

Sometimes the stories will have magic and other times they'll have madness. But as long we dance ballet, there will always be a story.

Just like my friendship with you; I think this but don't say it aloud. On good days you and I are magic, trading jokes at the barre and sharing confidences after class, as we hurry home through the cool evening air, so our muscles won't lose heat too quickly and cramp. On bad days you are angry for no reason, quick to judge and reprimand me for my mistakes. But that only makes me want to please you more, to win your approval, to feel special, chosen as the only girl qualified to be your best friend.

I am Scheherazade, she tells me. *I am magic because I know stories of love and betrayal.*

Sometimes, there might even be some madness thrown in.

Chapter Forty-One

"Have you heard the news?" Julie prances up to me in the dressing room. She's in her leotard, pointe shoes, tights, and leg warmers. A simple black ballet skirt is tied around her waist because she's convinced that she has a big butt so she always tries to cover it.

I drop my duffel bag onto a bench and take off my jacket. I wore my leotard here and my tights are hiding beneath my sweat pants. I'll want my change of clothes later, after everything I'm wearing now is sweat-soaked. I sit next to my duffel bag and remove my converse sneakers which are damp from walking through puddles.

Julie's forehead is pinched, both from the tight bun her that hair is pulled into, and from her electric smile.

"What news?" I ask.

"Ballet Institute East is partnering with that TV show, *The Standout*. This season, instead of using real models, they want to use ballet dancers instead!"

"Why?"

"It's their latest theme, so every challenge will be based off of a famous ballet, like *Swan Lake* or *The Firebird*. But it's incredible, right? We're going to be on TV!"

I lace up my toe shoes. "Really? Are we just automatically on?"

"Well," Julie says carefully. "I guess you need to be at least 5'4" and 18 years old, but we both are, so we're good."

"I can't believe it's that easy." I don't remind Julie that she's only 5'3" and three fourths, something she usually flaunts, because at 5'6" I'm a little tall for a ballerina.

I stand and stretch. "Don't we have to audition, or get selected somehow?"

"Who cares if we do?" Julie demands. "Nobody is going to beat us."

She loops her arm through mine and leads me from the dressing room into the dance studio, where we have spent thousands of hours over the past ten years. Julie and I tell each other everything. On the outside, she's like any other girl at Ballet Institute East; her light brown hair is always pulled into a tight bun and she's the right height. She doesn't stick out when we stand in a line. Because of my extra two inches, I'm always on the end or in the back, but Julie is always in the middle, where she will blend in, unnoticed, while everyone sees her.

I notice her. I see her. That's our unspoken deal.

"Do you think your mom will freak out when you tell her?" Her voice rasps like she has a cough. "Oh Zelda!" Julie always stresses her "ahs" when she's imitating my mother, "reality television is so common!"

We stretch at the barre and I'm already contemplating my walk home in the dusky evening. "Do you want to get coffee later?" I ask. "I have stuff to tell you."

"Can't. Wish I could, but I'm expected home. Tell me whatever it is now."

"It's not important. Just more about my dad."

Julie raises her foot onto the higher barre and rubs her blistered toes. "Is he still boning his assistant? God, that's so gross."

"Yeah..." my voice trails off as Yuri walks by. Actually, Yuri soars more than he walks and in his wake there's always the scent of ego.

Julie smacks her lips. "The Russian is mine."

I laugh and whack her in the shoulder. "Says who? Every girl here has claimed him."

"What do you know about it?" Julie's chin is quivering with irritation. "Just because you're a celibate freak doesn't mean I have to be."

I let the fire of her words scald me. You would think that by now, I'd be immune to Julie's sudden angry outbursts, but I'm not.

"Sorry," she mumbles. "Just kidding on that last part."

"No worries." I say it because I have to.

We skip over the moment, pretend it didn't just happen. Our eyes follow Yuri to the corner of the room, where he opens his gym bag and takes out a black crew-neck T-shirt. Muscles rippling, he peels off his white tank top. Julie is practically salivating and when he pulls on his black shirt she shakes her head and mumbles. "Guys like Yuri should only ever go around shirtless."

"He'd get pretty cold," I say.

"You just don't get it." Julie's tone is now affectionate.

Then the teacher walks in, the music starts, and class begins.

Chapter Forty-Two

When I get home Mom is there but Dad is not. As always.

"How was class?" Mom asks.

"Fine." I breeze towards my bedroom, where I take off my converses. Then I plop down on my bed with the black satin comforter that reminds me of *Swan Lake*. Mom follows and stands in my doorway, assessing the mess. She picks a book up off the floor, scowling like it's a dirty gym sock. "Why do you have an AP Economics textbook?"

"For school." We both know that by "school" I mean the online option I have chosen in order to graduate. Dance class and rehearsals take up too much time for me to be normal.

"Yes, but AP Economics? Wasn't there something easier you could take?"

I ignore her question, pick up my pastel colored pyraminx, and start turning, trying to line up the colors, keeping my gaze off Mom. When she's standing among my clutter of books, dancewear, and collection of Rubik's Cube type puzzles, she seems even more glassy and brittle than usual in her perfection. But she's still beautiful, which is only fair, since she spends a lot of time and money on her looks.

She sighs. "Zelda, why didn't you tell me that you're taking AP Economics? It could distract you from your dancing."

There is a little purple triangle in my puzzle that is out of place and I can't rescue it from a sea of pink. I turn it to the right, but that just makes it worse, so I turn it back and then down...

"Zelda!"

Mom snatches my puzzle away. "At least pretend to listen when I talk to you."

I sigh in defeat. "Mom, it's no big deal. I just thought it would be challenging. Economics is like a really complex puzzle, and someday I'm going to need a plan, you know, for when I'm no longer dancing-"

"Don't think that way! That's defeatism, and I won't accept it." Mom puts the puzzle and my book on my desk, but it's hard to find space amidst all my tiny model skyscrapers. "I know you like all this stuff, and it's good to have hobbies." She gestures to everything: the puzzles, the models, the school books. "If you would just focus, Zelda, you could be the best. You will get that internship you've always dreamed about and then you will have options. But you have to focus." She punctuates each word with emphasis.

I've been hearing the same spiel all my life.

And since we're talking about options, the last time I had one was when I was ten years old. I chose "ballerina" and now I'm tied to that, irrevocably. I mean, I love dancing. But there are other things I love too. "Mom, the economics class won't distract me from getting an internship. I promise."

Mom bites her lip like she's holding back, like she might say more, but she's not completely insane. Most parents want their kids to work hard at school, and she gets this. But her singular purpose is to make me the next, great prima ballerina. "It had better not," she says. Then she leaves.

Without asking if I've had dinner.

I pick up my phone and text Julie. *I want to audition for The Standout. Give me all the details.*

Chapter Forty-Three

Two trains get us to the audition and it's packed with models who have got to be European. I bet that they speak French and that they never go a minute with their hair uncombed. "Is that what we're supposed to look like?" I whisper to Julie, gesturing toward a tall, skinny girl with a sleek, jet black bob. Her full, bright lips are scowling poutily. Or pouting scowlily.

Julie gives her half a glance. "Speak for yourself. I do look like that."

In your dreams, I want to say, but Julie is in one of her moods today. The type where her nails will come out if I just look at her sideways.

I say nothing, but still that's the wrong thing, because she's quiet as we fill out our audition forms.

"Hey, Adrian!" Julie calls exuberantly to a girl from Ballet Institute East and talks to her like they're besties. But if I say anything I get the silent treatment back.

I almost leave because I feel so young. Inexperienced, like I'm a fourth grader who's with sixth graders because I'm good at math. And all the other kids think I have cooties.

But it would be so cool to have a real job. I'd have a sliver of independence. Maybe I could veer off the life path I've been barreling down for as long as I can remember. Maybe I could afford myself some options that don't include pointe shoes, sore feet, or being a minion in a tutu. Still, a thousand times I eye the exit sign and I almost make a run for it when my name is called.

"Zelda Lansing?"

"Here," I reply.

I hand the casting agent my headshot and resume'.

"You're from Ballet Institute East?"

"Yes," I tell her.

"Very good." She raises her eyebrows. "You're sure you're eighteen?"

Like I could be mistaken about it. I tell her yes, I'm sure. I climb up to the walkway and for a split second I close my eyes, remembering everything I've learned from *America's Next Top Model*. I lift my chin and saunter like I'm Cara Delevingne. At the end of the walkway I pivot, resisting the urge to pirouette or grand jete'. All I'm supposed to do is walk. Walk with an attitude.

"Very graceful" one casting agent says.

"Great posture" says another.

"Her feet were too turned out," says a third.

So that's it, I think. But no. There's murmuring.

"Come back tomorrow," says the first lady. "3:00 o'clock."

I can't help it. I do a little chasse' as I get off the stage. Julie is watching; I pretend she's not angry and I skip on over. "They want me to come back tomorrow!"

She's able to simultaneously raise one eyebrow, half her mouth, and one shoulder by just a fraction of an inch. "Great," she says, though her tone implies otherwise. She leans in and whispers. "I think they say that to everyone."

"Julie Harlow!"

She gets up and pretends that she isn't nervous. "How tall are you?" I hear the casting agent asks. Julie isn't ruffled and her confidence must earn her points. After she's done, she walks back over to me.

"See, I told you they tell everyone to come back tomorrow. Five o'clock, right?"

"Um, no. I'm at three."

There's a tense moment before I figure out what I'm supposed to say. She glares at me expectantly until I put the words together. "I'm sure they're saving the good people for later in the day?"

"Probably." Julie smiles. She's no longer angry. "Let's get out of here. I'm starving."

Chapter Forty-Four

A week later we're stretching before class and discussing ballet company internships. "Oh, Zelda," says Adrian, who is only ever nice to everyone. "Don't be modest. You know you'll get into either New York City Ballet or American Ballet. You're way too good not to get snatched up."

Julie is stretching with us, so I'm anxious to change the subject. Adrian hasn't mentioned how good a dancer Julie is.

Julie can get worked up so easily about this sort of thing, even though I always tell her that she's the best dancer in our level. I knead my left foot, flexing and pointing, flexing and pointing, and smile gratefully at Adrian. "That's nice of you, but nobody knows how this internship thing is going to go down. And I don't even know if I want an internship."

"Are you crazy?" Julie demands. "Of course you do."

"I might want to go to college instead."

She laughs shrewdly. "Your mother will never stand for that."

We've all got our phones out, but I'm about to put mine away because we're not allowed to have them during class. Then Adrian's phone vibrates with a text.

She picks it up and squeals. "OMG! It's the people from *The Standout*! I'm in!"

"Congratulations!" I cry.

"Let me see that!" Julie snatches Adrian's phone, reads the text, and checks her phone to make sure she didn't miss her own notification. Then another phone vibrates, but it isn't Julie's.

It's mine.

Congratulations! You have been selected as a model for the upcoming season of The Standout. Please contact us soon to sign your contract and to receive all the details.

I look up, and Julie's hard stare gives me a cold wave of anxiety. "I'm sure they're texting you next," I say.

She flicks her head to dismiss the idea. "Whatever. Like I care about that stupid show."

She gets up and puts her phone in her bag, proving how unconcerned she is. I do the same and we get through class without a huge amount of tension.

Yuri is here and Julie watches him. We do center exercises and I jump, trying to cross and uncross my ankles four times, midair, before I land. On my fifth try I achieve it, and when I smile at myself in the mirror, I spot a second pair of eyes on me. Our gazes meet in the reflection. Yuri grins, in this wide-mouth, caramel cream sort of way. Everything about him is warm and inviting, like the sun at the end of September.

Julie says something to him that I can't hear. Now his eyes are on her, and he's laughing and when she touches his shoulder, he touches her back. I'm glad there's something that will put her in a good mood.

After class is over Julie retrieves her phone and finds out that she's the understudy. So it's pretty convenient when, several days later, Adrian decides she doesn't want to be a model after all. She doesn't give a reason and I don't question it.

Now Julie and I can do the show together. That was always the plan.

Chapter Forty-Five

Several afternoons later I am super-hungry yet I don't head to the refrigerator when I get home. I don't have the chance. Mom hears the front door slam and calls out my name, high pitched and urgent.

"Zelda!"

My sore shoulders slump and my blistered feet drag into the living room. She's sitting on our white couch, which doesn't look soft because it isn't. She's facing away from the window, so the cityscape view is lost on her and there's nothing else in this room to occupy her attention. Our slab of marble coffee table is just a shiny lump that holds neither magazines nor remotes, and there's no television either.

Mom's sitting perfectly erect, as always. She wears a stylish black tunic and her perfectly tousled, wavy hair makes her look like she belongs in a glossy magazine.

"What's up, Mom?"

Her chest rises and falls. "How was your day?"

I press my lips together before answering. "Okay."

"Really?" Mom gets up from the couch and puts her hands on her hips. "That's not what I heard. It seems to me that you have some pretty big news."

"If you've already know then why are you asking?"

Mom, graceful as always, steps around the two-ton rock that we call furniture. "I ran into Meredith Andrews at Citarella today. We were in the cheese aisle when she told me about that reality show. I had to pretend like I already knew, Zelda!"

My entire body sags. "Look Mom, I'm sorry I didn't tell you sooner. I wasn't sure they'd pick me, and I wanted to wait until I knew."

Her gaze is intense, forcing us into a standoff. "Let's get to the real issue here, Zelda. Why did you sign up for it, when you ought to be focusing on an internship?"

"I don't know," I mumble and stare at the floor. Of course I'm lying.

"Well, your father is going to be BEYOND upset." Mom's voice borders on shrill. "All the work we've put in, the money for dance classes, and for what? So you can parade amateur fashion designs in front of that aging super model, Hilaire Kay? I mean, your chances for recruitment by one of the major companies is nonexistent now, you realize that, don't you?"

"Sorry, Mom."

And because I can think of nothing else to say, I spin on my balletic heel and glissade off to my bedroom, ignoring Mom's demand to come back, that we aren't done yet. "I won't let you throw away your future," she yells. "So forget about doing the show. It's not happening!"

I ignore her wailing but then it turns to a more guttural sort of cry. Concerned, I turn around and re-enter the living room. My mom is staring at her phone like it's the devil's pawn.

"Are you okay?"

She tilts her tearful face up, towards our track lighting. "He just texted that he's delayed his trip home again." She blinks rapidly, surrendering tears. "I know it's because he wants to keep screwing Janice. I think I'm really losing him this time, Zelda."

Dad is one of the most renowned set designers in the world. He and Mom met nearly twenty years ago, when he was designing the set for *Giselle* and she was the second lead. They fell into an intense, passionate, push-and-pull sort of relationship, the type where they couldn't live without each other one moment and were railing at each other the next.

Mom "accidentally" got pregnant and she gave up her career to have me. Dad married her on one condition: he would continue to travel to London and Paris for work and he'd have liaisons when he felt like it. I still don't know why Mom agreed.

And I really wish I didn't have to hear about it.

"Can I get you anything, Mom? A glass of water?"

Mom closes her eyes and winces, as if she's suffering from a migraine. "Don't worry about me, Zelda. I'll be fine."

"Okay..."

Her eyes snap open and she's suddenly alert. "But promise me you aren't going to do that show."

"Mom, be reasonable. It's a great opportunity! Julie and I got picked out of a lot of girls. You should be excited for me."

The corners of mom's mouth turn down. "I should have guessed that Julie is behind this. I don't trust her, Zelda. She's not a good friend to you."

"Julie's my best friend."

Mom shakes her head. "No, she's not."

Chapter Forty-Six

M om and I both got emotional and our fight escalated, until she threatened to kick me out if I do the show.

"Fine!" I yelled in response. "I don't want to stay here anyway!" And I slammed the door behind me.

Now I walk through the Upper East Side, tears blurring my vision. It's one of those cold spring days, when March has pushed April back, demanding the spotlight and pirouetting out sleety rain. But that's not why my face is wet.

I wipe my tears with the sleeve of my hooded Ballet Institute East sweatshirt, which gives me feeble protection against the soggy weather. I didn't think, I just grabbed a few things and ran. And I didn't text Julie to warn her I was coming.

When I get to Julie's building, the doorman rings her. Julie's parents are fancy, big-time lawyers who often travel or stay late at the office, so Julie pretty much gets the apartment to herself. I knock on her door and she answers, immediately noticing my sad face.

"What's wrong, Zelda?" She takes me into her arms. Silently, I hug her. Then, over her shoulder, I see him.

It's Yuri, in nothing more than a pair of tight sweatpants. And Julie is so warm, dressed in a tank top and leggings, baring her stomach every time she raises her arms.

I pull away. "God, I'm sorry. I didn't mean to interrupt anything."

Julie laughs and pulls me into the living room. "Don't be such a dork, Zelda. We were just practicing lifts."

"Is good you're here. Ve can vork on lifts together, yes?" Yuri smiles like he's proposing a threesome.

"You watch, okay Zelda? Tell us if we look okay."

I wipe my face and sit on the couch, while Yuri and Julie dance to *Swan Lake*. He lifts her because she's graceful, born for the air. His muscles strain underneath his golden skin and the two of them seem fused. They belong together and I'm here in the audience, privileged to witness to their beauty.

Chapter Forty-Seven

It's been several days of ignoring my mother's phone calls. I texted once, to let her know I'm safe and staying with Julie. Julie's parents have been working non-stop, so that gives us the freedom to do whatever we want.

And Julie wants to do Yuri.

Late Saturday night, I'm in the living room, headphones on, iPod tucked into my sports bra. I'm dancing around the hardwood floor, doing a pas de valse, waltzing to the steady beat of trumpets, my favorite sound. I need to drown out the noises coming from Julie's bedroom. My strategy works, because I don't even notice Yuri, not until he stands directly in front of me.

"You startled me!" I say, pulling my headphones down. I'm suddenly aware of my sweaty bangs matted against my forehead and I feel my cheeks burn. "Where's Julie?"

He cocks his head toward the hallway, toward the bedroom. "Asleep."

"Why aren't you sleeping too?"

"I am not good sleeper." His face scrunches in concentration. "What is word, when you are unable to sleep?"

I shift my weight. "Insomnia?"

"Ah, yes. I am insomnia."

"No, no," I laugh. "You are an insomniac."

"Ah."

Yuri blinks his grey eyes rapidly and twists his chin, which juts out of his perfectly sculpted face. But he looks so confused that I laugh even more.

"Me too," I tell him. "I've never been able to sleep for very long."

"How do you pass time?"

I lift my arms and let them float back down to my side. "Dancing, mostly. What about you?"

"I dance. I go for walk."

The way he says walk sounds like valk, which is charming and exotic but I choose not to be affected. "You go for a walk in the middle of the night?"

"In Moscow, best time for walk is in middle of night. I am krovel'shchik."

"Huh?"

He smiles and shakes his head slowly, like he's withholding something out of spite. But when he extends his hands to me, I sense only friendship. "You want we dance together? Show me what you are working on, yes?"

The rise of thick eyebrows—that grin of anticipation—they make me want to agree. But Julie is sleeping down the hall. She's claimed Yuri and he seems happy to be claimed by her. Still, it's just dancing, and that's innocent enough...

But how many dance partners does Yuri need?

"It's a solo, actually. I'm choreographing it, just for fun. I don't think anyone will ever see it."

"Then what is point?" Yuri asks. "We dance to share."

Gently he steps in and reaches for the iPod that's underneath my T-shirt. His fingers graze my skin and then they clasp the metal that's warm from my body heat. It feels as intimate and forbidden as a stolen kiss.

Yuri goes to the stereo and plugs in my iPod, selecting the song I was playing before he came in. When the trumpets blare his face lights up and he moves to the rhythm, his arms and shoulders swaying in celebration. I rush to turn the music down.

"You'll wake up Julie," I say.

"No, she is dead to world."

You would know, I think.

Silently, I dance. I am not self-conscious as I release a series of jetes, with the occasional pirouette when the bridge in the song occurs. I spin around four full times without breaking and Yuri claps.

"Excellent," he says. He dances too, matching my movements, and this dance becomes a pas de deux with an unspoken agreement: we move in and out of each other's spheres but we won't invade them. We will reach but we will not touch. Our bodies are in sync but our limbs will never meet.

Chapter Forty-Eight

The next morning Julie makes coffee and we all drink it black. Yuri finds a lonely bagel in the refrigerator and puts it in the toaster. "I will share, yes?"

Julie makes a disgusted face. "Are you kidding? I don't want that."

My stomach is gurgling with hunger. "I'll have half," I say.

Yuri smiles and his eyes widen. "I like peanut spread. Do you like it too?"

"Peanut butter? Yeah, sure."

Yuri glances at Julie in question and she points him to the right shelf. Then she takes a bold sip of her steaming coffee and glares at me.

"What?" I ask.

"You really want all those calories?"

I sit on a stool by the island in her kitchen. "I'm hungry. Coffee isn't enough for me."

She snorts. "Really? What is enough for you, Zelda? Tell me."

Yuri has found the peanut butter and he goes to the toaster, checking on the bagel's progress.

"Never mind," Julie says, before I can interpret her question, let alone answer it. "My parents will be home tonight, so you both need to find somewhere else to stay."

She walks away, clearly pissed. Yuri takes the bagel out of the toaster, oblivious to any tension. He spreads it with peanut butter and offers me half. "Delicious," he says, talking through a bite. "Do you agree?"

"Sure," I respond, chewing slowly. But honestly, I can't decide if it's the best bagel I've ever eaten, or the worst.

Chapter Forty-Nine

Later, we're at Ballet Institute East, before class. Yuri is stretching in the middle of the floor. I swear his muscles are made from rubber bands and there are secret suction cups on the bottom of his feet. He grabs his left ankle, and with his leg perfectly straight, he raises it up to his ear; he makes it look as easy as breathing.

"Where will you go?" Yuri asks.

I try not to stare in awe. Instead I press my toe shoes into the wooden floor, limbering up my arches. "I suppose I'll go back home."

I'm already dreading the apologies I'll be required to give to my mother, and the conditions to which I'll have to comply. "But if she says I can't do *The Standout* then I'm not staying. I'll be homeless." I laugh although, really, it's not funny. "What about you, Yuri? Do you have a place?"

He nods. "I share with four other peoples, but room is very small for so many. I have mattress on floor, part of closet and that is all."

"Well, at least you can stay with Julie some of the time. I think it's great that you two are together."

"I like Julie." Yuri somehow lowers his leg while looking deep into my eyes. The boy has skills. "But we are not together, like how you say. We have fun. Julie knows we are for fun."

Just then, Julie comes prancing out, her pink ballet skirt fluttering like a butterfly wing. She doesn't seem angry anymore and she squeezes one of Yuri's very firm butt cheeks. "Hey, Babe," she coos. Julie's face is flushed with pride and pleasure. Her smile can't be contained, and it reminds me of when she was cast as the Sugar Plum Fairy over all the other girls in fourth form.

"Are we going out after class?" she asks both of us. "We should go dancing at Murmur. I hear it's really hot."

For Julie, it's about winning. It's about being chosen by the sexy, straight guy that all the other girls want. It's about the glee of owner-ship. So she doesn't mind having me around, because that way I can be an audience member, a witness to their relationship.

I shrug, feigning indifference. "You have to be twenty-one to get in. Besides, tomorrow is the first day for *The Standout*. I want to get a good night's sleep."

And I need to figure out where that sleep will be.

"But you do not sleep," Yuri says. "You dance at night, yes?"

"Huh?" Julie glares at me, her temper on the brink of explosion.

"You were asleep," I tell her. "Last night, Yuri and I were both awake and we talked about how we dance when we have insomnia."

"Then we did dance," Yuri adds, and I want to hit him. "Zelda choreographs ballet to trumpets. It was very special."

I'm a fish, floundering and squirming, wishing to be thrown back into the ocean. "It wasn't anything. It's not like we practiced lifts, or—"

"Don't be such a freak, Zelda." Julie laughs a little too loudly and gives Yuri a proprietary back rub. "I don't care if you two were danc-ing." She wraps her arms around him, so his back is pressed into her chest, her chin resting on his shoulder so she can speak to me, "But don't worry about tonight. Yuri and I can go, just the two of us."

Yuri gives me a smile of apology, and then—Oh God—a wink that Julie does not see. He turns toward her and kisses her on the nose while I hold back my barf.

"Yes, we will go," he says. "Just two of us."

Chapter Fifty

I t's dinner time. I came straight home, right after class because I might need several hours to smooth things over before I can crawl into bed in hopes of a good night's sleep. Our apartment is quiet, dark, and cold.

It's like nobody has been around to use electricity. It's like one of those silly horror movie scenes. It's like when the young girl walks unwittingly into a room with a monster.

"Mom?"

No answer. I walk down the hall, towards Mom's bedroom, flicking on every light as I go. Her door is ajar. I slowly open it and peer inside.

"Mom?" My voice is soft this time.

Silence. There's a mom-sized lump lurking underneath her covers, so I sit on the edge of the bed. My pulse is pounding in my ears, which is silly. She's probably just taking a nap.

But Mom never naps. Naps are for the weak, she says.

With a tentative hand, I shake her shoulder. She grunts, turns over, and opens her eyes. "Zelda?" she rasps, not trusting her eyes.

She's alive and I'm relieved enough to breathe. "Are you okay, Mom?"

"He won't return my calls, Zelda. I don't know what to do. I gave up everything and now he's casting me aside."

In the dim light her face looks greyish and sweaty. I place my palm against her forehead and my heart skips a beat. "Mom, you're burning up. How long have you been sick?"

"Don't know," she mumbles, and her eyes flicker shut.

I go to the kitchen and call my dad. His voicemail picks up. There's no point leaving a message because he won't call me back. I look in the cabinets for soup but we don't have any, so I walk to the corner market, where I find Gatorade and Campbell's chicken-noodle. That's what Mom always gave me whenever I had a fever.

She lets me feed her and I give her Tylenol, and by the end of the evening she's better. We don't talk about tomorrow, when I'll abandon her again. Instead, we watch *Casablanca* on the TV in her bedroom, but she falls asleep before Humphrey Bogart tells Ingrid Bergman to get on that plane, so I turn off the television, get into my pajamas, and climb into my own bed. I'm wide awake, anxious, and staring at my ceiling in the dark.

Chapter Fifty-One

The next morning I slip out of the apartment before Mom wakes. I walk to *The Standout* with a spring in my step and a rock in my stomach. I've heard that modeling is even more cutthroat than ballet.

At least being Julie's friend has thickened my skin.

I tell myself that I need this. *Forget about how scared you are. Just remember the fun; remember the paycheck; remember that you're doing this with Julie.*

Julie.

She and I were supposed to show up for the first day together, but she texted me earlier. *Crazy night. Yuri is an animal. Don't wait for me.*

I texted her back: *You're still coming, right?*

She never replied.

I enter the lobby of The Clarkson School of Design. The lady behind the desk tells me to go up a floor and into the last door on the left. I find a room full of models and there's no way I can be one of them. My tongue feels large in my mouth, swollen, and so does my heart. Some of the girls here are from Ballet Institute East, but we're not friends; we just tolerate each other. There are also girls I don't recognize and they are so gorgeous that I can feel myself diminishing next to them.

At least I'm moving and acting like a person.

"Excuse me," I address a beautiful, brown-skinned girl with huge, mud puddle eyes and red finger nails like bloody talons. "Are you here for *The Standout*?"

She doesn't snarl, or spit, or even make a face. "Yeah." She points to a rack of shiny black slips. "You're supposed to change into one of those."

"Thanks." I pigeon walk over, feeling like I'm inching along a precipice, and I find a slip with a notecard that says *Zelda* pinned to it. And since other girls are getting dressed and undressed right here, I do the same.

Where is Julie? I look at my phone probably hundreds of times even though there's no possible way I could have missed a text from her. But the minutes tick by and she doesn't show. We're lined up backstage and the production assistant, who is wearing headphones, waits for some cue before she motions us forward and tells us to go. I'm fifth in line.

I hear a door open. "Thank God," I say, rushing forward and leaving my spot. "Where have you been?"

"I told you I'd be here," she growls. I take a step back.

"Um, actually, you didn't and I wasn't sure if you were okay."

"I'm fine. Stop being such a drama queen, Zelda." She somehow knows where she's supposed to stand and goes there. I do the same. The girl wearing headphones motions towards me.

It's my turn. I suck in my stomach and lift my chin. I try to recall why I ever thought I could do this. Then I remember; it was Julie. Julie made me believe I was capable of being a model.

When we are all on stage, one by one we're assigned a designer. My designer is named Robin. She's tall and blond and she could be a model herself, except her face is too open, too distinct. Once we get backstage, into the workroom, she fits me into this incredible dress. It's made of muslin, which I guess is the cheapest fabric ever, but the way she sewed it, it's like a silk evening gown. Robin's forehead has these deep creases as she stitches. Her jaw clenches more with each pin that she removes from between her teeth.

"You seem really nervous," I say. "Don't worry; your dress is the best one here." I look around the workroom and mean what I say. Julie is wearing a black cocktail dress, which is cool but not very original. Somebody else is wearing a biker chic sort of outfit, and another girl looks like Elsa from *Frozen*. None of the dresses compare to the one I have on.

Robin smiles through gritted teeth. "I'm having a really weird day," she says. "I mean, weird besides being on a reality show." She looks up and sees a camera looming over us. "I thought I'd be used to all this, but I'm not."

"I don't understand. Why would you be used to it after less than a day?" Everything about Robin—from her long, capable fingers to her intense focus over this dress—makes me feel like a kid, like I should be sipping a juice box before recess.

She raises both eyebrows. "I was on *The Holdout* before."

"Oh." My cheeks warm. I should know who she is. I've heard of that survival show but I've never actually watched it. "That's cool. Did you win?"

"Nope." She tugs on the hem of my dress, checking to see if it's even on both sides.

"Better luck this time, huh?" My stupid giggle-grunt combo embarrasses us both. "I love the dress," I offer, hoping I sound sincere, since I am.

"Thanks." She takes a deep breath. "Why do all the other girls here wear their hair back, in buns?" she asks.

I explain it to her, and soon, Jim Giles comes in and tell us it's time. There's a flood of activity and heightened voices. The designers make final adjustments on their masterpieces and we're all herded into place. I worry that my guts are exploding so vigorously that they'll seep through my skin and stain this amazing gown.

Robin smiles and squeezes my hand before she leaves me backstage. "Be brave, Zelda." So I try.

The runway lights are blinding. I keep my shoulders back, like I'm about to sweep my torso in an arc-like motion, but I stay upright, relying on the beauty of the dress for confidence. *You must rock the dress*, I tell myself. *Just play some trumpet music in your head and feel free, like you're jumping from somewhere high.*

One foot in front of the other. It's the longest walk of my life. At the halfway point, I pivot and it's all downhill from here. But I'm used to ballet slippers, not platforms, and I snag the toe of my shoe against the floor. I go flying, and the lights surrounding me are an endless crest of nothingness as the darkness bottoms out. It only takes a second to fall but it feels like an eternity. And when I land on my knees and palms, I hear the appalling rip of fabric.

I wish to melt, to disappear, to find a teleportation device and use it. Somehow I keep functioning, I'm not sure how, and I'm not really conscious of what I do or say until Hilaire's voice cuts into my brain.

"We can't judge a ripped dress." She says it in this spiteful, happy way.

Words eject from my mouth like a broken DVD. "It's not Robin's fault! Fire me if you want, but you can't hold this against her. That isn't fair."

Hilaire glances at me. "You are a model. Models do not talk."

My mouths drops open before I clamp it shut.

Sonofabitch.

I'm used to being silent. Models don't talk and neither do ballerinas: that's what's wrong with me, with my life, with my world.

I need to use my voice.

Chapter Fifty-Two

My first day of *The Standout* is finally over. I'm exhausted but I rush out before they can fire me.

Once I'm safely on the sidewalk outside of Clarkson School of Design, I search my overstuffed bag for my cell phone. It's wedged between a pack of chewing gum and some Chapstick. I find three texts from Mom.

5:12: When are you coming home?

5:38: Zelda, we need to talk about your participation in this show. I still do not approve.

5: 56: Have you talked to your father recently? Did he mention Janice?

I drop my phone into my bag, wishing I could hurl it to the ground. Mom always gets clingy right when I'm trying to assert my independence. But if dad is leaving her for real this time, then I'm terrible for not being more sympathetic.

"Zelda?"

The Russian inflection of my name makes me jump. I turn towards him, semi-air borne, which has to be comical. It's no wonder that Yuri laughs. "All right?" he asks, but it sounds like "alvight."

"What? No. Fine. Bad day. How are you? Are you looking for Julie? I think she left already. Did you miss her?"

Yuri's glowing face dims. "I am not sure which question I answer first."

"I... ummm... sorry. Where's Julie?"

Yuri bites his lip. "Julie is very mad. She and I dance last night, after we return from club?" I nod, showing my understanding, urging him to go on. "We do lift," he holds his hands out, as if to demonstrate, "and she jump into my arms but I am not ready, and my hands, they slip." His arms drift sadly to his side. "Julie fall, and land bad on her ankle. Now she will not return my texts so I look for her here."

"Oh." I am careful in my reply. "Julie knows how to stay angry. I'd just give her some time to miss you."

He steps close. "Julie is not talking to me. I have no other choice."

"Okay." I run my fingers through my hair, contemplating my next move. I don't want to go home, and Julie didn't wait for me, so what's next? "What are you doing now?" I ask Yuri.

He gives me a dangerous smile of encouragement. "We could eat? And after, I take you for walk?"

It's the worst decision ever, to spend the evening with Yuri, but the day I've had calls for a little bit of bad judgment. "That sounds perfect." I tell him.

We find a diner and order cheeseburgers and fries. I could never eat this way in front of my fellow ballerinas, but I'm completely comfortable devouring my food while Yuri bears witness. After I finish, he scoots the rest of his fries towards me. "You eat these."

"No, no," I say, shaking my head. "I'm just stress-eating at this point. I should stop."

"What is 'stress eating'?"

"You know, when you've had a bad day and you just want to stuff your face and forget about it? Don't boys do that?"

Yuri draws his eyebrows together and rubs his chin with a single finger, contemplating. "When I have bad day I do things to forget. But not usually eat."

He's clearly a physical creature. Yuri probably dances, or works out, or finds a willing sex partner to relieve his stress. Maybe he does all three at once. I picture Yuri twirling around with a barbell in one hand and a naked girl straddling him in the other, and it's both funny and sort of hot. I try to shake it off.

"Do you have bad days very often?" I ask.

He nods. "Da. I get sad for home. I miss sometimes my family."

"So are you planning on going back soon?"

He swirls a fry in ketchup. "Perhaps. Or perhaps I stay and become big star."

"Really? Is that what you want, to be famous, like the next Baryshnikov?"

"Is time for a new one, yes?" Yuri laughs but his face goes serious. "I wish to work hard and make big progress. I will practice and be success and bring my mother here when I have fame and money."

Under the bright lights of the diner Yuri's face is in clear focus and without guile. "That sounds nice," I tell him. "You must love your mother a lot."

His grey eyes grow dreamy. "Do we not all love our mother?"

I catch myself thinking something ugly and exhale a pint of guilt.

"Do you not love your mother?" He asks.

"No, of course I do. But it's complicated. She wants me to be what she once was, and I don't think I can, so then she gets angry and invents some new drama to make me feel bad, usually about my father. Seriously, they're always flirting and fighting, even though they're like, late middle age. When he comes home they make up, but that's the worst, because of the disgusting sounds that come from their bedroom." I tap my fingers against the Formica table and let myself ramble. "I should be feeling bad for her but I don't. All I feel is resentment." I take a breath, and see that Yuri's head is cocked and his jaw is crooked, again like he's contemplating. "Sorry, I'm not making much sense, am I?"

He rises from his chair and extends a hand to me. "We go for walk now. I show you what I do when day is bad."

"Why don't you just tell me instead?"

He flicks his head back, knocking his bangs out of his eyes. "In Moscow we find tall buildings and we climb. Is fun, to tempt death and win."

I imagine him scaling a building like Spiderman, and this seems as natural as if he told me that he likes to skateboard or play video games.

"I'm sure it is fun to win," I say airily. "But it's probably not so fun to lose."

I'm aware that I'm flirting, but as long as we don't touch, it's okay. I'm not Julie or any of the other girls at Ballet Institute East who have fallen for Yuri. We are just friends. "I've never been afraid of heights so that sounds cool."

"Then we go."

We leave the warmth of the diner and go into the chilly spring night. I don't tell him that my mom expects me home and I force Julie from my mind. She doesn't have to know about this.

"This way," he commands. We take a subway to the financial district, talking very little, which isn't as awkward as you would think. He leads me to an un-extraordinary skyscraper.

It's not hard to sneak past the security guard and through the locked door that Yuri knows how to open. We climb up steps, along railings, higher and higher, up the side of the building and I think, *I could be home, eating egg whites and salad, watching* America's Next Top Model.

Then we're up as high as we can go. I look down. The street is a mile below and it might as well be a world away. The difference between life and death is in the balls of my feet.

"This is your idea of fun?" I ask. The impossibly thin air is rushing through my ears.

"You feel alive now, yes?" he yells over the wind.

Sunday morning low-carb brunches, hollow holiday dinners, and false smiles from false friends instant-replay in my mind.

"I do," I tell him.

We break the no touching rule when his warm, strong hands clench mine, and we walk along the narrowest of beams. I could skim an airplane if it happened to fly by. I dare to look down and the city is a swarm of movement and light, safer at this distance than it's ever been before.

I forget that my dad is having an affair, that my mom doesn't accept me, that nothing I do pleases them. It's just light, air, and adrenaline. It's just Yuri's hand holding mine, in a place I never thought I'd be.

"Is even better than dancing," he says.

"Yeah," I answer.

One false step could send me to my death, which isn't unlike any other day. It's like executing a quadruple pirouette while airborne, like having wings, like defying gravity.

Yuri takes out his phone and points it at me. "Now smile."

Right now, that's easy to do.

Chapter Fifty-Three

The next morning I wake to the buzzing of my phone. A text from Yuri: *When can I see you again?*

I put my phone back on my nightstand and turn off my alarm. It was about to go off anyway. In the shower, I let hot water course over my head and down my back as I try to form coherent thoughts.

Seeing Yuri again is out of the question.

Too bad I'm not more experienced. Dancing fulltime and not attending high school doesn't help me meet guys, not straight ones anyway. It's kind of embarrassing that I haven't even had my first kiss yet, unless you count the one from my cousin, Powell. We were at his Bar Mitzvah, he was drunk, and we never spoke of it again.

The worst part is I can't talk to Julie. As I rub conditioner into my hair, images of last night come rushing back, and I feel how much I want to be with Yuri. But I know I should go to Julie as if we're all good, and never mention or think about last night again.

I get out of the shower, dry off, and get dressed in a pair of jeans and a T-shirt. Nothing fancy, but I don't have dance class today until 3:00 and I don't need to be at *The Standout* until tomorrow. All I need is some coffee and a protein bar and I'll be on my way.

In the kitchen I'm rooting around for the instant coffee and the Nature's Valley box, when I hear a shuffle and a cough. There's Mom, looking like death warmed over, like maybe she patted white talc on her face just to enhance the effect.

But that's a terrible thing to think.

"Where were you last night?"

The lie slips out quick and easy. "I went out with some girls from the show."

"Didn't you get my texts?'

"Sorry, Mom. But when I got home you were asleep. I checked your forehead and you didn't seem feverish." Maybe she won't notice I didn't actually answer her question.

"I'm not well, Zelda." Her glazed eyes bug out. "And I need you to spend some time with me. I was thinking we could have a spa day. I really need a massage."

"Why can't you go alone?"

Mom's mouth goes slack and wounded. "Because nobody should have to be alone when their marriage is falling apart!"

This is true. She's right. I'm selfish.

But I'd rather get an ear infection than a massage with my mother. "I need to go see Julie! She hurt her ankle and I didn't even realize it and she struggled through modeling yesterday."

"But I need you!" Mom wraps her bathrobe tightly across herself as if she's trying to hide. "I'll get dressed and then we'll go, and we'll discuss your involvement in *The Standout* too. Don't think I've forgotten."

Mom heads down the hall, to her bedroom to get dressed. That's when I do something unspeakable. I leave before she can hear me go, before she can command me to stay.

Chapter Fifty-Four

I stop and buy Julie a pack of Twizzlers, *The National Enquirer*, and a bottle of bath soap. There is no problem so big that it can't be cured by soaking in a bubble bath, eating Twizzlers and reading about the screwed up lives of celebrities. Those magic three items have been our consolation gift to each other for years.

But Julie barely cracks a smile when I hand her my bag of presents. "Thanks," she mumbles, and she adjusts her ankle, which is propped up on a pillow.

"Why didn't you tell me about your ankle yesterday?"

"I didn't want to make a big deal out of it," she replies.

"It must have been hard for you, walking in high heels."

She smirks. "Not as hard as it was for you."

I let her comment roll off me. "I'd feel even worse if Robin had been kicked out. I bet they're going to fire me today." I scoot closer to her on the couch. "Seriously, it's for the best. Now Mom and I won't have to fight about it. She's already going to be furious ..."

I trail off because Julie's not listening. She blinks back tears. "Are you okay, Julie? I mean, other than your ankle?"

She shakes her head. "He hasn't even called to see how I'm doing. What an asshole, right?"

Obviously she means Yuri. "Maybe he thinks you blame him and that you need some space."

"Maybe I do! But he's my boyfriend! He ought to call!"

I should tell her about last night. I should tell her about what Yuri said the other day. I should tell her and I'm an ugly coward for keeping my mouth shut. But Julie will get angry, call me a liar, and accuse me of stealing him away. I love her like a sister but I know how flawed she is. She can be intensely loyal but if you cross her she'll rip you to shreds.

"Hey, forget about Yuri. Let's watch *Sound of Music* with the volume turned down, and make up dirty song lyrics. Okay?"

Watching musicals while singing our own, twisted lyrics has been another mainstay in our friendship, but I guess not anymore. "God, Zelda. I'm not twelve, okay? I need more than candy and stupid games to cheer me up."

It's like I'm some fungus growing in her pointe shoe. "We're the same age, Jules."

"Whatever," she responds.

My cell phone vibrates. I'm sure it's Mom, but no. Yuri has texted me again. *Please meet me today.*

My decision comes so easily it doesn't even feel like a choice at all. "I have to go, Julie. It's Mom. She's sick and I need to take care of her."

"Whatever," she says again.

Yuri and I spend the day walking around Brooklyn, exploring parks and eating fresh-baked scones from a bakery, until it's time to go to class. Julie isn't there; she must be resting her ankle, so Yuri and I dance, side by side. When class is over he doesn't walk off to the dressing room, but taps my elbow instead. "I must rehearse now, but we go out tomorrow, yes?"

Every part of my brain is saying no. "Yes," I tell him.

When I get home Mom is waiting for me, all reproachful eyes and grimacing lips. "Did you get a massage?" I ask.

She says nothing. So I'm getting the silent treatment. Guilt tightens my chest and it hurts to swallow. "Mom, I'm sorry, but I'm doing the show. You can kick me out, but I'm eighteen now and I can do what I want."

I just need to figure out what, exactly, that is.

Chapter Fifty-Five

Giselle is a peasant girl who is head over heels for her boyfriend. He's actually a nobleman disguised as a peasant. He doesn't reveal his true self to Giselle because she doesn't trust guys with money. Giselle's mother warns her that dancing with him will turn her into a "Wili" – a maiden who dies before her wedding night.

Of course, Giselle doesn't listen.

When she finds out that her boyfriend has betrayed her, her mother gets to say "I told you so." Giselle dies of a broken heart and she joins the ghostly gang of the Wilis, just like her mom said she would.

Eternal dancing is her fate. She will dance every night, alone, but with a group of other brokenhearted brides. If she ever finds a real partner, she must make him dance until he collapses from exhaustion, and dies.

You don't want that, she tells me.

But I'm tired of being told what I want.

Chapter Fifty-Six

The next day Robin fits me into her latest design. I try to thank her for giving me this unexpected second chance, but my brain is so muddy, it weighs down my tongue. But when she demands that I do a pirouette, my execution is perfect and I feel my confidence return. However, the moment is short-lived.

I see Julie and give her a smile and a wave. She waves back but her grin is false and I'm now certain that Julie is mad at me. That guilt-induced sore throat from last night comes back, and it's even worse than having strep. What if Julie knows about Yuri and me?

Would it change anything?

Several hours later I'm done at *The Standout*, I meet Yuri, and we board a train to Queens. Yuri says he knows of a construction site where we can climb. It's not super-busy, so we don't have to wait until dark.

"How did it go today?" he asks. We are seated on the train. It's not crowded but there are a handful of people. A mom is reading her novel while her son plays on a Nintendo DS, with little grunts and pops emanating out. There's an oldish lady who has taken off one shoe. Her socked foot is in her lap and she absently rubs it as she stares out the window, which shows nothing but dark. There are a couple of business people and a guy in a hotdog-stand T-shirt.

And, of course, Yuri and me.

He's sitting close to me even though we have room to stretch out. I'm worried that I smell. Nervous sweat is much stinkier than exertion sweat, and today was full of nervous sweat. "Today was interesting," I tell him. "The dress my designer made was amazing, and she almost won, but they told her she needs more of a vision."

Yuri scrunches up his forehead. "What do you mean?"

"Umm..." I search for words as the train suddenly lurches. My arms shoots out, trying to grab onto a pole, but the nearest one is still too far away. So I sort of tip over into Yuri. My shoulder meets his arm, my hair brushes his chest, and I can feel his breath against my cheek.

It is the opposite of unpleasant. It is the opposite of smart.

I sit up straight and ignore the tingly rush.

"You were talking about vision?" Yuri asks. I nod and he continues. "Yes," he says, "I understand. Is what I look for, you know? In Moscow, we are called 'krovel'shchiki'." I shake my head, not understanding, and Yuri furrows his brow. "Roofers," he says, "that is our term, and there is many of us, because city does not know how to keep us away." He runs one hand through his hair, pushing it back so it sort of stands up, like it hasn't been washed in a while. But his smile is so charming that I forgive him for dirty hair. "We climb one time and we must go back. The rush, the feeling of grabbing all from life? I cannot stop."

"I understand." I shrug, suddenly self-conscious. "It's why I'm here." I shouldn't be here, after all. But I couldn't get it out of my mind, climbing up so high, balancing on thin pieces of metal with no net, no rope to grab; it was just me, the city below, and the sky above.

And I had never seen the world so clearly. "Up there," I say, "I was no longer looking for something."

Yuri pinches his chin while he thinks this over. Is he trying to interpret, to get past the language barrier, or is he just a really deep thinker? "I see," he says, slowly. "Yes, you are looking for something. The first moment I see you, I think, 'she needs more.'"

I laugh, unsure of what to say. "I'm not exactly malnourished, Yuri."

I expect him to smile and be dismissive, but he turns all serious. "Zelda, you must take your share."

"My share of what?"

"Life."

The train hurls itself blindly down its path, grunting and groaning like a caged animal. I blink, tempted to look away from Yuri or to move away a fraction of an inch. That will show him I'm not interested, that even though he's parting those soft, warm-looking lips as if he's about to press his mouth to mine, I will flinch and tell him no. But I'm paralyzed because my body is on fire. Yuri is leaning in and this train, the people in it, and the world outside are a blur, just like the dark streaks that appear through the windows.

Then the train squeals to a stop and the spell is broken.

"Ah," says Yuri. He stands with his usual composure. Does that little tick in his left hand mean that he's shaken, like me? "We are here. Come. Let's go."

I follow him to the construction site and we climb, and I know these are the moments I'll remember, even before they're over.

Chapter Fifty-Seven

The next time Yuri and I go roofing we are in Brooklyn and we're not even up that high. We're at another construction site and it's just after 9:00 PM, but it's not super busy so Yuri says it will be fine. We climb along heavy, steel planks and round patches of concrete, which will eventually be covered with wood, or more metal, or both. But right now they make a random, fun-house kind of staircase and getting to the top is a challenge.

When we reach the highest point there are three-foot wide spaces to stand. There are also wide gaps where I could fall into a mess of timber and cement.

Yuri is balancing on the same board as me. "I have surprise," he says, grinning like the Cheshire cat. In the haze of darkness, light, and oxygen, his grin is the only highly visible thing.

He takes out his phone, swipes a few times, and trumpet music plays. "You like?" Yuri asks. "I downloaded, just for you." He moves closer, making it easier to hear. "Now we dance."

I realize why we're at this location; he chose it because we'd be able to hear the music.

You would think I'd be harder to impress. But the idea of Yuri, thinking about me, planning something to make me happy: it is the best gift I've had in a really long time. "Thanks," I say, softly.

Yuri places his phone down, so it's balanced against a steel beam, then he holds out his hands to me, a *let's dance* gesture. I let my arms and legs move in tandem to the trumpets, to Yuri's dancing, to the rhythm of everything I never knew I needed.

The no-touching rule has died. His warm, flat palm is against the small of my back and our stomachs press together. I put my arms around his shoulders and he places both of his hands against my hips. Yuri bends his knees and lifts me and I am propelled into nothingness, into infinity. We're defying the laws of nature and gravity, merged together in this beautiful, precarious way. Never has anything felt so right.

I'm not sure who leans towards whom first, maybe it's just a mutual decision for our mouths to meet. But before I can process anything we are kissing, and it's apples and honey and flying in a dream.

Then we wake up.

"You there! Stop where you are!" A voice broadcasts itself over the tinny trumpet music that's still playing on Yuri's phone. "This is the police and you are trespassing on private property. Come down, now!"

Yuri's face is a mask of horror and panic. His eyes turn into wide, dark, infinite circles and his jaw drops about a foot. He stares into me for a moment, as we are both paralyzed.

He shakes his head and says, "I am sorry, Zelda. But I cannot get caught."

Then he flies away.

Okay, he doesn't actually fly, but he makes a comic-book villain exit, bounding off with super-human force before I can even register that he is abandoning me. I don't know how he gets down but he doesn't take the route we used to get up, which is the only route I know. It leads me directly to the policeman, who is waiting at the bottom like an angry parent, pleased with the prospect of punishment.

Chapter Fifty-Eight

My first phone call is to my mother, but there's no answer.

"Can I try another number?" I ask the clerk at the police station.

She sips from a mug that reads "*Life is short. Do stuff that matters.*" "Make it quick," she tells me.

I call Julie.

"Hello?" She sounds confused, probably by the unknown number that popped up on her cell.

I speak in a relieved rush. "Julie, thank God you answered. Can you come get me? I'm in Brooklyn and I've been arrested."

There's a pause. "You're joking, right?"

"No, I'm serious! Please?" I inhale the smell of stale coffee and sweat. "And bring some money so you can post bail, okay? It will probably be around $300."

"Come on, Zelda. I'm not in the mood for this. I don't know why you even think it's funny."

"I'm not joking. Please, Julie!" I lower my voice so I don't sound so frantic. "I'm at station #65, in Brooklyn, on Mitchell Avenue."

I can hear her silent struggle over whether or not to believe me. Meanwhile the clerk uses her pudgy hand to motion that my time is up. "Julie," I cry, one more time, "I'm totally serious. Don't make me spend the night in a holding cell with prostitutes."

I'm forced to hang up and then I really am put in a holding cell with prostitutes, plus a few drug dealers and an old woman named Marlene, who I share a bench with. She tells me she's been arrested for indecent exposure.

Marlene looks sort of like my great-aunt Trisha, who lives in the mountains with her dogs and has grown plump from eating a lot of cherry pie. I'm trying not to picture how Trisha would indecently expose herself, and I'm also trying to stay clear of an argument between a woman named Coco and another lady, whose name I didn't catch, but Coco is using some very colorful terms to describe her. Then, mercifully, I am released from the cell and led down a hall, where Julie is waiting for me, hands on her hips, looking like she might vomit.

"You totally have to pay me the bail money back," Julie says.

I don't answer. I'm too blinded by tears of relief to do anything but hug her, which is awkward, because she only sort of hugs me back.

"Careful!" she cries. "Don't make me injure my other ankle. That's the last thing I need."

"Sorry." I balance her and myself so we're steady. "Let's get out of here. I'm starving."

We go to a diner with shiny plastic booths, a 50s style jukebox, and an unapologetic pride in its predictability. I stare at my water glass as beads of condensation dribble down, forming a soggy mess that eats away at the paper placemat beneath. Julie just has coffee and I have a slice of cherry pie; thinking about Aunt Trisha made me crave it. I'm wolfing it all down: the bright red cherries, the buttery crust, and the vanilla ice cream that's saturating and turning it all pink. I'm not even concerned that Robin might have to let out the seams of tomorrow's dress. I also don't care that Julie is watching me, almost as if she's the anthropologist and I'm the rare, exotic survivor from the stress-eating tribe.

"I should never have gotten involved with Yuri," Julie says, unprompted. She waits for me to respond.

My brain stammers for a second as I swallow down some pie. "You blame him for your ankle?" I ask.

Julie bites her lip in contemplation. "Yeah, but it's not just that. There's something weird about him, Zelda. I wish I'd stayed away."

"What do you mean? How is he weird?" I reach for a joke, some quip to lighten the mood and detract from my panic. "Does he have three nipples, or something?"

Julie doesn't even crack a smile. "I can't explain it, so just trust me, okay? There's something weird about Yuri."

"All right."

She takes a sip of coffee, I wipe my mouth with my napkin, and tension hovers above us. "Aren't you even going to ask me what happened?" I ask. "It's not every day that I get arrested for trespassing."

"Okay. What happened?"

I summon all my courage to tell her the story, feeling safer in a public place than I would somewhere private. Sure, she'll get mad, furious even, but the lashing will be controlled. Nonetheless, my words feel heavy and sluggish as they exit my mouth and my body temperature rises from the strain. "...and," I struggle, "then he kissed me. It was the first time, I swear, and we were interrupted by the police. Then he ran. And, well, that's it."

I expect her to be blinded by rage, so I'm caught off guard when her eyes stay wide, barely blinking and deadly calm.

"He's gone too far," says Julie.

For the first time I notice a wide scratch starting at her left temple and extending all the way down to her chin. It's covered by makeup and I can imagine Julie's nails drawn; perhaps she wounded herself. Now her eyes dance and her dark pupils seem unnaturally large, like she's in shock, like she's soulless.

"What happened to your face, Julie?"

She doesn't answer, doesn't even register the question. "I'm not going to let him hurt you again."

The gravity of her voice makes the hairs on my neck stand up. "It's okay, Julie. He hasn't really hurt me that much."

She pounds a fist on the table, causing a mini-earthquake, upsetting the salt and pepper shakers and rattling the silverware.

"Everything that's wrong with your life is his fault. And it's time to stand up, Zelda. Stop being such a pushover."

I feel my nostrils flare. "I'm not! I just don't think we need to make some big statement against Yuri."

"I'm not saying we should kill him." Julie's shoulders slacken with strength. "We'll just rough him up. Problem solved and nobody is a murderer."

Out of me escapes a distorted little laugh. She has to be joking. This is her twisted payback for me kissing Yuri.

Julie's mouth turns down. "Something funny?"

"I know you're only kidding." I engage her in a stare-off, like when we were ten. Back then she never blinked first and now she's stoic, plastic, like an ancient Dutch painting where the subject seems dead.

A waitress sets down a thermal carafe of coffee at the table next to us. Her behind bumps into the back of my chair and I'm propelled forward, enough to make me look away for a split second. Julie's probably glowing with victory but my phone lights up with a text from Yuri. *I am very, very sorry, Zelda. Are you okay? When can I see you?* My chest feels hollow and like it might explode.

Somehow Julie knows. "Say that you'll meet him," she demands. "I'll come, and when he's distracted, I'll whack him in the knees with a crowbar."

I study her face and she studies mine, and we're simply two best friends making a major decision. For a moment we could be contemplating where to go after prom or do we want to go to the same college? If only life were that simple...

Julie fractures the tension with a frenzied laugh, loud enough to startle the coffee drinkers nearby. "Of course I'm not serious, Zelda. You didn't really think I was?"

Airways that I didn't know were closed, open up. "No...But you're not coming with me to meet Yuri. I'm not even going to text him back."

Julie flinches like I just ran my nails down that scratch on her cheek, like I caused tiny spheres of blood to resurface. Long ago she established that "no" was a word I was not allowed to say and I never rebelled, not until now.

"You'll regret this," she tells me.

And then, there's nothing more to say.

****

In her version she is always the white swan. That doesn't mean I'm the black swan. No. I'm just a feathered member of the corps de ballet.

Swan Lake is a tragedy. There's this prince who is bored at his own birthday party, so he ditches and goes hunting. He's about to shoot a swan when she transforms into a beautiful woman, right before his eyes. They fall in love faster than you can say "Put down your crossbow."

The swan lady is Odette, and an evil sorcerer has cast a spell on her, so she's a swan by day and a human by night. Until, that is, someone falls in love with her and breaks the spell.

Problem solved, right? Wrong.

The next night there's another party. The prince invited Odette, but she's running late because she has to wait until nightfall to become human again. The evil sorcerer shows up with this Odette-look-alike named Odile, who is wearing a black tutu instead of white. The prince is easily duped, dances and falls in love with Odile. Meanwhile, Odette finally arrives at the party, but when she sees her prince dancing with Odile, her heart breaks. Once the prince realizes his mistake, his heart breaks too.

Of course, they both die, because people always die after their hearts are broken. I'm sure the same rule applies to swans because they notoriously mate for life.

I am meant to play Odette, she tells me. *It's my role.*

I don't question her sense of entitlement.

Chapter Fifty-Nine

"Robin, tell us about your look."

We're standing on the runway. Robin's outfit has either gotten one of the highest or the lowest scores, but she doesn't know which. I wish I could reach out, grab and steady her shaking hands, but my job is to stand here like a mindless mannequin. Robin's job is to explain her design, and she does so in a trembling voice.

"Well, Robin," Hilaire breaks into a cover girl smile, "I loved your look. You are on the top."

I feel like Robin's win is my own. I'm not taking credit for the success, but I still feel proud, so much so that I forget, for a moment, about all my problems. I am bone tired, and once we're done filming, all I want is home and a hot bath.

But it's not to be.

The moment I open the apartment door I encounter Mom, standing in the entryway like she's been there for hours, letting time inch away until I get home.

"Holy Crap!" I yell. "You startled me, Mom!"

But if I was scared a moment ago, now I'm really freaked out. In the fading evening light Mom looks so pale that her freckles, which usually come out only after a day at the beach, are this colony of pink smudges up and down her cheeks and chin. Her forehead has double, no triple, the amount of creases, and her eyelids and mouth look so heavy that they might just fall off her face.

"I got a call today, Zelda." She is speaking from somewhere deep and hidden, like maybe her kidneys. "A lawyer from one of those places that advertise on television wants to know if you need representation."

My head starts to pound. "Mom, I can explain. Let's go into the living room and sit, okay?" I tap her shoulder and I swear that cold blood is running through her veins. "Mom, are you okay? Are you still not feeling well?"

"Your father finally returned my call." Her voice is barely a whisper. "He wants a divorce so he can marry Janice."

I let her statement settle over me and now I feel cold too. Dad is never coming home.

"Oh, Mom. I don't even know what to say."

She points down. There is a suitcase at her feet. "You're his problem now."

"What?"

"I gave up everything: my career, my dreams, my identity, to have you and marry him. And he's never taken responsibility. It's always been me. But I am done." She picks up my suitcase, extends it toward me, and my hand just automatically reaches out to take it.

But when she opens the door I stay rooted, paralyzed in my spot. "Dad's in London. I can't go live with him."

"I guess you should have thought of that earlier."

"Mom! Please! I'm sorry, okay? Can't we talk about this?"

For a moment she's statue-like, and I wonder if she's even heard me. I'm about to repeat the question, when she speaks in a soft voice. "I could have been great, you know. But I blew it. I made all the wrong choices after I met you father. So forgive me if I can't just sit by and watch you make all the wrong choices too. Think of this as tough love, Zelda."

"No, Mom! Please! I really am sorry."

"Oh, Zelda." She scolds me and I'm just a toddler who spilt her milk, but this mess is not so easy to wipe up. "You're only sorry that I'm kicking you out. But you'll be fine; you're eighteen and you have a job."

"I don't get paid for another two weeks!"

"Well if Julie's the good friend you insist she is, she'll let you stay with her again." She leans in, keeping her voice low and secretive. "Otherwise, you'll learn to be on your own, and then maybe you'll stop taking me for granted."

Mom is so calm that she could be reading off a grocery list. Meanwhile, panic rises in my stomach like sushi gone wrong.

"But you don't understand! Please, can't I just explain?"

Her lips stay pressed shut and her eyes hold no sympathy. She gives my arm a tug and I'm out in the hallway. "Good luck, Sweetie," she says, right before she closes the door, slowly and methodically, and I hear the deadbolt click into place.

Chapter Sixty

I head to the place that is as familiar as home. Rehearsal is just getting out at Ballet Institute East when I arrive at the doors. The company dancers give me a strange look for going inside, but I just say, "I'm meeting Yuri. He wanted to rehearse the new piece he's choreographing."

This is a total lie. But Yuri is always choreographing something new and since he' the current golden-boy at *BIE*, I get away with it. Whatever Yuri wants, Yuri gets.

I go upstairs, to one of the smaller dance studios. I flick on the lights, stretch and dance around, because that's what I'd do if I was actually waiting to rehearse with Yuri. When I glimpse at my reflection in the wall of mirrors, I remember that I'm in my street clothes.

I crouch down and unzip the industrial sized zipper of the canvas bag that Mom packed for me. There's a slim toiletries bag with a travel toothbrush and toothpaste, face scrub, and a mini deodorant. There are also a couple pairs of underwear, some jeans, my Ballet Institute East sweatshirt, pajama pants, and three pairs of tights, three leotards, and my pointe shoes.

And on the very top, like it was an afterthought, is my favorite Rubik's Cube, its stickers peeling at the corners. One hand reaches for it and the other hand pulls my phone from my backpack. I try to solve the puzzle while I call Dad.

He actually answers, but when I tell him that Mom kicked me out, he just groans. "That is so like your mother," he mumbles, like I'm not supposed to hear.

"Dad, she's taking her anger at you out on me. Why can't you come home and patch things up?"

"Because it's always something with her. She's not happy unless she's miserable."

Harsh words pool on my tongue. *That must be why she's stayed with you for so long,* or *you're incapable of making anyone happy.* But silence is my only answer and he senses the pressure change. "Look, Zelda, I need you to handle things this time. I can't get away."

"You're never coming back, are you Dad?"

His breath hums through the phone. "I'll always be here for you, Sweetie."

I should just ask him for his credit card number, but my lungs labor in my chest as if I stepped into sub-zero temperatures. I want to reach through the phone and kick him where it hurts, because life is unfair and he can have a trophy wife while mom just gets a nervous breakdown. "Dad, the only thing worse than a cheat, is a liar."

It takes a moment for my statement to register, but it does. "Excuse me," he coughs. "Where do you get off—"

"Goodbye, Dad."

After I hang up, the silence of the empty dance studio is deafening in its creepiness. I go downstairs to make sure the outside door is locked, and then I trudge back up, all the while feeling like someone might jump out at me.

I'd almost welcome the company.

I keep my phone by my side, and at around midnight it vibrates with a text. *Forgot to tell you. Your hearing is tomorrow morning at 9:00.*

I text her back. *Thanks, Mom. I really do need you.*

She never responds and the rest of the night is filled only with my own tossing and turning.

I wake early because the last thing I need is to get caught squatting at a dance studio. I dress, wash up, and manage to shove my suitcase into my locker. Then I scuttle out and go to a coffee shop, where I inhale caffeine and kill time before I need to be in court.

My hearing goes okay. It's almost an out-of-body experience, walking into the courtroom and standing before the judge. Am I simply observing a good girl who has lost her way, watching as her assigned attorney manages to swing a three-hundred dollar fine? That will be the bail money that Julie already coughed up.

But this girl, this unrecognizable version of me, will still have a smudge on her permanent record. Plus, I have to pay Julie back as soon as possible. When I get to Clarkson School of Design she's the first person I see. She's standing in a tight circle of girls, laughing while cigarette smoke settles above their heads in a toxic, protective cloud.

"Hey," I call, more out of habit than friendship. Julie gives me an uninspired wave back. And as I walk past them and through the door, their laughter rings out. There's a hitch in my chest and I'm sure that the joke is on me.

A long time ago I decided to be one of the few, uncool ballerinas who doesn't subsist on diet coke, cigarettes, and the occasional sniff of cocaine. I guess it's just one more way that Julie and I are different. I trudge up the dimly lit stairwells, and enter the bustle and noise of the workroom, with its purple walls, long dark tables, and harried designers.

Robin looks hung-over, like there ought to be a cold compress on her head and a hot mug of coffee in her hand. "Are you okay?" I ask.

"I'm having a rough couple of days." She holds up the dress. It's dark blue but the fabric is so sheer and delicate, it's nearly see-through. It's printed with large white flowers and randomly placed red circles, and the design is simple: long and straight, with a conservative scoop neck and large, flowing, bell sleeves.

"This is lovely," I say.

"They're going to say it's too simple." She bites her chapped lip and shakes her head. "I wanted to drape the back so that it hung really low, but there wasn't time."

"Should I try it on?" I start to undress, having long gotten over my modesty at changing clothes in the workroom.

"Wait!" Robin notices something on one of the sleeves, but I don't see the problem. "I need to fix this. I'll be right back." She rushes off to the sewing machines, and I'm left, holding my shirt over my bare chest. Then Julie comes up.

"How are you?" She asks.

"My mom found out I got arrested and she kicked me out."

"And are you going to jail?"

"Nope."

I shift my weight, wishing for Robin to hurry back. Julie places her cold fingers on my bare shoulder and I shiver. "Look, Zelda. You should know, Yuri and I got back together last night. And you can't be mad because I had dibs."

"I don't care about Yuri." But I'm reminded of what I said to my dad just hours ago, about cheats and liars. I suppose I'm both. I lift my chin and look her in the eye. "You two deserve each other."

She flinches like I hit her. "When did you become such a bitch?"

Thankfully, Robin reappears with my dress, and she's oblivious to our conflict.

"Here." She hands me the dress and I put it on.

Julie stands back, leering. "Did you want it to be so baggy?"

Robin focuses her scalding eyes on Julie. "Who are you?"

"I'm Julie – Nadia's model."

"Then go find Nadia!" Robin turns back to examine the dress. Julie takes her sweet time sauntering away. Once she's gone, Robin whispers under breath. "... has a lot of nerve....*saved* her design... and now I'm being sabotaged...her model criticizes me?"

It's true that the dress doesn't fit quite right, but if I mention it Robin's head might explode. "Robin, is there anything I can do to help?"

"You are helping. Just stand still."

She works her magic quickly, so the dress looks pretty decent by the time the runway show starts. I actually really like it, but I can never predict what the judges are going to think. So I'm not sure if Nadia, Julie's designer, is on the bottom or the top. The dress is cute, if not a little short, but maybe they like that.

When the runway show is over, Robin stalks away, angry about Hilaire's criticism of her design. I decide to get going, but on my way out I realize I've forgotten my phone. Cursing to myself, I head back. I bound up the stairs, taking two at a time, rushing because I know they'll need to use the workroom soon, so the kicked out designer can be filmed cleaning out his or her space.

The lights are all off but there's somebody in here. I see the closing of a tablet, some scurrying, and then the figure ends up at the workstation I was headed towards.

"Robin?" Isn't she supposed to be downstairs, getting filmed with the other designers while they speculate on who will be eliminated?

She's nervous and out of breath. "Hey. What are you doing up here?"

I turn on the lights. "I think I left my phone on your table." When I pick it up and swipe, I see that only Yuri has been trying to get a hold of me. "My head hurts," I say, more to myself than to Robin.

"Tell me about it," Robin utters.

I can't look at Yuri's texts right now. They're probably just condescending apologies for his picking Julie over me. Maybe I'll just delete them all. I don't need one more destructive force in my life. I have enough of that with my parents.

"Zelda," Robin uses her lower register and I'm diverted from my thoughts. "Can you keep a secret?"

"Sure. What is it?"

She looks around, over her shoulder, at the vacant room. "Come on, not here." She grabs my arm and drags me to the dining room, where trays of pasta and wilted salad have been picked through and sitting for hours. The residue smell of garlic and ranch dressing still lingers and I realize I'm ravenous. When was the last time I ate? I can't even remember.

Robin points to a chair. "Sit," she says, and she takes the seat across from me. "It's a long story and I'll try to go fast, but bear with me, okay?"

She launches in, telling me about her botched affair and her friendship with Clara, the notes and the *Rotten Robin* website. "But it hasn't stopped," and she provides more detail. Somebody pushed her on the treadmill; somebody dumped water on her dress; somebody is for sure trying to sabotage her.

"And I thought I saw her on the train," Robin exclaims. "She's supposed to be dead or missing, but I swear it was her and I swear she saw me too."

"Who?" I ask, confused.

"Clara! Of course, Clara!" Robin wrinkles her forehead like she's a million miles away.

"There you are!" We both turn, startled by the bark of Gabe the camera man's voice. His face grows red and his volume grows too. "Everyone is looking for you! Nadia got kicked out and they need you downstairs, saying goodbye and looking sad, NOW!"

Robin shoots up and rushes out, barely remembering me before she goes. "Zelda, everything we talked about is confidential, right?"

"Absolutely."

"Thank you, Zelda." And she disappears into the dark hallway.

It hits me how tired I am. My limbs feel so heavy I don't know how I'll get up from this chair. I haven't had a good night's sleep since before I was arrested and that feels like a lifetime ago. What I wouldn't give for my flannel pajamas, my bed, and a steaming bowl of noodles. I could watch TV and try to solve my newest puzzle toy, until my head drops to my pillow and I drift off to a deep and dreamless slumber.

What if I just go home? I can refuse to take no for answer. If I yell and bang on the door and scream and cry, my mother will have to let me in, because otherwise, what would the neighbors think?

Once I'm outside, I button up my jacket and orientate myself towards the subway station. Then someone grabs me from behind. Thoughts of Robin's sabotage story invade my head, and I scream.

"Relax! It is me." *Relax* sounds like *velax* so I know instantly whose arms are holding me. I break away and he lets me go.

"What do you want?"

"Just to talk." For the first time ever, I see Yuri use bad posture. His shoulders slump and he hangs his head. "I want you not to hate me, Zelda. I want for you to understand."

"You caught me at a bad time." I stomp away, towards the subway station, but Yuri follows and easily keeps up with me.

"Did you receive my texts?"

"I deleted them."

"What is delete?"

"I erased them." His face is still confused, so I sigh. "I did not read them before they were removed from my phone." I fish for a token in my pocket and move through the subway's turnstile, but Yuri just leaps over it. "You're a thief for doing that," I say. "They should arrest you, a million times over."

"Zelda, I am not hoodlum, I promise."

He knows *hoodlum* but not *delete*? Who is this guy?

I am walking fast enough that he has to make an effort to keep up, and as we're dodging through a crowd of commuters, it's difficult for him to talk. But he follows me all the way down the stairwell and onto the platform for my train, which pulls up right as we arrive. I jettison myself on, and again, Yuri follows. "I don't know what you think you're doing," I say, as we both grasp the same bar. "But you're not coming over to my apartment, and I'm going home."

Yuri nods. "Then we talk here."

The subway doors close and the train lurches forward. Many passengers adjust their footing as the floor beneath us tilts and sways, but Yuri and I have such good balance that we are unfazed. He's like a statue, with a moving, talking head, which he lowers toward my ear. I don't have much choice but to listen.

"Julie told the police to have us caught," he says. "I am sure."

I squint, grasping the bar and keeping my gaze on my shoes. "What are you talking about?"

"I see her, after I get down. She was waiting and is surprised that I am alone. But she laughs and says, 'I underesticate you.'"

"Do you mean 'underestimate'?'

He nods and I try to internalize this new information but it's hard because the pieces don't quite fit. "Are you saying that Julie followed us the other night, told the police where we were, and then waited down below while we tried to escape?"

"Yes," Yuri answers simply. "And I did not know how to find you after, and Julie is walking with me and yelling, using angry words. I should not be with you and she will have me sent back to Russia." He uses his free hand to run his fingers through his hair. "I am sorry I leave you behind. So, so sorry."

I sort of want to accept the apology, just so I can leave it in its wrapping and re-gift it later. "How did Julie possibly follow us? We would have seen her on the train to Brooklyn."

"Julie looked at my phone." He takes it out and scrolls to a text that he shows to me. "I know other roofers and we share address of good places. Julie sees and knows where to find us."

An idea startles me. "Are you the reason she got that scratch on her face?"

Yuri meets my eyes. "Yes. It was accident. We were walking and she was yelling, and we are still on construction site, and she uses both fists to hit me. I step away, quickly, and she loses balance and brushes against sharp beam."

I close my eyes, trying to put everything together. So Julie had been aware of what's been going on between Yuri and me from the beginning, but she took the time to cover her face with makeup and feign ignorance on the night she bailed me out of jail. Why? What's her endgame? Has she just been crazy this whole time, and I refused to see?

And there's still a flaw to Yuri's story. "Why did you get back together with her?"

Yuri blinks rapidly, like he needs me to repeat the question and I know now that Julie was lying. The train pulls to a stop. "Never mind," I say, "this is my stop."

He follows me onto the platform. There is a lot of noise; a street musician belting out a bluesy song, people bustling around us, and the subtle roar of trains coming and going. But none of it compares to the rushing in my head. I don't know my best friend anymore; maybe I never knew her at all.

"Thanks for the information," I yell to Yuri. "I guess I'll see you around."

Some emotion dances across Yuri's face but I'm too exhausted to try and read it. "I walk you home."

"You don't have to. I'll be fine."

He reaches out, but he lets his arm fall to his side before his hand touches me. "Is getting dark. I walk you home."

"Really? You're going to get all protective now, after everything?" I can tell he doesn't completely understand and I shake my head. "If you walk me home, I'm not inviting you in."

He nods and I feel we have another silent pact. We move from the noisy platform up to the much quieter street, and Yuri keeps pace with me as I navigate the Upper East Side sidewalks, towards home. My neighborhood, with its pristine streets made from old money, has to feel worlds away from his Brooklyn apartment and galaxies away from where he's actually from, in Russia. I realize how little I know about his true home and I want to ask him, but doing so would mean I forgive him and that we're friends.

"This is me," I say, pointing to my building.

He laughs. "No, you are not apartment building."

"That was a joke. I just meant—"

"Yes, I know. I joke too." His smile is lopsided and self-deprecating. "There is only one Zelda, and she is beautiful girl, standing in front of me." When he meets my eyes I feel an unwelcome tide of heat. Flustered, I search my bag for my keys, wanting nothing more than the safety of my bedroom, and heavenly, blissful sleep. Yuri's fingers graze my shoulder. "Good night. I hope you hear trumpets in your dreams." He takes my hand and presses his lips against my knuckles.

"Good night, Yuri."

I turn to go inside and Yuri slowly backs away, but neither of us gets very far. "I'm sorry," the doorman says, "I've been instructed not to let you through."

"What?" Panic pounds inside my head.

The doorman's face turns bright red. "I really am sorry, but your mother said that under no condition am I to let you through, and I should report you for trespassing if you try. She said..." he clears his throat self-consciously, "she said that you need to take this seriously, because another trespassing charge will be very, very bad for you."

Yuri comes back and stands next to me. "Is there problem?"

I shake my head violently and swallow back my dismay. "Never mind." I bolt down the sidewalk toward some unknown destination but Yuri catches up with me instantly.

"Zelda," he says, "tell me what is wrong."

I can't keep the tears from coming. They pour down and I hiccup and sob. "My mother kicked me out. I have nowhere to go and I am so, so tired."

I don't resist when Yuri takes me into his arms. My face is smashed against his shoulder and he rubs my back while he makes soothing noises. "Is okay," he says. "You stay with me."

"I can't."

He pulls away, keeps both hands on my shoulders, and gives me a soulful gaze. "I sleep on floor. You sleep in my bed and get rest. Then you will feel better, and tomorrow we figure out new plan. Yes?"

I don't think I can take another night of hardly sleeping on the couch of Ballet Institute East.

"Maybe just for one night," I concede.

We go back and get my suitcase from my locker at Ballet Institute East and then Yuri takes me back to his cramped apartment in Brooklyn. He makes me a peanut butter and jelly sandwich, I use his shower, and then we watch television while his roommates come in and out. They mostly go out, which is great because by ten o'clock we have the place to ourselves. Yuri shows me to his mattress.

"You don't have to sleep on the floor," I tell him. "There's plenty of room for both of us."

"You are sure?" he asks.

"Yes."

So we sleep side by side, and in the middle of the night I wake to find his arm draped over my stomach. I fall back asleep, warmer and safer on a mattress on a floor in Brooklyn, than I was in a bed in the Upper East Side.

Chapter Sixty-One

I get the sleep I longed for but the peace that came with it evaporates the moment I turn on my phone. There's a text from Julie.

I was a bitch. Can I make it up 2U? Plz TMB.

I can count on one finger the amount of times Julie has apologized to me over the course of our friendship. I don't even know how to respond.

Yuri turns and makes noise, letting me know he's awake. "You want we get breakfast?" he asks. "I am hungry for pancakes."

In the dim morning light his face is lined with sleep, but still he looks simultaneously bright and dreamy. "Pancakes sound good," I say.

He smiles and blinks at me, unabashedly peering into my eyes. His right index finger reaches out and traces my lower lip. The fleeting moment of physical contact sends a rush of warm shivers through my entire body, so I throw common sense to the wind, lean down, and kiss him.

His response is enthusiastic. Yuri wraps both of his strong arms around my waist, pulls me down onto my back, and lowers himself onto me. The dance our mouths do together is more intricate than the ones our bodies have already done to trumpet music. I pass my hands over the warm skin of his bare shoulders, and as we kiss and strain against each other, I feel him grow hard against me.

I'm so overwhelmed that it takes me a moment to remember two things: one: he has four roommates and absolutely no privacy, and two: I have no idea what I'm doing. What if I'm really bad at sex? This is definitely not the time to find out.

"Pancakes," I mutter, as I push him away. "I thought we were going to get pancakes."

Yuri is breathing hard but he manages to speak softly. "Yes." He runs a hand through his hair, and then points to the bathroom. "You wash up first?"

At breakfast I ask Yuri about his home in Russia, and he talks and talks, which is great because it means I don't have to explain why my life has turned into a cautionary tale. Plus, listening to him really is interesting, and I pretend nothing has changed and that I'm still the only girl in New York who thinks of him as just a friend.

When we exit the cafe he says, "You call me later," and then he pulls me close. His gentle kiss leaves the lingering taste of maple syrup. "You stay with me again tonight. Or not, but call and tell me, yes?"

I nod and pass my fingers over his finely chiseled cheekbone. Pretending we are just friends will only become more and more difficult. "I'll call you later. And thank you, Yuri. For everything."

One more kiss. "Last night made me happy, Zelda. I talk to you later, yes?"

"Yes."

I travel on a cloud rather than the train, but when I get to Clarkson School of Design I'm thrust quickly back to earth. Julie is standing outside the building, smoking a cigarette, alone this time. I see her before she sees me, but her face lights up once she registers my presence. She launches her cigarette to the ground and stomps it out, and then comes barreling towards me. Before I have time to say anything, she throws her arms around my shoulders and hugs me, hard.

"I am so sorry about yesterday," she says. "I was such a bitch. Are you okay? Have you made up with your mom yet?"

I take a step back. "I'm fine. Yuri let me stay with him last night, so I wasn't homeless."

Something flashes on her face. Maybe anger? Maybe concern? "Stay with me tonight, okay? You can stay for as long as you want."

"I don't know."

"He's not a nice guy." Her nicotine breath reaches my nostrils and I wince, but she must misinterpret my reaction, because she takes on a soothing tone. "You're so inexperienced, Zelda, that it will be hard for you to understand. You want to trust him, but trust *me*, you shouldn't."

So she's already given up pretending that she and Yuri got back together. "What are you even doing here?" My voice is as abrupt as my question.

She smiles. "One of the models has mono. They called me this morning and told me to come in."

I move my head around, searching for the right response. "Well, we should get inside."

Julie puts her arm around me, all buddy-buddy like, and I let her guide me towards the door. A production assistant is waiting for us and looks way too stressed for this early in the morning. "Hey girls, there's been a change," she taps a pencil against her clipboard. "Zelda, you're with Amos now, and Julie, we don't need you. You can go home."

There's a tense, silent moment and Julie sets her mouth into a grimace. "What are you talking about?" Each word comes out so tightly that it could be its own sentence. "They called me this morning and said I would be with Amos."

"That was before Robin got kicked out."

"What?" Now she really has my attention. My stomach clenches and I grab onto the edge of the reception desk. "Why would they kick out Robin?"

The PA shrugs but I can tell she's savoring the juiciness. "I guess she got caught bribing the judges. *And* she stole Kyla's scissors. Can you believe it? She seems so nice."

I grip the desk's smooth, rounded wood even harder and my hand slips away without enough traction. "No. No! That can't be right." The world is spinning too fast, but Julie's feet are planted, firmly and defiantly.

"Let me get this straight," she says, "you guys are picking Zelda, over me?"

"Yeah," The P.A. says. "I mean, it's not my decision, but they are definitely choosing Zelda over you."

"This is all a mistake," I struggle out. "Robin wouldn't bribe the judges." I turn to my best friend. "We can work this out, Julie, I swear."

"Fuck you." She's so measured and controlled, like that expletive has been brewing for years and it's now finally dripping out. "You fell on the runway. You're a disaster, Zelda. You wouldn't be here if it wasn't for me, yet they pick you? Everyone always picks..." She shakes her head, refusing to finish the thought.

If I try to respond I'll just sound hurt and whiny. No, staying silent is the only way I can choose strength. So I'm standing here, like the mannequin I've become, as Julie storms out. I don't follow her; there would be no point. Instead I rush to find Robin.

She's in the workroom, packing her stuff, keeping her head down. Everyone stares at her with accusatory eyes, and the injustice of the situation overwhelms me.

"But you're innocent!" I cry, speaking to the entire room.

Robin looks only at me and not at Gabe, who has a camera shoved in her face. "I'm sorry. I know this totally screws you over too."

I almost laugh at her concern. "Don't worry about me. Amos's model has mono, so I'm not out. They're shifting me over to him."

"Oh." Robin puts some spools of thread into her sewing kit. "Well, good. Amos's great, so that should work out."

"But I want you." My urgency is a tidal wave ready to crest. "Don't worry, Robin. I'll do some snooping, and I'll catch the person who's behind it, and then they'll bring you back."

Robin seems to be in a daze as she pulls out her phone and reads a text. But when she looks back up at me, her expression is grave. "Don't snoop around, Zelda. We don't know what this person is capable of. I don't want you getting hurt."

"Somebody pushed you. Somebody framed you. And I'm finding out who!" I yell this, hoping everyone hears and everyone knows how serious I am. I even meet eyes with several of the designers. Who knows who the saboteur might be? "Don't worry, Robin. This isn't goodbye."

We hug, she gives me a silent, shaky, farewell smile, and then she picks up her stuff and is gone.

But I'm still here.

Part V

Chapter Sixty-Two

Robin

I'm outside the Clarkson School of Design, gripping my cell phone. My possessions are at my feet and the people walking past have to dodge around me and my stuff. It's windy and my hair whips into my face and sticks to my eyes, but I manage to dial the right number, despite my shaking fingers.

Nick picks up on the third ring. "Robin?" His voice is tentative. "They're letting you call me?"

There's no time to revel in the sound of his voice or to say how much I've missed him. "I was kicked out, Nick." I talk fast so he doesn't have the chance to assume that this is just about me getting eliminated. "They think I sent one of the judges $40,000 as a bribe, so I've been asked to leave."

His breath catches. "Hold on. That stuff about the bribe was slander. Monty got it taken off the website because it's all fake."

"Fake?" I wish I had something to smash right now. "This is real, Nick! Why the hell aren't you taking this seriously?"

"I am taking it seriously." His voice is the type of deadly calm that comes in the middle of a tornado.

But I'm done being calm. "Someone put $40,000 into your bank account to use as a bribe for my success on the show. Someone accessed my computer and posted that slutty montage of me online. Oh, and *someone* miraculously filmed us having sex and she posted that too! So in other words, this person is systematically ruining my reputation while you bury your head in the sand!

"My head has not been in the sand!"

"You promised you would take care of this for me and you didn't!"

"I've been trying, okay? It's not so easy!"

I brush my windblown hair away from my face and I already regret what I'm about to say. "It's only difficult because you refuse to believe that Andrea is involved!"

There's a fatal pause before he answers. "We are not arguing about Andrea again." I can't decipher what, if any, emotion fills Nick's voice. He sounds like he could be a customer service representative looking into my inquiry. I hear the clicking of his keyboard, so I imagine him, sitting at his desk in the real estate office he's trying to escape, half a cup of coffee by his computer and a pile of contracts waiting to be filed.

Make this day go away. "So," I finally ask, "did you check? Is there anything in your account activity?"

"This makes no sense."

"What do you mean?" My throat is tight with tension.

"Who would put forty thousand dollars into my account? Who would even have access to that? I don't get it."

I could splinter apart from stress. "So it's all there? The transfer in and the transfer out?"

"Yes, but—"

"Nick, how could you let this happen?" For some strange reason my voice is level and self-possessed, but my stomach is roiling and runny.

Nick will probably assume that I enjoy blaming him. Yet it hurts like I'm pulling out all my teeth, sans Novocain.

I clench my free hand into a fist, telling myself that this all a misunderstanding, that it has to be one. But I can't hold back what I'm about to say. "Do you realize what this means for me? I will be a laughing stock! I'll be a notorious cheater! Nobody is going to want to work with me or buy clothes from me. You have turned me into a joke!"

Nick's voice is a low tremble. "This isn't my fault. I knew nothing about it!"

The sidewalk is crowded and someone accidentally grinds her spike heel into the edge of my toe. For a moment there is searing pain and I don't edit myself; the words fly out like crazy, quacking ducks. "But Andrea knows all about it, Nick! She has to because there is no other explanation!"

"Watch what you say, Robin!" Nick's incredulity burns my ears. "Andrea would never do that and there's no way she has forty thousand dollars just lying around!"

I don't like his tone so I do my best to emulate it. "No, no of course not! I forgot that Andrea is an angel who can do no wrong."

"Andrea would never purposefully hurt you!" Nick rarely raises his voice but now his decimal level is at least a seven. "I know my sister and it's just not possible. If you want someone to blame, blame your ex-lover's dead wife! Or blame some other ex-lover of yours, one whose wife is still alive. That's a lot more plausible than blaming Andrea."

Oh no, he didn't! "So I've slept around so much that I deserve this?"

"You said it, not me."

His words are a punch in the gut. "Wow. If that's how you feel, maybe we're making a mistake, getting married."

Nick breathes in and out. I bet he's closing his eyes, trying to stay calm. The idea infuriates me.

"I can't talk to you about this right now." His voice is so still that I want to shake the phone like it's a bottle of pop and make it erupt with his anger. "I have to go."

"Fine!" My answer is boisterous enough for us both. "Call me when you have time, Nick. The last thing I want is to be a nuisance."

He ignores my sarcasm. "Okay. I'll talk to you later."

And then he hangs up.

How did I manage to ruin my career and my relationship in the space of an hour? Only I could manage this level of self-destruction. And now I'm on a New York street with nowhere to go, my one saving grace is there's no camera stuck in my face. Since I wasn't eliminated in the normal way, I'm not expected to stay at a hotel with the other ousted contestants, but my options right now are pretty crappy and pretty limited.

So I do the only thing I can think of to do. I call Ted.

Chapter Sixty-Three

Robin

"I still don't understand why I didn't come to Philadelphia," I say. "I need a place to stay, not a chaperone."

Ted emits an exasperated sigh. "It's complicated, okay? But if you want my help, here I am."

How can anyone be such a mess of contradictions? My big brother sits atop the hotel's brown polyester bedspread, trying to figure out who is behind the *Rotten Robin* website and he's helpful but unco-operative, considerate but thoughtless, protective but self-involved. I simultaneously love and hate him. And of all my friends and family members, he is the last one I would choose to have by my side during a crisis. Yet, here he is and I should feel grateful but I don't. "I never said I wanted your help. I said I wanted a place to stay."

"And now you have one." Ted gestures around the dim, airless room he booked for us, with its two queen-sized beds and windows that will need a crowbar to pry open. He sits cross-legged, Bud-dha-style, swiping at my tablet. "At least they let you keep this," he murmurs.

I'm just not strong enough to contain the bitter sarcasm. "Yeah. My career and my engagement are both over, but hey, I get a free tablet, so everything is okay." I want to sob, or yell, or pull out my hair because never has my life been less okay than it is right now. I pace, trying to ease all my crazy energy before I explode from anxiety, but I give up, collapse onto the free bed and stare at the textured beige ceiling.

Ted glances in my direction. "Don't knock the tablet. It's the only way we have to do research."

"I don't care about the tablet. I think Nick is done with me." I lay my arm over my eyes and welcome the darkness.

"He's not done with you. He's just reeling from all the drama."

I uncover my face and sit up. "How do you know?"

Ted rubs both eyes with one hand, using his thumb and his index finger, like he's in pain. "Look, I'm the last person you should talk to about this. Any advice I give you will be wrong." There's a deep line of concentration creasing his forehead and his jaw is a spring that could snap. I think back, to how unhappy both Ted and Tina seemed that morning at breakfast before I left for the show.

"Are you and Tina splitting up?"

Ted lets his hand fall to his lap. "I really don't want to talk about it. We should focus on proving your innocence."

Well, I guess that answers my question.

After a couple of seconds he speaks. "I wonder if there's any chance someone broke into your house and stole Nick's passwords."

"You mean someone other than you?"

He jabs the air with his index finger. "I only told you that story so you'd realize my credibility. You're not allowed to hold it against me."

"I don't care that you broke into our house. But I do care that you just automatically accuse Nick."

"It turned out I was right!"

The words explode from my lips. "It wasn't Nick!"

"Then who was it, Robin?" Ted matches my volume and tone. "I'm sure I don't know, but I'm guessing it's not a dead girl who was last seen boarding a bus in rural Greece."

I close my eyes and see Clara, mounting the steps of a Greyhound and unknowingly walking to her death. But that image soon morphs into something else - Nick, Andrea, and me, having a backyard picnic, celebrating a March heat wave.

Is everything about my life a lie?

I open my eyes and exhale a big burst of air. "Let's try and prove something, okay? I need real evidence before I talk to Nick again."

Chapter Sixty-Four

Zelda

"I had nothing to do with it and you can't prove otherwise," says Kyla. She pushes her large, dark-rimmed glasses up her nose. They're hipster/nerd type glasses, which I've only ever seen her wear while she's sewing. Maybe Kyla is a hipster but she's way too snarky to be a nerd. I've been talking to her for around thirty seconds and already she's snapped at me four times.

"You never tried to hide how much you dislike Robin," I retort.

Kyla swings her long mane of hair from one shoulder to the other as she pins pleats into the skirt she's creating. "If I was going to frame her for something, don't you think I'd be a little more subtle about it?"

There's a reason I'm a dancer and not a detective. I suck at this. Meanwhile, Kyla's body language states that I'm dismissed and I don't have the chutzpah to challenge her. Yet as I start to walk away Kyla interrupts my exit. "Hey," she croaks, "you know who you should ask? Your friend... Nadia's model."

"Why? What do you know?"

Kyla speaks through a mouth of pins. "I don't know anything and if you say I do, I'll destroy you, got it?"

"Umm...okay?" I square my shoulders and straighten my posture. Even if I'm completely intimidated, I can still act like I'm not. "But why should I ask Julie about Robin?"

Kyla spits the last of the pins onto her work table and stretches her jaw. "The other day I saw her going through Robin's stuff."

"What do you mean?"

Kyla explains, and I realize that everyone here is out for themselves. They are all glad Robin is gone. She's one fewer person to compete with and that's the nature of reality television. Maybe that's the nature of life.

But I text Julie. *So sorry about everything! You're right about Yuri and I'm a total disaster. Can I still stay with you?*

She must have calmed down in the hours since we talked, because she texts back and tells me to come over after I'm done for the day. I tell her that I will, and then I text Robin with Julie's address. *Come by at around 8:00. I have a feeling you'll get all your answers.*

One way or another, we will get to the bottom of this.

****

The doorman lets me in, alerts Julie, and I take the elevator to the fifteenth floor. My stomach is like a snow globe: shaken, upset and waiting to resettle back into reality. I have no idea what kind of Julie I will find on the other side of her door.

Her shiny face is the first thing I see when the elevator doors open. "Hey!" Her voice is perky, her smile is bright, and even her hair is in a swishing, energetic ponytail. So this evening she's playing the part of happy best friend. I step onto the solid floor and she loops her arms through mine, guiding me to her apartment. "I bet you haven't even heard!"

"Heard what?"

"They posted the summer repertory roles today!"

I can't believe I'd forgotten. Weeks ago, Julie and I and every other girl at Ballet Institute East auditioned for a part with the summer repertory program that partners with New York City Ballet. Getting cast means opening a door for an internship with one of the best ballet companies in the world.

Julie's happy demeanor must mean she got good news. "What part did you get?" I ask.

"I didn't get anything." As she speaks her shiny expression expands, like Pinocchio's nose when he's telling a lie. "We both knew I wouldn't. But you did, because you get everything you want, don't you?"

"I... I wouldn't say that." We're in her living room now, and I plop down on the plush, heather-colored armchair that I've always loved. "I mean, who even cares, right? It's not the end all, be all."

Julie is leaning against her couch's armrest, unwilling to sit down. "You don't have to pretend, Zelda. I know how much you wanted it and I know you're already dying to call your mom and tell her." She widens her eyes in insincere wonder. "Maybe you've finally done something that will make her happy."

"So they posted a list? I'm surprised I didn't hear about it from the other BIE girls at *The Standout*."

I stare and she stares back. The smile hasn't left her face but Julie's eyes are cold and hard. "If you don't believe me, ask Yuri. He got cast as Albrecht. He'll tell you when he gets here."

"What? Yuri is coming over?"

"I mentioned the idea of a threesome and he was all for it. He should be here soon." She does a fake yawn and stretch movement. "Do you want anything to drink? I could really use something to take the edge off."

She strolls toward her parent's liquor cabinet and I get up and follow her. "Julie, I'm sorry about Yuri. I only meant to be friends with him, really. But you and I need to talk."

She's kneeled down, pulling out bottles, sorting through and rejecting each one. "I think I'm in the mood for vodka and we keep that in the freezer." Julie meets my eyes as she stands up straight. "Yuri will like that. Vodka will make him feel at home."

I follow her into the kitchen and speak to her back as she digs through the icebox. "Julie, I'm serious. I need to know what's going on with you."

She wrestles out the vodka bottle, which was sandwiched between a box of Boca Burgers and a bag of frozen peas. "I'm fine Zelda, really. I mean, why should I care that you stole my boyfriend, my modeling job, and now my repertory spot? I've only been working towards it for my entire life, but everything happens for a reason, right?" She tightly grasps the frosty bottle and refracted light shines through it. "Do you want ice in your drink?"

"I...um, no thank you." I mean no thank you for the drink itself, but Julie assumes I just want it iceless, so she pours a healthy portion of straight-up vodka into a martini glass and hands it to me. I take a tentative sip, and warmth, both soothing and sickening, travels from my lips to my limbs.

Meanwhile, Julie fills her own glass with ice and a larger amount of vodka than she gave me. As she boldly drinks I marvel how she can take such a big swallow of this medicine-like stuff.

"Anyway," she continues, waving her vodka around so that some of it sloshes down to the floor, "there's always a solution, right? Maybe I'll pull another Adrian."

"Huh?"

Julie takes a contented sip before answering. "It was easy, convincing Adrian she didn't want to be a model on *The Standout*." She sets her glass down on the kitchen counter. "Crazy, really, how little you have to do to make someone feel scared."

Oh yeah. Julie was only cast as the understudy, but she got the job after our Ballet Institute East classmate mysteriously dropped out. "You threatened Adrian?"

"I did what I had to do to get what I wanted." Julie spins, faces the kitchen counter, and lifts one leg so her foot rests on top, as if she's standing at a ballet barre. She raises her arm over her head and arches her back. Her head is upside down, peering at me. "I tried to do the same to you. I thought if I could get your designer out, I could get you out too."

Her confession just slides out, graceful, effortless, and nearly beautiful. I don't even know what to think. "But why, Julie?"

She straightens up, calmly lowering her leg like she can't be bothered to rush her answer. "Because I wanted to beat you for once."

I don't always win. I don't get everything I want, far from it, and everyone knows Julie is a better dancer than me. "You sabotaged Robin just to punish me?"

"I wouldn't call it sabotage. I just tried to undermine her confidence, which was easy, because let's face it, she's a mess."

Suddenly I realize I am squeezing my glass of vodka, harder and harder, with every word Julie says. I loosen my grip and it shatters to the kitchen floor, little shards of glass amidst a puddle of white alcohol.

Then a buzzer rings.

Julie steps over my mess and into the foyer, where she presses a button on her wall. "Yes?"

The doorman's answer is full of static. "Yuri is here for you."

"Send him up." She marches back into the kitchen. I have grabbed some paper towels and am crouched down, attempting to clean up. "Don't worry about that now, Zelda," Julie barks. "Come on, we're meeting Yuri at the elevator."

I can barely orient myself around any of this. "Huh? Why?"

Julie taps her foot, too impatient to explain. "If you care about what happens to him, you'll come with me."

Blindly, I get up and follow her out to the elevator. I am silent, though my head is drowning in unasked questions. Meanwhile, Julie is on a diatribe. "Everything comes so easy to you and you just throw it away! I mean, seriously, Zelda! You're thinking about college? How mediocre can you be? What are you going to do, study economics at some third tier school, like Penn State? I bet you'll get date raped at your first campus party, drop out, and become a certified accountant. Then you'll be fat and ordinary, while you waste away in some office building, when you could have had it all. And meanwhile, Yuri chose you, a virgin with no vision. God, it's such a waste!"

All I can think is: *She hates me. My best friend hates me and she's right. I didn't have the vision to notice.*

The elevator doors open and before Yuri can get out, Julie grabs my hand and pulls me in.

"What is happening?" Yuri asks.

Julie presses the very top elevator button. "We're going to the roof." The doors close, the three of us are contained, and the air feels so thick I'm not sure I can breathe.

"I thought," struggles Yuri, "I pick up Zelda to bring her home."

"You really believed that?" Julie laughs. "I don't care what you do later, but first we're roofing."

"What do you mean?" I ask.

Julie turns sunny again, pasting on a smile. "You guys have been holding back on me! I know how fun you think roofing is, and I feel so left out!" She drapes an arm around each of our shoulders. "I'll finally get to see what all the fuss is about."

The elevator dings and the doors open. Julie uses her key to gain access to the roof. She runs out first and Yuri and I follow with heavy steps.

"I know this isn't hardcore enough for the two of you," Julie cries, dancing around the flat surface atop her building. "Not enough of a challenge, right?"

"Is fine," Yuri answers. "But I am not in mood."

"Oh really?" Julie sticks her face in his. "How convenient. You always used to be in the mood to do stuff with me, Yuri."

"I am sorry you had wrong idea," he answers, but she just laughs.

"No," he continues, "is not meant to be joke. Zelda and I go now." He uses his eyes to motion to me, asking me to get back on that elevator, and I almost say yes before my phone vibrates with a text.

It's from Robin. *We're here. Where are you?*

On the roof, I text back. *Hurry.*

Then Julie cries out.

"Hey!" she calls. I am shocked at how quickly she managed to jump up onto the railing that surrounds the edges of the building. She is balanced and unmoving, her center of gravity deep. "Now what do you think? Is this dangerous enough for you?"

"Julie, get down!" I run toward her. "Please! I'm sorry about everything, okay? Just please, please get down."

"No. This is too much fun." The wind is whipping her hair and she raises one leg into an arabesque. Only the ball of her other foot, planted against the thin, round rail, keeps her from falling to her death.

Yuri doesn't hesitate. He jumps onto the railing and holds out his arms. "Dance with me?" he asks.

I know Yuri is trying to be kind, thinking if she gives him her hands, he can ease her down. But Julie sneers. "I don't need your pity!"

The wind billows her shirt and makes her hair fly. I cling to the fact that Yuri hasn't had the large drink of vodka that Julie did. His hands are still outreached, hoping to grasp onto hers. "I know you are excellent dancer," he yells over the wind. "This is what roofers do. We balance and we dance."

"And you take selfies, right Zelda?" Julie glances at me. "Better yet, you should film this, okay?"

"Sure," I shakily take my phone from my pocket. I turn on the video camera and point it at them. "And once we get some really great footage, you can come down."

Julie looks skeptical, but she takes a tiny step in Yuri's direction. Then she does another arabesque. "Can you do this, Yuri?"

He nods. "Sure," and he models her movement while I film them.

"Julie," I say, still pointing the camera at her. "What did you do to Robin?"

She keeps her eyes on Yuri. "It wasn't just me. Nadia and Gabe were very easily convinced; they both believed that bringing Robin down would help them get ahead. So I told Nadia to access the internet on Robin's tablet, and to distract her while Gabe dumped water on her dress. Oh, and I took Kyla's scissors and put them with Robin's stuff. I can't believe something so stupid got her kicked out."

"Did you push her on the treadmill?"

Julie raises her arms over her head and for a breathless moment I think she's going to attempt a pirouette. But she just laughs. "Of course I didn't push her. The bitch went crazy paranoid. She probably just tripped over her own clumsy feet."

My eyes have been on Julie and too late I realize that Yuri is reaching for her. She pushes him away which causes them both to lose their balance and slip.

"Yuri, watch I out!" I yell, but it does no good.

Yuri's feet fly from beneath him, but he catches the railing with one slick palm, leaving his body to hang over the vast expanse between sky and sidewalk. Meanwhile, Julie's ankle becomes wedged between two rails, and that is the only thing that stops her before she falls forward, head first toward the ground.

They are both hanging between life and death, and if I take the time to try and save one of them, then the other will surely die.

I think fast. Yuri is the easier save. If I give him my hand, he will have the strength to pull himself up and then maybe he can rescue Julie. So I drop my phone and go to him first.

"Help me, Zelda!" Julie's screams like a terrified, wounded animal, and it pierces right through me. "I'm your best friend! You have to help me!"

I climb onto the railing, not to the top bar but in the middle, and I pitch myself forward, arm outreached. Yuri's face is bleached white and his lips are shaking at an extremely high velocity, but he manages to take my hand. I literally hold on for dear life, using every ounce of strength to both anchor him and to pull him forward. He's strong but this feels impossible.

"Please pull harder," he grunts. Heart pounding in my ears, I close my eyes and see him fall, landing on the ground in an unnatural, bloody mess; his beautiful body meant for dancing turned to wreckage. That image summons some extra reserve of power. I give him one last tug and I fall back, onto the floor of the roof. He mounts the railing like a gymnast on a vault, and then propels himself back onto safe, solid ground.

"Zelda!" Julie cries.

"Yuri, help her!" I yell, but he's already rushing forward.

He climbs up onto the railing over where she hangs and he uses one hand to grab the ankle that isn't caught while he uses his other hand to wedge out the ankle that is. He gets her unstuck, but Julie is screaming and writhing in terror. Her body is already propelled forward, but when Yuri tries to pull her up she slams herself back. I hear a sickening thump when her head hits the side of the building at an angle, and then her ankles slip from his grasp.

Seconds later there are screams. Automobiles screech. The world ends.

Horror hits me at full force. "She's dead."

Yuri looks over the railing and winces. "Yes."

I sob. Yuri, in an effort to console me, places his hand on my shoulder, which is hot with pain from trying to pull him up.

"Don't touch me!" I yell, and Yuri recoils as if he's been burned.

Everything around me becomes noise: the street below, the wind rushing past, and the pounding in my head. Surely it will all come together in a big explosion and this sick spinning will stop. But somehow I differentiate and realize that the pounding and the yells aren't coming from within my eardrums but from behind the rooftop door.

"Robin," I say to myself, and move to let her in.

"Zelda, wait!" cries Yuri. "We should not be up here."

"It's a little late for that!"

And then I open that door.

Chapter Sixty-Five

Ted

Robin's model, Zelda, is hysterical. A Russian guy tries to explain what happened, something about dancing on the railing, and I try to understand.

We hear sirens. "That must be the police," Robin says. "They'll want to talk to you."

"And to her parents," I add. "Where are this girl's parents?"

Zelda uses her sleeve to wipe away snot from her nose. "At their office, I bet." Her chin quivers as she dares to glance toward the sounds on the street below. "I'll call them. It's better coming from me than the police." She has calmed down enough to speak coherently so she turns to the Russian, who I am assuming is her boyfriend. "You should go," she tells him.

"No. I stay," he answers.

"They'll deport you for sure," she answers. "They'll suspect foul play and they'll make it your fault. You have to go."

Robin asks them both questions, but I can't decipher the words because I'm fixated on a ledge. I don't actually make a decision to stroll over but my legs move me there, nonetheless. I look down to the street, where emergency vehicles' siren lights are flashing and paramedics work to erase what happened.

But can it be erased?

She was here one moment, gone the next, and there's no physical evidence of it on this roof. How is it possible that we are so fragile, that even in the act of being rescued, one wrong move can instantly end a life? The railing is still rigid, with no scratches or scuffs that would indicate she was thrown over.

Nope. She was just a girl goofing around; they tried to save her, and now she's dead.

I'm on the middle bar of the railing but now I stand up straight, look out at the city, and I'm hit with the strongest sense of deja vu I've ever had. This is my dream, the one where I wanted to fly from the top of that building. I'm reliving it, if it's possible to relive something you've only ever dreamt about. But the notion that it's possible to be free, to be airborne, settles into me like a wave washing away sand, and the peace I didn't even realize I was seeking is suddenly found. There is no more stress from a job I can't handle, no wife who no longer loves me, no family members who merely tolerate me. I'm alone up here and the world is at my fingertips. I can touch it if I just reach out, so I climb up onto the top rail.

Balancing on the highest rail is easy; my stance is wide and my center of gravity is low. Even the fiercest of pushes wouldn't make me fall. I spread my arms as if they're wings and I'm ready for a launch. I remember Mom's note: *Get yourself together, don't be afraid, and jump.*

So this is what she meant.

Chapter Sixty-Six

Robin

I wasn't prepared for any of this. And though I never liked this so-called friend of Zelda's, I still feel a crushing sense of remorse, like it was my fault and I could have prevented it if I'd just made better choices.

Zelda and Yuri exit through the rooftop door, ready to call Julie's parents and to talk to the police. Only then do I think to glance around for Ted. When I see him, I have to bite my lower lip to keep from screaming.

He's balanced on the railing like he's a superhero.

I walk up with soft, slow steps. If I startle him from behind he might fall. Yet with every inch forward, anxious fear pulls me back. My heart is in my throat and I need somewhere to put my hands, like maybe on a doorknob out of here. Walking to that ledge is the stuff of nightmares and I realize that I am acting out my dream from last night. I am on the roof and I'm trying to save someone when I can't even save myself.

But I had no idea that the person I'd be saving is Ted.

I force myself right up to the railing, so my face is parallel with the back of my brother's knees. I have one shot at this and I move quickly.

There's no time for talking him down. I just wrap my arms around his legs and lunge back.

When we land I feel crushed, like a splattered, rotten tomato. The wind is knocked out of me and my lungs don't work. For a moment I'm dying. But then Ted climbs off of me and I realize that anyone as angry as I am has to be alive.

"Son of a bitch!" I yell, once I regain my breath. "What the hell was that, Ted? Did you think that was funny?"

"Sorry," he mumbles. "Are you okay?"

I move my arms and legs, my head and torso, and other than a bruised bottom I am fine, but I'm not telling Ted that. It would be letting him off the hook.

"What were you thinking?" I push him in the chest. "You have two sons! You're not allowed to make crazy moves, Ted!! You of all people should understand what it's like to lose a parent! God, what would Mom think?"

When I mention Mom, Ted's face crumbles. "I don't know," he says with a sniff. "I wasn't thinking about Miles or Mason." Tears moisten Ted's cheeks but he swats them away. "I wasn't thinking at all. My life is kind of screwed up right now, and I just..." he buries his head in hands, and when he continues to speak, his voice is muffled. "Don't tell anyone, okay?"

My brother is broken and I have no idea why. I put my hand on his shoulder and move in for a hug. Surprisingly, he hugs me back. "After we talk to the police, we're taking the train back to Philly," I tell him. "I won't tell Tina what happened, but only on the condition that you do."

I feel his ribcage move up and down as he takes a deep breath. We just hold each other, closer than we've been since I was a little girl. "I wasn't actually going to jump." Ted speaks into the top of my head.

"I'm not saying that standing up there was a smart thing to do. It wasn't, but I liked how free I felt. I never feel free anymore."

Simultaneously, we let each other go and I look into his glistening eyes. They're naked with honesty, just like each line and crease that his face has earned over the years. "I know you have a lot of responsibilities now," I tell him.

"I've always had a lot of responsibilities," he answers. "I'm not complaining; that's just how it had to be, so you and Ian could…" he breaks off, thinking and scratching his chin. "I won't say it's what I chose, but I never tried to choose anything else, either. I guess I felt important, being in charge when Dad needed me. But now…" he rubs the back of his neck, "…now, if you took all my responsibilities away, I wouldn't even know who I am. There's just nothing left."

"That's not true." A picture pops into my mind: a teenaged Ted as my babysitter, following a treasure map I drew of the backyard, humoring me, trying to find the bubble gum I had planted as the prize. How many more moments have I stored away and lost? "You are more than just your to-do list, Ted. Maybe you just need a vacation, or something."

"Like what?" he asks wryly. "A Carnival cruise?" His laughter at my lame suggestion sounds cynical, but at least he's laughing.

The moment is broken when the police come through the rooftop door, followed by Yuri, Zelda, and the building manager.

Hours later, after we finish giving our statements to the police, Ted and I take the train to his home in Philadelphia. It's past 3:00 AM when our taxi from the station pulls up to his house, and he leads me around to the back, where he pulls a spare key from the nozzle of their garden hose. "I keep the spare key at our house in an almost identical spot!" I say.

"I know."

We walk in through the back door and Ted punches in the security code. Then he quietly leads me to the guest room that I stayed in before. "I don't think I've ever been so exhausted," I say.

"Yeah, me too." But instead of wishing me goodnight, Ted goes to our mother's first run print and gazes at it. "Robin, do you believe in ghosts?"

I have to force myself not to collapse into the soft mattress by my side. "I don't know," I answer. "I think they're possible. Why?"

"The other day I found a piece of paper in Mom's handwriting. It fell from behind the Mats Gustafson."

"Okay..."

"It said: *Get yourself together, don't be afraid, and jump.*" He rubs the back of his neck as he veers himself towards me. "I know it wasn't there before. I hung that picture myself."

It's a struggle to process my unformed thoughts. "Are you sure Mom wrote it?"

Ted shakes his head. "Of course not. We can't be sure of anything, right? But I kept every birthday card and every Valentine Mom ever gave me. That note was in her writing."

"And you think Mom was telling you to jump from the ledge? Why would she do that?"

"No... I don't know." He scratches his head and breathes through his nose. "Maybe she somehow knows that I'm lost, and she's trying to help me..." he shakes the thought off. "Forget it. It sounds stupid when I say it out loud."

Get yourself together, don't be afraid, and jump. That could apply to all sorts of situations and I have no doubt that Ted needs guidance. I'd also love to believe that Mom is capable of writing us notes, but if so, where is mine? I'd certainly like to hear from her.

I don't say any of this and Ted sinks to the bed. The quiet settles around us, beautiful and precarious. Ted sighs. "I don't know how Tina will react, once she knows that I'm home."

"You have to talk to her, Ted."

"Like you'll do with Nick?" He asks gently.

I close my eyes and my head finds its way down to a pillow. "I can't think about that right now. I need sleep."

A moment passes before I feel Ted's hand briefly rest on top of my head. "Good night, Robin."

Then things fade to black, like the end of a scary movie that I hope won't give me nightmares.

Chapter Sixty-Seven

Ted

I find Tina's skinny form in the twisted blankets on our bed. I sit on the edge of the mattress and tenderly touch her shoulder. "Tina," I whisper. "Hey, wake up for a minute."

Her eyes flicker open. She's always been a light sleeper. "What are you doing here?" The question isn't exactly angry but her voice holds no elasticity.

"Tina, I'm so sorry."

She rolls over, away from me. "Whatever, Ted. I want to go back to sleep."

I inch closer and put my hand on her back. "No, not whatever; I have something important to say." She doesn't respond so I just hope that my words reach her. "Tina, I had this moment tonight, where I was so close to... to jumping off a building. A really high building."

My confession is a mild temperature change, an excuse for her to shiver, to wrap that blanket more tightly across her body. But she sits up abruptly, shedding the covers and exposing her skin to the cool air. "You're not serious."

In the dark I can still make out her features that I know so well. I can still see the girl I fell in love with. "I wouldn't joke about something like that."

"Because you never joke about anything."

My ears had been ringing but her comment stops the annoying sound. I'm reminded of a conversation long ago:

"Of course your family likes you," she'd said. "Why wouldn't they?"

"They think I'm no fun. Seriously, I'm not joking."

"Because you never joke about anything?"

For years afterwards, every time I told her I was serious, she would laugh and reply, "Because you never joke about anything." Then I'd laugh and somehow she taught me to have a sense of humor about myself.

But she stopped using that line on me years ago, which probably was when she also stopped loving me. So I can't laugh now, but I offer her half a smile. "Do you ever have moments when you just want to let go?"

"Only two or three times a day." She says softly, but loud enough for me to recognize that her unhappiness mirrors my own.

"You can't let go. I... I don't know how to let go of you. So what do we do about it?" I'm desperately hoping she'll have an answer, or at the very least, that she won't flinch at my assumptive use of "we."

"I don't know, Ted."

Dejection threatens to settle over me, but then my crappy expectations explode through the roof, because Tina leans in, presses her warm, skinny body against mine and her lips find my lips in the dark. "But it's going to be okay," she whispers in my ear, "because I'm not ready to let go of you either."

I grab onto her like she's that railing along the rooftop. Then I'm crying and my tears land in the balmy curve of her neck, but instead of pulling away she only holds me tighter.

Chapter Sixty-Eight

Zelda

Please pick up, I pray as I call my mother. There's a ring and another ring and I lose hope after the third ring, but on the fourth ring, a split second before voicemail is about to pick up, she answers.

"Yes?" is all she says.

"Mom, I need you." My whisper is a shout. "Julie died and it's my fault."

She takes three deep breaths before answering. "Where are you, Zelda?"

"At the police station. I just got done making my statement."

Another deep breath. "You should have called me right away—*before* you gave a statement."

I don't respond. What's there to say? I could write volumes about all the "should haves" I've left unfulfilled recently, but it wouldn't change anything. Julie would still be dead.

"Do you want me to come to the station to get you or would you rather just come home?"

"I just want to come home."

Yuri insists on taking my train and walking me to my building. When we get to my door it's so late, or so early, that the doorman isn't there, so it's just Yuri and me and the stillness of the night. Yuri was silent for the entire journey, from the police station to my front door.

"Are you going to be okay? I ask.

He flicks his head ever so slightly. "I worry they think I kill Julie on purpose."

"No." I shake my head adamantly. "You were trying to save her. I know what I saw." I take his hand. "You did everything you could. This is not your fault, and I'll swear it up and down if I have to."

"You always see best in people, Zelda."

"I see what's really there."

He just looks at me, blinking away tears but unafraid to meet my eyes. And for the first time ever, I feel like someone is looking at me and seeing what's really there too.

"I call tomorrow," he says, right before he gives me a chaste kiss on the forehead. Then we say goodnight.

When I get inside Mom is waiting in the living room, wearing an old sweatshirt of Dad's. "Tell me what happened to Julie," she says, her flat voice rising to my ears.

There's a lump of regret swelling my throat shut. "I wish I didn't have to," I struggle out. "Mom, I really messed up and there's no way to fix it."

She stands and leads me to the couch so we're sitting side by side. "Tell me what happened to Julie." The second time she says this is a gentle, insistent nudge towards something I must do.

I try to breathe normally but I can't, not if I have to think about this. "She was so angry at me, Mom. The ballet and the modeling jobs and I sort of stole her boyfriend...and she wanted to go up to the roof, but...she'd... I couldn't stop her from..." I can't finish the thought because I'm crying too hard, but Mom lets it go.

"It's not your fault, Zelda." She hands me a tissue which is way too thin to absorb all my tears.

"You can't say that," I moan. "You weren't there. You don't know."

"But I know you," she insists. "So whatever happened, I know without a doubt, that it simply wasn't your fault." Mom sounds like she's going to cry too.

"I thought you hated me," I tell her.

"No." Mom tucks a strand of hair behind her ear. "I could never hate you, Zelda. I love you, more than anyone, but I just get so angry and hurt sometimes. That's on me, I guess." She rolls her eyes toward the ceiling. "There should be a personal standard that parents are forced to meet, but I always fall short."

"I feel like I'm always falling short too."

"No, Zelda. Don't feel that way."

She takes me in her arms and as we hug I become her little girl again. It's not everything, and it's probably not permanent, but this regression feels like a start.

Chapter Sixty-Nine

Robin

The next morning I wake to Ted urgently tugging on my shoulder. "I can prove that your phone was spoofed!"

"Huh?"

Ted explains that he got up early and snooped around on my phone until he figured out at least part of the mystery. He shows me my phone's history, something to do with the settings and downloads, and says it's enough that we can contact Jim Giles. "But we still don't know who's behind the bribe," I say.

"It doesn't matter," Ted insists. "This proves that it wasn't you."

That, and Julie's taped confession about Kyla's stupid pair of scissors, gets me an invitation from Jim Giles to come in for "a little chat."

I have to take the first train to NYC, and I'm assuming it's so I can take part in the next challenge. I try calling Nick, over and over, but he never picks up. Finally I just leave a message, detailing what happened last night.

"Nick," I say, after my long explanation, "I still don't know who is running that website, but I do know she's not going to stop until we break up. So look, I'm probably going to be unreachable again, and obviously we have to talk, but..." I sigh, procrastinating and not wanting to say this next part. "I think we should go on a break, say that we're no longer engaged, because I'm kind of at a loss and I think you are too. I love you. You know that...." *but you won't even answer my calls,* "but it's probably better if we take some time to think."

There's a knock on the guest room door. Ted's standing in the entrance, tapping his watch. "Are you ready?" he mouths.

I nod and gulp back some tears. "I have to go, Nick. I'll call you as soon as I'm done with the show."

Chapter Seventy

Zelda

Yuri is given one of those terrible choices that's not a choice at all. He can leave now, go back to Russia and enjoy his supposed freedom, or stay in the U.S. and face involuntary manslaughter charges.

"But that's so unfair! You were trying to save her!" I pace around my living room while Yuri just sits still, his feet propped up on our marble slab coffee table. Good thing my mother is out meeting with a divorce lawyer. The feet on the coffee table would be an instant deal breaker.

"Julie's parents decide to press charge," he answers.

"Just on you? Not on me?"

"You were not in video like me."

"But that video is all the proof they need..." I gnaw on my knuckle and think. "I'll call and explain. They will listen to me."

"No." He is calm as he lowers his feet from the table, gets up, and takes me by my shoulders. "Some fights we cannot win. They lost only daughter. If I must go back to Moscow so they do not mourn so much, then I go."

"But you got cast as Albrecht in *Giselle*. I thought you wanted to stay and be a big star."

His lips part so that he's almost smiling. "I wish to stay for many reasons," he says softly, "but I will still be big star. And I come back someday." Yuri's hands drop from my shoulders down to my waist. "When I return, I will look for you, yes? I will not forget."

It's probably just some line he's feeding me; that's what my mom would say. I shouldn't believe him, especially since he'll soon be half a world away.

But life is short.

Chapter Seventy-One

Robin

"Robin, I hope you will accept my whole-hearted apology." Jim sniffs emotionally. We're surrounded by all the remaining contestants on *The Standout* and of course, a bunch of cameramen, though Gabe is conspicuously absent. The workroom clock is ticking away and time is running out before the next runway show. Jim looks at me but his words are meant for a much larger audience. "After last night's tragedy involving two of our models, some truths have come to light, and we know now that you're innocent." He places his palms against the lapels of his double-breasted suit and takes a deep breath. "Will you please return to the show?"

My reply is choked with emotion. "I'd be honored." Everyone claps, even Kyla, but when no cameras are on her she squints and makes that *I'm watching you* sign, pointing to her eyes and then to me.

At first I'm stepping into another role. *Tonight, the wronged reality show contestant will be played by Robin Bricker.* I finish up my plaid tutu dress in record time, and it miraculously scores in the middle, even though I have a substitute model and my crafting was super-rushed.

But during the next challenge I know I won't get a free pass. I just keep my head down while I sew pleats into a sheer Wili-inspired camisole. The Wilis are this crazy gang of dancing phantom girls from the ballet *Giselle*. Since they're all abandoned brides who died from heartache, I create this alternative sort of wedding dress, with tulle and wire, giving the image of constant, weightless movement.

"It's certainly ambitious," Jim places his finger against his chin. When it becomes clear he can think of nothing else to say, he pats me on the shoulder. "Keep working." Then he moves on to Amos.

Jim and Amos confer over Amos's dress which has golden embroidery and bugle beads. I overhear Jim's effusive praise and wish I could work like Amos, unencumbered by emotional baggage. But I'm glued to this wedding dress, unable to detach from everything it represents.

Oh well.

I'd rather create a wedding dress for a dead, heartbroken bride than talk about my feelings.

Chapter Seventy-Two

Zelda

On his last night in New York, I come to Yuri's apartment, and by some miracle he is alone when I get there.

"What do you want to do?" I ask. "We could go out dancing, or to some touristy place that you haven't seen yet? Maybe ice skating at Rockefeller Center?" I purposefully don't bring up the Empire State Building. No more rooftops.

He shrugs. "I wish to spend time with you."

His grey T-shirt clings to his broad shoulders, his jeans have a slight rip in the knee, and just looking at him makes me warm. If I were to touch him, it would be the strongest, most delicious warmth I'd ever feel.

"Well, we could just get dinner," I answer.

"Dinner. Yes." He grabs his jacket, which is lying atop a packed bag. The finality of his impending departure hits me with a nauseating punch to the stomach. Yuri stands by his apartment door, waiting for me to join him on our way out. I walk over and wrap my arms around his shoulders.

Then we kiss. I thought it would be a mild kiss, more perfunctory than passionate. Nope. He holds me like I'm the black swan.

When I pull away, his cheeks are pink with anticipation and his hair is tussled. I remember him and me, our first time on top of a building, and I am sure.

"You look strange," he says. "What is wrong?"

"I'm not ready to let go of you yet."

He gives me a sad smile. "It will not be goodbye."

Even though I'm shaking, I reach behind and lock the door. Then, praying he won't laugh at my inexperience, I gaze at him with slow, seductive eyes. "Dance with me," I whisper, holding out my arms. His face softens and he pulls me in.

After a moment he turns on music and we sway to it. It's a soft and rhythmic orchestra and a vibrant chord is struck inside me. Moving together, touching constantly, I breathe a sigh of relief as I become a different version of myself. I bury my face into the curve of his neck and feel myself lifted into the cradle of his arms.

Our dance becomes something more, something precious, something I'll never forget. It's dreamy and intimate, better than how I'd always imagined it would be.

We are reaching, climbing, hearts beating in the hope that this moment will not end.

Chapter Seventy-Three

Robin

When Zelda comes back we don't speak about what happened on the roof. I worry that she is just a broken Wili now, heartbroken, dancing in misery but not for joy.

Or maybe I'm just projecting.

My Giselle dress gets chosen as one of the highest or lowest scores, and my heart trips but I regain my composure almost instantly. "Robin," Hilaire asks, "do you think your design is on the bottom or the top?"

"I have no idea," I tell her. "I can never predict what you're going to like. If that means I don't have vision, maybe you should send me home."

Hilaire tilts her chin in her charming, ex-supermodel sort of way. "Are you sure about that?"

"No" I reply. "I mean, I want to be here very much, but I can't apologize for creating something I believe in. And if that's what you're asking me to do... well, I won't, even if it means I'm going home. "

Hilaire's gaze is as thoughtful and soft as I've ever seen it. "I understand, Mon Cherie. But I thought your design was both skilled and highly original. You are on the top and you are not going home—at least not tonight."

There's a hitch in my chest and my knees threaten to buckle. With all the turmoil and drama, I've been wondering if doing the show is worth the price. But Hilaire's praise is like the designer clothes she wears, so beautiful and stylish that I want to keep it on forever. I win the challenge and I'm in the top for the next two challenges after that. Then I keep landing in the middle but never in the bottom, and I stitch away, my vision and my design concepts clear.

The final challenge is on *Swan Lake*.

"It's a nice story," I say to Zelda. "But I don't buy it. People's hearts break all the time and yet they stay stubbornly alive."

"That's the part you don't buy?" Zelda shakes her head. "Forget the broken heart bit, he falls in love with a bird. Twice."

Zelda and I are waiting for the stylist to do her hair and makeup. Kyla and her model are hogging up our time and I should demand that my consultation start. But there's no hurry; for now I'm happy watching Zelda scuff her tattered Converses across the floor in large, balletic loop-de-loops.

"Sometimes I think the characters in these timeless tragedies are better off, just keeling over once they've lost the love of their life. They don't have to deal with the tedium of getting over it."

"You don't mean that," replies Zelda. "Think about Julie."

"Sorry." I shift in my seat. Zelda is standing above me, too energetic to sit. She arches her back and does this twirly little jump that I don't know the French term for. I'm glad she's dancing again. I've been worried that Zelda's love for ballet died along with her friend.

"You know who I feel sorry for?" Zelda rolls her shoulders back and arches her neck, looking very swan-like. "Odile. She was under the sorcerer's spell when she made the prince fall in love with her. And who knows, maybe she loved the prince just as much as Odette did. But everyone thinks she's this evil black swan when really, she never meant to hurt anyone."

"Yeah."

For the millionth time today there's this weird pressure in my chest, and my pulse quickens while my heart turns to lead. It happens whenever I'm reminded of Nick, or my stupid mistakes, or how my feelings have been hurt. "I guess we're a sisterhood: you, me, and Odile."

Zelda raises an eyebrow and I can't tell if she agrees or not. "I wish we got to find out how Odile's story ends. She leaves the party and that's all we know."

"Maybe she goes to college, starts a career, and marries a nice man with a bird fetish."

Zelda laughs, although I would have missed it had I been blinking. Still, it's progress.

I tap my foot impatiently. "Seriously, how much longer is Kyla going to take?"

"She is so inconsiderate," Zelda says. "I don't care if you take me to Fashion Week, but if Kyla gets to go and you don't, I will forever lose faith in reality TV."

"You don't care if I take you to Fashion Week? But you have to be my model! I couldn't do it without you."

Zelda regards me, hands on her hips. "Of course I'll come. But you *can* do it without me, Robin. We both know that you can do anything you set your mind to."

After her hair and makeup are finally done, I fit Zelda into a dress that is all black, with an empire waist and lace sleeves that end at her elbows. Lace also covers her neck and part of her chest, and the solid, beaded material plunges into a deep-V neck that ends just below her bosom. Zelda stares at herself in the mirror as if she's never seen her reflection before.

"I think it works," I say, but I'm more confident than I sound.

I know it works.

Chapter Seventy-Four

Robin

Amos, Kyla, and I are the three contestants who make it to the end. That means we get to show at Fashion Week, which is like the Holy Grail for designers. We're given eight weeks back home to create our collections, and then we'll return to show at Fashion Week, where the winner of this season's *The Standout* will be announced. I know everyone will be rooting for Amos. Heck, I'm practically rooting for Amos. He doesn't pulse with negativity like Kyla, and he isn't a drama magnet, like me. Plus, he's super-talented and he really wants to win.

But I want to win, too.

Ted offers to let me stay in his basement, saying I could set up a studio and just focus on my work. I'm probably stupid not to take him up on it, but I have to go home. I text Nick with my flight information, and I say we should wait to talk in person. He responds right away with, *Okay. I'm excited to see you.*

When I emerge out of the ticketed area and into baggage claim, I see him instantly, his hands shoved into his jeans pockets and his eyes darting nervously around. When his gaze lands on me, his face breaks into a hesitant smile and I can't breathe.

We walk towards each other and my body is already flushed in anticipation of his touch. We're at a high-traffic, crowded spot in the middle of the room when we meet and I drop my purse to my feet as he clutches me in a ferocious hug. "No," he says into the side of my head.

I pull away. "No, what?"

"No, I reject your idea of not being engaged. I still want to marry you."

I tilt my head down and he kisses my hairline. All these weeks of not knowing he felt this way, of crying in my sleep, of thinking we were done. He could have just told me. "Why didn't you ever pick up when I called?"

"I had no idea you'd called. I lost my phone and by the time I found it you were back on the show and I couldn't get ahold of you."

"I don't understand," I reply. "You lost your phone? But..."

"I know it sounds lame, but I swear it's true. I looked everywhere and I tried calling myself a dozen times, but my battery was completely drained. I was just about to report it missing, when I found it in the pocket of these jeans I haven't worn in months."

I don't say anything because I don't have to. Nick knows what I'm thinking. "Maybe," he says carefully, "but I really don't think Andrea hid it. She felt so bad for me, like she always does when I'm miserable. Andrea wants me to be happy, Rocky. You have to believe that."

"I do." I kiss him and he kisses me back, with a combination of gentleness and passion that makes me wish we were alone so I could rip his clothes off. But I'm aware that we're surrounded so I break away and compose myself. "Hey," I smile broadly because I can finally share my success with the person who matters most. But I lean in and whisper in his ear, cognizant of the confidentiality agreement I signed. "I'm going to Fashion Week!"

"There was never a doubt in my mind that you would!" Nick's laugh is joyous. "I'm getting married to a winner!"

"Yeah, Nick, but about that..."

He wrinkles his eyebrows together. "Come on; tell me you weren't serious about calling off our engagement."

"I want to marry you. I just think we have a lot to talk about."

"Like?" Nick crosses his arms and broadens his stance, unconcerned with all the people who are stepping around us.

"Maybe we should wait until we're in the car to discuss it."

"Just tell me. I've been waiting weeks for this conversation and I can't take it anymore."

I sigh. "I did well on the show. What if I'm offered some fabulous job in New York?"

He shrugs. "We'll move to New York. I just need to finish school and then I can teach music anywhere."

"What about Andrea?"

"Andrea's almost as old as I was when I took her in. She'll figure it out." He pauses, thinking carefully. "But I'd like to always offer her a bed to sleep in. If that bed is in New York, so be it."

I scuff my foot along the linoleum floor. "And the cyber-stalking? If we get engaged again, it will start back up."

"Look," he says, "I get that you're the one being hurt by all this ..."

"No, that's not it," I interject. "Whoever's behind it knows that the best way to hurt me is by hurting you. If we get married, you're setting yourself up for more."

Nick raises one eyebrow and the side of his mouth at once, arching his face in irreverence. "What can I say, Rocky? Bring it on."

His laugh is sweet music that goes right to the softest, most vulnerable spot in my heart. I reach for him and Nick lifts and twirls me around. The happiness I feel in that moment, the surety that we fit, that we're right, that we're meant to grow old together, doesn't go away after he puts me down and the world stops spinning. It stays with me that night as we have the house to ourselves and enjoy a sweet reunion, and even the next morning when I wake up and find Andrea in the kitchen, scrambling eggs before she leaves for her job at the rec center.

"Is Nick still asleep?" she asks.

"Yeah." I am dressed for a morning run, in shorts, my Hoyt College T-shirt, and sneakers, and I pull my hair back as I head toward the kitchen cabinet. I grab a water glass and fill it up at the sink. As I take a sip I can feel her watching me, so after my last swallow I place my glass down and face her. "It's good to see you."

"Good to see you too," she says, her back now to me as she cooks eggs over the stove.

"Andrea..."

Keeping her eyes averted, she turns off the burner and uses a spatula to scrape her eggs into a dish. "Nick has been going crazy, so seriously, it's great that you're back."

"Thanks." The coffee she put on to brew gurgles, and the aroma of French Roast is like a courage injection. "Look, I know how much you love your brother, and I also know he'd do anything for you. That's how Nick is built; he protects the people he loves. And I expect that if he was forced to choose, he'd choose you over me, because all he's ever done is take care of you and he doesn't even know how to stop." I pause, giving her a chance to disagree, but I realize she's waiting for me to finish the thought. "Plus, he loves you more than anything. So please, Andrea, for Nick's sake, don't make it a choice. Let him have both of us."

Andrea places her dish of eggs on the table as if she can longer stomach them, and then she meets my gaze. "You still think I'm involved in...whatever is going on with you?"

I shrug. "I don't know. But I do know that it's not over, and I know that once Nick and I re-announce our engagement, whoever has been harassing me will start back up. But it won't change anything. As long as he'll still take me, I'm going to marry Nick."

Andrea crosses her arms over her chest. "You broke up with him."

"To protect him, but that was stupid." I can't look at her anymore; it's just too tight, those brown eyes that are exactly like Nick's boring into me. The faucet is dripping and I place my thumb against the spigot, letting the water pressure build and leak out from behind my skin. "I know what's it's like to lose someone, you know. We have that in common. And I also know what it's like to live in fear, that feeling that once you finally find the love and happiness you've been looking for, it could all disappear in a second, because life is dangerous and only naïve people believe in happily ever after." I sigh. "But after a while you're faced with a choice. You either take the gamble or you protect yourself from the inevitable, which is just as fruitless, because bad stuff will happen no matter what. Protecting yourself will only keep the good stuff from happening too."

I take my thumb from the faucet and wipe it against my shorts. When I look back at Andrea I see her lip is trembling. "Yeah," she whispers. "Protecting Nick from you *is* stupid. You're, like, the best thing that's ever happened to him."

Tears of gratitude prick at the corners of my eyes. "You really think so?"

Andrea nods, her face squished with emotion. "You make him so happy. And you probably won't believe me, but I really want that for Nick. Even if it means I have to go away."

I step towards her. "Andrea, can't we just be a family? I want you to stay, so we can be sisters."

Now she's crying. "You won't feel that way once I tell you the truth."

An alarm bell clangs inside my ears as I realize how much I was hoping to be wrong. "Just tell me." My mouth is suddenly dry.

Her chest rises and falls. "You have to promise that you won't tell Nick."

"I can't promise you that."

"Then I'm not going to tell you!" She slaps her hands against the counter and pushes off, propelling herself out of the kitchen, taking with her any last spec of good will between us.

"Andrea, please don't leave like this!"

"I'm going to be late for work!" Andrea cries.

"What's going on?" We're both startled by Nick's voice and we turn, finding him standing in our hallway, wearing his morning sweatpants and undershirt, his hair disheveled and his face in need of a shave.

I say nothing.

Nick looks imploringly at Andrea. "What don't you want me to know, Andi?"

Just the hint of kindness and sympathy in Nick's question makes his sister dissolve into tears. Blubbering, with her hands over her face, she says, "I am so, so sorry!"

Nick and I exchange a look: disbelief on his part, horror on mine. "So it was you who posted all that stuff about Robin: the bribe, and the website, and the... the sex tape?"

Andrea lowers her hands from her face and collects herself. "No, Nick. It wasn't me. It was Dad."

Chapter Seventy-Five

Robin

Andrea calls her work and tells them she'll be late, and then we sit down and she tells us the whole story.

"At first I didn't realize, I swear." Andrea picks at her cuticles while she talks and I try to look away from her. Then maybe she won't feel the intense, burning gaze that this situation actually calls for. "He'd take me out for dinner and ask me all this stuff, like what I'd overheard you guys talking about, so I told him because I pretty much overhear everything. And it felt like gossiping with a girlfriend, you know? Like, 'Oh my God, can you believe that Robin had an affair with a married man?' And he'd be so interested, wanting details, and it was like, the closest we'd been in forever."

"When did you realize what he was doing?" Nick asks.

"After the first handwritten note showed up at our house. I snuck down into the basement and read it while Robin was upstairs. Later I called Dad and told him what I knew, and…"

"And that night he texted and said that he was disowning you?" I ask.

"Right," Andrea answers. "So I didn't say anything but I tried to stop helping him. I told him he couldn't come over and mess with your computer any more. And I found the first note and taped it back together." She looks at me eagerly. "I kept it, in case you wanted it as evidence some time, and that's why I tried to keep the second one too. I swear it was to protect you." Her large brown eyes shift towards Nick; then to me; then back to Nick. "You have to believe me; I knew nothing about the spyware or the phone spoofing or your bank account stuff. And by the time he told me about it, Robin had been kicked off the show. That was the weekend he spent all day over here, watching TV. I'm pretty sure he hid your phone, Nick, but I didn't know where."

"Andrea, you still should have said something." Nick stares at the floor, clearly horrified. "You had a million opportunities and yet you just stayed quiet."

She nods, tearfully. "I know. But he convinced me that if you and Robin got married you'd lose interest in me, that once you have a family of your own, you wouldn't be there for me anymore. And it made sense! Plus, all the stuff he was digging up about Robin, made me think, that, well, you could do better." She inhales sharply and throws her gaze at me, only for a second. "Sorry."

"It's okay," I tell her.

"No!" Nick cries. "Not okay! It's definitely not okay!" He gets up and circles our small living room, pacing. "My father was sabotaging you, out of selfishness and greed and just general craziness, and you—" he spins towards Andrea, pointing a finger like he could shove it down her throat, "you *helped* him!"

"Nick," I start, but he waves me off, still addressing Andrea.

"You and Dad should just kill me now. I mean, heaven forbid I have a life of my own, or some small morsel of happiness. God, no! I'll probably die taking care of the two of you."

"Dad thought he was doing you a favor. 'Robin's too pretty for him. She's been with too many men. She'll steal his soul for sure.'" Andrea glances toward me. "Those were his words, obviously." She redirects her words to Nick. "He thought he was helping you."

"That is not an excuse! Do not EVER defend him to me again!"

Andrea is shaking like her world is about to collapse. I have to step in.

"Nick, calm down. None of this is fatal."

Nick looks at me like he'd forgotten I was in the room. "You should run, Robin. Go now! You definitely don't want to marry into this."

"I can make that decision for myself, thank you."

He shakes his head in incredulity. "You should hate me! I doubted our relationship when you accused Andrea, and you were right! I'm serious, Robin! Go while the going is good!"

Now Andrea sobs while she curls up on the couch, like if she just scrunches her body up enough she might disappear. Meanwhile, I've never seen Nick angrier; his hands are literally shaking with the urge to smash something. "I'm not going anywhere," I say, my voice as level as I can muster. "Yes, your dad is crazy and he can consider himself disinvited to the wedding, but there's still going to be a wedding."

Nick throws out his arms in frustration. "You were willing to end it before, Robin. Now, after everything that's happened, you should just let go!"

Deep sentiment bottles up in my chest. "I will *never* let go of you."

Nick rolls his eyes toward the ceiling, breathing hard and trying not to break down. I place my hands on his shaking shoulders and he captures me in a hug, squeezing me so hard it becomes difficult to speak. "It's going to be okay," I whisper into his ear. "We'll get through this. I promise."

I feel his body relax, tension escaping through his skin as he exhales. He tilts his head back and his lips find mine, brushing them with a quick, gentle kiss. Then he breaks away and speaks to his sister. "You're coming with me to Dad's," he says. "Now."

"I'll come too," I say.

"No." Nick squints, rubbing his forehead and trying to find the right words. "Please, let me take care of this. I can't handle giving him any more chances to hurt you."

I swallow roughly. "Fine," I tell him. "But I reserve the right to confront him later on if I feel like it."

"Understood," Nick answers. Then he gestures toward Andrea, signaling it's time for them to go. She stands, wipes her face with the back of her hand, and looks at me.

"Thanks for being so understanding."

I just nod.

"We'll be home soon," Nick tells me.

"I'll be waiting for you when you get back."

Chapter Seventy-Six

Ted

"How did it go?" Tina is standing in the middle of our kitchen when I walk in, eating a salad from a deli container and drinking juice. I notice that the salad has feta cheese and bacon bits, which I consider a victory. There aren't any croutons, but Tina would need a gun held to her head before she'd ingest carbs.

"I think I did okay," I answer, standing next to her and giving her a kiss on the cheek.

"Did he ask you all sorts of probing, self-reflective questions?"

"Of course," I laugh. "Isn't that the point?" Tina and I started couple counseling two weeks ago, but as soon as our therapist heard about her eating issues and my rooftop episode, he insisted that we also come individually. Today was my first solo session.

Tina throws her fork in the sink, closes the lid to her salad container, and places it in the refrigerator. "During my session he asked me about the kids, like he was sure that all my issues stem from motherhood."

"Huh. No, he didn't ask me much about the kids."

"See, that's so sexist. I suppose you talked about your career."

"Or my lack of one?" I am now officially unemployed but I still have health insurance, for a few months anyway. Tina and I are going to bleed our mental health fund dry.

She flicks away a stray blonde hair that is clinging to her fitted black T-shirt. "Well, we didn't talk about *my* lack of career, and it's something I've been thinking a lot about."

"So talk to him about it next time," I say.

"I'm talking about it to you." Tina leans against the refrigerator, arms crossed. "I really liked working at Robinson Health before the kids were born." She looks off, like she's envisioning her days as a physical therapist, helping people rehabilitate after major accidents. "So I called them and they actually have openings. I have an interview tomorrow."

"Tomorrow?"

"And it's with Angie Sampson, who still remembers me. It sounds promising." Tina crosses her fingers, then looks around our kitchen, trying to find some wood to knock upon and settles for our granite countertop.

"That's great," I say.

"Ted, if they hire me, the hours will be long. You'll need to be available for Miles and Mason. But I was thinking...maybe you could use the time? Decide if you want to be a P.I. or... I don't know; whatever it is you want to do."

I run a hand over the back of my neck, making the tiny hairs along my skin stand up. My mother used to rub along the top of her spine in the same way, whenever she was deep in thought or feeling tense. I can hear her now; "You can decide, Ted. Whatever it is you want to do." We were standing at the gate to a roller coaster ride during a family trip to an amusement park. Ian, who barely met the ride's height requirement, was already eagerly in line but I hung back, unsure.

My mother, with her unconditional love and acceptance, stood there, rubbing her neck and letting me choose, letting me find the strength and courage to take the plunge.

"Tina..."

She looks at me sideways. "What's wrong?"

"Nothing. Thank you, Sugar. I'd love to have time to decide." I hug her and she hugs me back. It's one of those magical moments when the world has slowed down. "Hey," I say. "Do you mind if we move that watercolor of my mother's? It's so pretty; I'd really like to see it every day."

Tina shrugs. "The Mats Gustafson? How about into the living room?"

I smile. Yes, it's time to let some memories live again, to bring that shadowy lady into the light.

Chapter Seventy-Seven

Zelda

I can't stop thinking about Julie, and that hurts. The blow she took to her head must have been an explosion of pain. And the loss that her parents feel? It has to be a knife twisting endlessly in their hearts. Still, I tell myself that I did the right thing, that I shouldn't feel bad about choosing Yuri or letting Yuri choose me.

I imagine Julie alive, dancing as a Wili in *Giselle*, dressed as a dead spurned bride and pirouetting her anguish away. But it's actually me who is doing that, performing in my summer repertory role and watching my weight by eating cauliflower for carbs and egg whites for protein. And it's nonproductive, wishing that Yuri was here playing Albrecht, wishing that we rehearsed together, wishing that we spent our free time together too.

Refusing to move on is a form of self-betrayal. I can't miss him; that's practically sacrilegious, because it tarnishes the indiscernible bottom line of who I am. If I've learned anything, it's that life is just a series of small choices combined with big choices, and I must try to make the right choices.

So I am starting now.

I grab my course guide and find my mother in her bedroom, reclined in her new sleigh bed and reading a tattered copy of *Anna Karenina*.

"What's up?" she asks when I enter.

"I applied to Penn State," I tell her, without prelude. "And I got in. I want to live on campus this fall and study economics with a dance minor."

I actually applied months ago, that's how long this has been in the works. Julie must have seen the brochures in my dance bag, which is why she chose to tease me about it. But I don't plan to get date raped at my first college party. Besides, losing my virginity that way is no longer possible. Yuri took care of that. I make these arguments inside my mind but what I'm really doing is bickering with a dead girl.

Now my mother looks at me. Her mouth and nose are twitching, arguing with her eyes over what emotion to communicate. She inhales deeply. "What about your internship with American Ballet? Do you know how many girls would kill for that?"

I sit beside her in her bed. "So let someone else have it! Mom, I love dancing, but I'm tired of all the backstabbing, and the dieting, and the sore, blistered feet. I want to dance for fun, because I love it, and if that means I can't do it professionally, then I'd rather do something else."

She closes her eyes like she's praying. "Do you have any idea what you're giving up? This is your only chance to be a dancer, Zelda. You are so close—but if you quit now and then change your mind, it will be too late. Meanwhile, it's never too late to go back to school and study economics."

She says "economics" like it's something distasteful, smelly, not worthy of consideration.

"I want to be normal, Mom. And pretty soon it will be too late to enter college as a freshman, to live in a dorm and meet people, to go to parties and join clubs. I want to make friends who know more than the calorie count in a tablespoon of peanut butter or the best way to wrap their feet."

"You want friends who are different than me? When you say normal, what you really mean is, you don't want to turn into me."

Shame burns my cheeks when I can't contradict her. She sits up and grasps my shoulder. "Zelda," she says. "'Normal' doesn't exist. That's lesson number one in your advanced education."

I nod, staring down at her satin comforter instead of into her sad blue eyes. "I still want to go to school."

I can feel her studying me; perhaps she's looking for some sign that I'm her daughter, like I bite the inside of my cheek when I'm nervous, just like her, or we breathe in the same irregular rhythm. There must be some deep, blood connection, or maybe she just loves me and that, in the end, negates all our petty disputes. With a sigh of resignation, she takes my course guide and leafs through it. "Then we'd better start choosing your classes. I don't want you taking something stupid, like 'Dumping Ground 101.'"

I laugh. "Mom, you just made a joke!"

She smirks, not letting go of her pique. "I used to be a lot of fun, you know. Blame your father if I lost my sense of humor."

I reach across carefully, like she might break, and gently capture her in a hug. "Thank you, Mom."

Chapter Seventy-Eight

Robin

Ted and I sit out on his deck, swatting away mosquitoes and drinking beer. Tomorrow he will drive me to NYC, with my entire collection draped across the back seat of his car. The fact that he's willing to brave that kind of traffic for me is either testament to how much he's changed or to how little I knew him in the first place. Either way, Ted's still a stranger but I'm glad we're becoming acquainted.

"I can't believe you're selling your house." I look around their gorgeous yard. The twilight only enhances its appeal, with the big oak trees, stone circled fire pit, meticulous garden, and manmade stream that ends at a bubbling fountain. "I feel like I'm at an exclusive resort."

"Exactly," replies Ted, draining his beer. "We don't need all this and we really can't afford it. We're going to find something smaller, same school district and all, but the change will be good."

"And Tina's okay with it?"

"It was her idea." Ted stretches in his patio chair, letting his legs extend like two straight poles. "Ever since she's gone back to work the weight of the family rests on her shoulders. Her practical side is shining through, which is good, because my practical side has sort of disappeared."

I laugh. "See, I didn't know you had any other side besides practical."

He peals back the label from his beer, examining it like it's an artifact that holds some ancient truth. "Don't get lost in all the crap, Robin. It's the easiest way to lose yourself, or your marriage, or just…" he trails off, unable to finish the thought.

I take a moment, really considering Ted's advice. "I'm more worried about Nick getting lost than myself. He's the responsible one. I can see him getting buried by all his obligations and forgetting who he is."

"Don't let him," says Ted. "You'll balance each other out that way. He'll keep you steady, and you'll keep him…" he waves his arm around, searching for the right word.

"Unsteady? With all the drama I seem to attract?" I lean forward and rest my feet against the seat's rim, hugging my knees to my chest.

"I guess this time the drama was Nick's fault. Are you guys going to be okay?"

I scratch at my ankle, where I think a mosquito got me. "Yeah. I mean, I'm still coming to terms with a father-in-law who hates me; that this angry man is partially responsible for creating Nick. So I can't hate Saul and I'm trying to forgive him, even though he never asked me to."

"I wouldn't hold your breath, waiting for an apology."

I nod. "But I'm glad we're not pressing charges. It was Nick's idea, making Saul use that $40,000 for Andrea's dorm expenses. In a way, it's counter-intuitive, like she's being rewarded for her involvement in the whole thing. But Nick said that it's time to cut the cord, and living together, just the two of us, will be really nice."

"I'm sure it will," Ted murmurs.

For a moment we're silent, listening to the cricket's nighttime serenade, but my chest feels heavy with unsaid words. "I never really thanked you for all those years that you looked after me. I was probably pretty bratty about it."

"You weren't so bad. And it's not like we didn't have Dad, looking after all of us." Ted rubs along the back of his neck. "We all did okay, given the circumstances."

"Yeah." I swallow back a burst of nostalgia. "So I noticed you moved the Mats Gustafson."

"Yeah."

"Any more notes fall out of it?"

Ted shakes his head. "That'll probably always be a mystery. Maybe I imagined the whole thing. Because, for the life of me, I can't remember where I put the note. It's just gone."

"Get yourself together, don't be afraid, and jump." Ted's eyes meet mine after my recitation of Mom's words. "You don't need the note," I tell him. "Her advice is pretty easy to remember. Just don't take it too literally." I get up, stretch, and then go over and give my brother a kiss on the cheek. "I should probably turn in. Big day tomorrow!"

"Good night."

I go upstairs to the guest room, which now has a big blank space on the wall where the painting once hung. I get ready for bed and fall asleep easily, but in the middle of the night I wake, open my eyes, and see the Mats Gustafson hanging where it once was. The shadowy lady is walking towards a dream, so I let myself drift back to sleep, thinking of her.

In the morning when I wake, she's no longer there.

Chapter Seventy-Nine

Robin

Ted pulls up to the curb at The Empire Hotel, where a camera crew is waiting to capture my arrival. Luckily, they're not so interested in me hauling garment bags onto a luggage cart, so I can hug Ted and thank him in relative privacy.

"You'll be there for the show, right?"

"Are you kidding?" he asks. "I can't wait."

I got to invite a half dozen friends and family to sit in the front row during my showing at Fashion Week. Nick, my dad and Catherine, my brother Ian, and my best friend Isobel are all flying out. Ted will take the train into the city. The idea of having everyone there feels like eating chili, warm and gassy all at once.

When I get up to the posh hotel suite I share with Amos and Kyla, there is a bottle of champagne on ice with a congratulatory note from Hilaire and Jim. Since I am the last to arrive, we pop it open and engage in the perfunctory round of fake hugs and smiles, while the cameras film us being happy for each other.

"What's your collection about, Amos?"

He modestly sips his champagne. "I did a modernized take on Venice in the 1800s, using a lot of glass beads and a masquerade theme."

"Wow. I can't wait to see it." And I almost mean that. Of course Amos is going to win. I know this the way I know that stomach crunches don't really reduce belly fat, yet I keep doing them anyway. I turn to Kyla, who dips a strawberry in her champagne and sucks on it. "What about you, Kyla? Does your collection have a theme?"

She juts her lower lip to the side in a semi-sneer. "Of course. It's about animals. Each piece represents an animal on the endangered species list, and everything was made with eco-responsible materials and technology."

"Neat," says Amos. "I bet the judges will love it."

Her shrug says *of course they will* and Amos and I exchange an eye roll. "So how's your collection, Robin? Did you find a through line?"

"I think so," I say, stepping away from a camera that's a little too close for comfort. I walk towards a window that looks out on the cityscape and press my hands against the glass, reminding myself that I'm inside so I can't fall.

"What do you mean, you think so?" asks Kyla.

I close my eyes and see Ted balancing on that railing, Julie's dead body several hundred feet below. Heights make me more nervous than ever before. "It's about memories," I tell her. "How they sort of blur in our minds, but a few details remain in sharp contrast. Each piece is a reworking of some previously made garment, and they're all muted and soft, except for one detail that stands out."

"Interesting concept," Amos says. "I'm sure you made it spectacular."

"Thanks."

Kyla laughs in this throaty way that some people find likable, but to me, she sounds like she needs to cough up phlegm. The cameras turn to her and she slides her gaze, tucks her hair behind her ear, and chortles in a way that's straight from the reality TV star playbook. "That's so *brave* of you, Robin. I can't believe you simply reworked thrift store items. They'll either love it or hate it, right?"

"Right," I answer.

I didn't "simply rework thrift store items." They were all just a starting point and I gave them a new life. I made them my own. I started by thinking of the song Nick sang me when he proposed: all the memories of people, of moments filled with love that I'll never lose affection for.

Each piece is a snapshot of a person or a moment that's important to me. Only I will ever know that the beige trench-coat mini-dress represents my dad, or that the strapless silver jumpsuit is for my best friend Isobel. It's not important if people don't get that the vintage, pleated cocktail dress is about that time when Nick and I went ice skating last February. I have it all stored away, so who cares what Kyla thinks?

But I feel dizzier than ever, and the view from the window is only part of it.

The next two days is a whirlwind of hiring models, meeting with stylists, and putting the finishing touches on my pieces while listening to Jim Giles' critique. Zelda comes down on the afternoon before the show and I fit her into the signature piece in my collection: a reworked wedding dress that's now an evening gown. I dyed it a sepia tone, gave it a plunging back with a collar that slopes at the base of her neck, and a poofy skirt that trails in the rear but is knee length in front. The sharp, contrasting detail is the red satin lining underneath the skirt that will peek out as Zelda floats down the runway.

"I wanted you to be the white swan this time," I tell her. "But then I thought, *nah*. The white swan dies of a broken heart, and that's not Zelda. She's a fighter. So I tried to make a dress that communicates how awesome you are; both inside and out."

"This is gorgeous," Zelda says, her huge eyes cast down, focusing on the skirt. "I know I always say that, but this one is really special. You should wear it when you get married."

"I made it for you," I reply. "And after the show is over, it's yours to keep."

As Zelda looks up at me, her face crumples and she pinches her eyes shut. "I don't deserve that."

"Of course you do." I place a finger underneath her chin and prop it up so that she's forced to look at me. "I know you think Julie's death is your fault, but the only person who blames you, is you. Accept that you did the best you could, because really, most of it was out of your control."

She nods. "Thank you for saying that." After an emotional sniff, Zelda pastes on a smile. "Most of the time I'm so busy with school, I don't even have time to think about Julie. I guess being here brings it all back." She brushes the skirt with her hands and spins around, reminding me of a little girl playing dress up. "I can't believe you're giving me this dress."

"I hope you'll find somewhere fancy to wear it."

"Well, there's a campus formal coming up, and there's this guy..." Zelda shrugs. "Who knows? But I'll figure something out. I'm not going to let a dress like this hide in a closet. It deserves to be seen and appreciated."

"Just like you."

****

Backstage is like an amusement park on the day of the fashion show. Models are standing in these weird, random lines that seem to have no beginning or end, and I can't tell what purpose they serve. All the noise forms this collective rushing sound that I can't escape and there's this consistent, heart-pounding panic, like someone is going to forcefully strap me into a roller-coaster. I can't find the right pair of shoes to go with my evening look and I'm searching underneath every countertop in a 200-foot radius when I see her.

Clara.

My head snaps back and the floor shifts beneath me. What's she doing here? My stomach tosses and turns as she breezes past, like she belongs, like she's going somewhere, with her auburn hair brushing against her shoulders and her bangle bracelets tinkling down her wrist.

It's harder than you think, to leave your husband when he's cheating on you. Her words echo in my ears and suddenly I get it. She left Robert and came to the one place that made sense. She came to New York, to reverse the fate her grandmother suffered with a philandering spouse in Des Moines. So what if she had to supposedly die to live out her dreams?

"Places, Robin!" Jim straightens his tie as hurries to me. "You're up next."

I have to find her, to chase her down and see if she's real. I wave my hands around like I'm checking my pockets or grasping at air. Maybe what I'm really doing is chasing a ghost. "I'll just be one minute, Jim."

"Wait! Where are you going?"

I don't answer. I rush past, in pursuit of Clara. It can't be some strange coincidence that she is here, now, right before I face the masses to be judged for my supposed vision and skill, for the part of myself I want most desperately to be real. Clara will judge me first, for the part of myself I want most desperately *not* to be real.

I squeeze around other people, dodging every little obstacle in this huge space, following her cloud of red hair as it moves further and further out of reach. When I get to the door I push it open; I'm sure she will be waiting for me on the other side, to give me no more or less than I deserve. But all I am met with is open sky and a round observation deck with a low railing that could be too easily mounted. That is how someone gets hurt. That is how someone falls.

I am not falling apart but my heart is pounding as if I just finished running an eight minute mile. I look around, aware of my nerves vibrating beneath my skin. She's got to be hiding up here, ready to jump out and confront me, and I am overwhelmed with black-swan guilt.

They are waiting for me inside. Now is my moment. Now is my chance. Don't I want to take it?

I do. I just need one more minute.

I can't walk away yet. I hear the clanging of stilettos against metal. Clara is climbing up the ladder that runs along the wall to the roof. Blindly, I follow.

One rung after another, I make a point of not looking down and soon I have reached the top of the skyscraper. I've seen YouTube videos of people parachuting off buildings this tall, or they're using zip lines to enter a swimming pool on a roof that's a quarter mile down. It's a crazy death wish, and up this high, with no barrier to catch my fall, my ability to reason evaporates in the oxygen-thin air. There is nowhere to hide and nowhere to go, except, of course, down.

Crap. Going down means using sweaty palms and hesitant feet to navigate unstable pieces of metal, hoping I won't slip or that gravity won't win. I cover my forehead, using my fingers as a visor, convinced that with a bit of shade I'll see Clara and everything will make sense. She'll be wearing one of her gramma's wrap dresses, the blue and black one, with perfect accessories, because she was bestowed with an impeccable sense of style. But she is nowhere and panic zips through me. I hurl myself toward a protrusion of concrete, wishing to attach myself to the most solid looking thing I see.

"Clara!" I yell, my voice raspy and panicked. "Where are you, Clara?" I run around, searching and not paying attention to my footing or to where I go.

"Robin?"

At first I think Clara is answering my call but no, the voice belongs to Zelda. I peer over the edge, past my feet, down to where she is. "I'm right here," I yell, relieved to see a friendly face. Relieved to see any face at all.

"What are you doing?" she calls. "It's time. You have to come, now. Everyone is waiting for you."

My pulse is hammering away and strands of hair cling to my damp forehead. "I thought...I saw someone I know." I hear my words and know they sound unbalanced. I guess I have gone crazy.

"Nobody is up there, Robin," Zelda shouts. "You're just nervous about showing your collection and your mind is playing tricks on you."

Everything is dream-like and I'm not even completely sure I'm awake. The sun is a peaking from behind a cloud, shooting out rays of light that bathe Zelda in this impossibly beautiful, iridescent way. My mind takes a photo of her, in her sepia toned ball gown with the red lining, and I know already that this is a standout moment, one I will see in my mind's eye for the rest of my life. I close my eyes and I still see her but I see my mother's Mats Gustafson print too; they are one and the same.

"Robin," Zelda calls. "Come down and introduce your collection."

"Yeah, okay. Be right there." I look for the ladder, but when I realize where it is, alarm clutches at my heart. In my frenzied search for Clara I must have jumped from one protrusion to another, because the only way back to that ladder is by leaping over a foot-long gap. A gap that hangs over the sidewalk several hundred feet below.

Zelda peers up at me, understanding. "If you got over there, you can get back."

I violently shake my head. "No. No, I can't. Just go in without me. I'll wait for a fireman to come."

"No, you won't!" I startle at the unique sound of Zelda's raised voice. "There's no time, Robin. You worked too hard for this and your family is waiting. Hell, your future is waiting, and I'm not going to let you throw it away because you chose *now* to have a meltdown." She takes a deep, patient breath. "If I thought there was any chance you would fall, I wouldn't tell you to do it. But you'll be fine. So get yourself together, don't be afraid, and JUMP!"

Her words are a slap in the face, the kind where people are being cruel to be kind, the kind that forces you to wake up. "What...what did you say?"

"I said get yourself together, don't be afraid, and jump."

"Yeah, that's what I thought you said."

So Mom's note wasn't just meant for Ted.

Right now, the way the light hangs over Zelda, putting her in shadow while illuminating her from behind, I swear to God: she has become the illusive lady that Mats Gustafson once painted, the lady my mom once loved, a physical manifestation of the beauty and truth I have looked for my entire life. Only now do I realize that I've had it all along.

I take a moment. I look to the sky and offer a silent apology for all my mistakes. I thank my mom for looking out for me. I give up the ghosts and remember the living, the people who are waiting for me, the opportunities I can always create whether I win or lose, and the unconditional love I vow never to take for granted.

I get myself together. I tell myself not to be afraid.

I jump.

The End

*****

Dear Fabulous Reader,

Thanks so much for reading The Standout. If you'd like to stay in the loop about my other books and get bonus content (like my contemporary rom-com, Jane Austen-inspired novella, *I Bet You Think About Me,*) subscribe to my newsletter on Laurellit.com.

Or, keep reading for a glimpse of how Robin's story began, in *The Holdout.*

Acknowledgements

Big thanks to Lynn Osterkamp, Matthew Corey, Shauna Slade, Allan Press, and Brett Carter for your help with this book. I would be lost without your friendship, feedback and support.

This books if for Rich, Eli, and Pauline: thank you for your patience and support while I'm always writing, for your enthusiasm at my success, and always, for your love. For you, I will always jump!

Chapter Eighty

Other Books by Laurel Osterkamp

Favorite Daughters

Beautiful Little Furies

The Side Project

Just Like the Bronte Sisters

The Holdout

The Next Breath

Starring in the Movie of My Life

Following My Toes

Keep reading for a glimpse at how Robin's story began, in *The Holdout*!

Preview Chapter of The Holdout

My only mistake was falling in love. Other than that I played a nearly perfect game. But it doesn't matter. Do you remember Janet Jackson's halftime performance during the Super Bowl back in 2004? It was stunning but nobody will ever recall the actual dance because at the end of it, she showed her nipple on national television. Well, Janet and I have something in common. I didn't think things through, I exposed myself to the nation, and now that is what I'll be remembered for.

Except it hasn't happened yet.

I filmed the current season of *The Holdout* months ago, but it's still airing. There are three episodes yet to be broadcast, and my most humiliating moments are still to come. Right now I only occasionally get spotted on the street, but I was edited out of a lot of the earlier footage. I'm not naïve enough to believe that will be the case later on. What happened was devastating but it will undoubtedly make delicious TV.

So I'm wondering if anyone will recognize me today, and if so, will that increase or decrease my chances of being dismissed? I park my car and walk from the lot to the federal court building, clutching my jury summons in my hand. If I'm chosen, it will be the second jury I've been on in a year.

Inside, I give my bag to the security guards and walk through the metal detectors. They give me my bag back on the other side, and I take the elevator to the fourth floor, which is where my summons said to go. When the elevator doors open I immediately see a desk and behind it stands a perky brunette wearing an adorable suit jacket with bell sleeves and a Peter Pan collar. She totally pulls it off.

I pull on the edges of my oversized sweater and smooth out my skirt. My outfit seemed reasonable when I left this morning but I've never worked downtown and I've never owned a pair of heels. What do I know?

"Hi," she says, with a floating voice. "Can I help you?"

I hold up my summons. "I'm here to report for jury duty."

She takes the summons and looks it over. "Robin Bricker. Great. Please sign in." She gestures toward a clipboard with a sign-in sheet. Mine will be the fourth signature.

"Here's your card." She gives me a new piece of paper, and it has a stamp with today's date on it. "Hold on to this. If you're selected for a jury, you'll present it every morning to be stamped and that will be documentation for your boss."

"Oh," I stammer. "I'm sort of between jobs right now, so there's no need." I tilt my head to the side, trying to stretch away the tension. Who cares if I don't have a regular, nine to five gig? I'm not obligated to explain how I support myself.

She nods and oozes sincerity, and even though she's wearing heels I tower over her. She's the sort of girl I wanted to be when I was in high school. "Well, then you'll get paid for your time here!" Her perfect brown bob curls just so, right under her ears. Maybe if I blow-dried my hair every morning I could get my hair to do that too. "You're a little early, but go ahead and have a seat in the lounge. There's coffee, juice, and muffins, and in about half an hour, we'll get started!"

I thank her and walk into the lounge, a large room with oversized windows and strategically placed tables and chairs. Although I've had breakfast, I grab a chocolate muffin because I'm still hungry, and besides, it's my policy never to turn down anything chocolate. I lost a lot of weight while filming *The Holdout*, but even if I gain it all back I'll still be thin. For the first eighteen years of my life I hated that I was always the tallest, scrawniest girl in my class. No cute curves for me. But once I went to college I appreciated that I could eat cafeteria food and still fit into my size six jeans, while my friends all struggled with the freshman fifteen.

I sit down in one of the many cushy chairs, take out my book, and settle in to read while enjoying my muffin. Who said jury duty has to be awful? But then the television that's mounted to the ceiling switches from the morning show to commercial, and an ad for *The Holdout* comes on. My castmates are walking along the beach, some wearing teeny tiny bikinis, others shirtless in swimming trunks. Joe Pine's voice can be heard over it all, loud and clear.

"This week, on *The Holdout*. The stakes are high, loyalties are tested, and hearts are broken." Then it switches to a close up of Grant. He's sitting and smirking; even the way he blinks seems self-satisfied while the waves lap the shore behind him.

"*The Holdout* is a game," he says, "and I'm not here just to play. I'm here to win. I'll do whatever it takes."

Then – oh my God – it switches to a shot of Grant and me, locked in an embrace. But even worse, it switches again, and now Grant and Klemi are making out. Finally it switches back to Grant, sitting alone on the beach, laughing to the camera and clapping his hands. Joe

Pine's voice comes on again. "Will lover boy Grant endure? Will he persist? Will he be The Holdout?"

The commercial ends and I shrink down in my seat. I look around the room and see that others are all busy on their phones or reading the paper or nodding off as if they're practicing sitting in the jury box. Nobody seems to recognize me, which is my goal. I've cut my hair since the show and I dyed it a darker blonde. I'd have gone more extreme, but contractually I'm only allowed to make minor changes to my appearance. So I'm wearing thick rimmed glasses with fake lenses, and I dress in ways that will hopefully help me blend into the wallpaper.

All my life I've wanted to be famous. Now that my day has arrived, I'm clinging to my old, faceless existence like J.D Salinger gone into exile after writing *Catcher in the Rye*. Except instead of publishing a groundbreaking classic novel, I got duped by a pretty boy and his girlfriend and cheated out of a million dollars. What's worse though, is soon the world will see it all play out on national television.

****

To keep reading, click here.